Praise for

Blind Dates, Bridesmaids & Other Disasters

"*Blind Dates, Bridesmaids, and Other Disasters* is adorable. It's a fun story with just a bit of sass. I smiled the whole way through!"
—Jennifer Moore, author of *The Shipbuilder's Wife*

"Well-written, funny, and optimistic, *Blind Dates, Bridesmaids, and Other Disasters* is the perfect escape for romance fans. I loved the characters and dove right into their world. The one is definitely worth reading!"
—Rebecca H. Jamison, author of *Chemistry Lessons*

"*Blind Dates, Bridesmaids, and Other Disasters* is a fresh romantic comedy that you'll want to curl up with for an entertaining escape."
—Melanie Jacobson, author of *Perfect Set*

Also by
Aspen Hadley

Simply Starstruck

Blind Dates, Bridesmaids & Other Disasters

ASPEN HADLEY

SWEETWATER
BOOKS

An imprint of Cedar Fort, Inc.
Springville, Utah

© 2019 Aspen Hadley
All rights reserved.

No part of this book may be reproduced in any form whatsoever, whether by graphic, visual, electronic, film, microfilm, tape recording, or any other means, without prior written permission of the publisher, except in the case of brief passages embodied in critical reviews and articles.

This is a work of fiction. The characters, names, incidents, places, and dialogue are products of the author's imagination and are not to be construed as real. The opinions and views expressed herein belong solely to the author and do not necessarily represent the opinions or views of Cedar Fort, Inc. Permission for the use of sources, graphics, and photos is also solely the responsibility of the author.

ISBN 13: 978-1-4621-3595-0

Published by Sweetwater Books, an imprint of Cedar Fort, Inc.
2373 W. 700 S., Springville, UT 84663
Distributed by Cedar Fort, Inc., www.cedarfort.com

Library of Congress Cataloging-in-Publication Data on file.

Cover design by Shawnda T. Craig
Cover design © 2019 Cedar Fort, Inc.
Edited and typeset by Kaitlin Barwick and Heather Holm

Printed in the United States of America

10 9 8 7 6 5 4 3 2 1

Printed on acid-free paper

For Eliana and Cadence
My intelligent, strong, hilarious, and beautiful daughters
Never lose faith in your happily ever after
Even if you have to kiss a few frogs along the way

My heartfelt gratitude to the women of Facebook who shared with me their "interesting" dating stories and allowed me to use them in this novel. Every date Rachel goes on is based on a true story from you. Thank you!

Love doesn't make the world go 'round.
Love is what makes the ride worthwhile.

~ Franklin P. Jones ~

Chapter 1

Who, being loved, is poor?

~ Oscar Wilde ~

Few things are as annoying to me as an attractive, twenty-something woman with a good job and a solid group of friends who complains she can't get a date. I am not that girl. Sure, I fit all the parameters, but the difference is, I don't want to date. At all. In fact, I never complain about my love life. Given my history, it would be hypocritical.

Yet, even girls like me, who look good on paper but aren't looking for love, get lonely. It sure doesn't help things when Valentine's Day rolls around and you realize you've been daydreaming about how many cats you'll own.

My roommate Val's loud huff interrupted my pondering of fuzzy sidekicks. Our other roommate, Hannah, was giving her a haircut, and Val, as usual, was not taking things well.

"You know I hate my life, right?" Val sat stiffly upright, hands clenching the sides of her kitchen chair as Hannah cut her some new choppy bangs.

"You do not," Hannah retorted around the comb she was holding in her mouth. Hannah was used to making drastic changes to people's appearances and the worrying that sometimes occurred. Hannah was also used to Val.

"I'm going to look ridiculous, all for the sake of your experiments."

"You'll look amazing."

"Ouch! Do you really need to pull my hair so hard?"

"I ran a comb through your hair." Hannah pursed her lips in a very mom-ish way, her voice remaining calm. "You can get nailed by the flying limbs of distressed people in the ER, but someone combing your hair is just too much?"

"What color is that dye on the counter?" Val's voice went up a notch when she saw the box. "That had better not be for me."

"Blonde, and it is." Hannah leaned back and framed Val's face in her hands. "It's going to be perfect."

"Blonde where? My hair is so brown. I'm not meant to be a blonde. Nature made me this way."

"Just your bangs. I'll leave the rest of you as nature intended." One side of Hannah's mouth pulled up in a teasing look that Val missed.

"Just my bangs?" Val started to stand, but Hannah stopped her with a touch on her shoulder.

"I'm kidding. I'm thinking kind of an ombré look. It'll be great."

"Am I supposed to know what ombré means?" Val sat back down with yet another huff.

"You should. It's all she talks about these days," I joined in, switching to a ditzy voice. "Like, totally, everyone who is anyone is doing it."

Hannah glanced at me with a grin. "I can't help it if you two are helplessly out of date." I grinned back at her.

"I seriously hate, hate what's happening right now." Val reached up to finger her now chin-length hair. "Big girls like me aren't supposed to have chin-length hair. It makes us look like we have square, strange faces."

"Your scowl is what makes your face look square and strange," Hannah retorted.

"I read in a magazine that if you measure from your chin to your earlobes it will tell you if you can pull off short hair or not," I commented helpfully as I laughed at their arguing from my safe seat on the couch across the room.

"Don't believe everything you read in a magazine," Hannah replied with a slight shake of her head.

"But it was an online magazine," I replied with a straight face.

Hannah's eyes rolled. "Even worse."

"What were the measurements?" Val wanted to know. "Because I truly believe this haircut is going to look awful on me."

"Anything two and a half inches or less is great for short hair—" I began.

"Stop!" Hannah threw me a look that informed me exactly what she thought of my help.

"Bring me a ruler, Rachel!" Val insisted. She turned to look at me, and I found myself under the loud stares of two strong women.

Their heavy glares in my direction didn't have the effect they were going for. Instead, I giggled out loud, truly enjoying the picture they made. Watching Val sitting there in her hospital scrubs, fresh off a shift and feeling grumpy, while Hannah massacred her hair, was the total highlight of my week.

Hannah had already taken her turn with me the week before. I'd been adamant that she not touch the length of my hair, because I'd been growing it out since my twenty-first birthday, and now, over six years later, it finally reached my bra strap in the back. This was a big milestone in hair growth. The bra strap equaled the goal line. Many women set the bra-strap goal, but few are able to muscle through to the end. I wanted to revel in my victory.

Hannah had left the length alone as promised; however, my naturally light-brown hair was now such a dark black that it sometimes pulled blue in certain lights. My second-grade students had asked if they could call me Miss Fairy, because the hair color combined with my unusually blue eyes and tiny frame made me look like a creature from a storybook. I had firmly declined. That didn't stop them from continuing to ask.

"If you don't stop laughing at this, I'm going to sic her on your eyebrows." Val raised one of her own eyebrows as she sent me a look.

I clapped my hands over my mouth in mock horror and opened my eyes as far as they'd stretch. My face finally cracked Val, and she chuckled.

"You know, Rachel, that's actually not a bad idea." Hannah looked away from Val for a moment and zeroed in on my face. I couldn't help but notice how perfectly sculpted her eyebrows were as they drew down in concentration. "Mine look so much better now that I've let the girls at the salon work on them."

My only reply was to pull another face. In my opinion, and really anyone with the ability to see, Hannah always looked great. She was one of those girls with a long, graceful, athletic body that everyone envied. With medium brown hair full of red highlights, high cheekbones, and a generous mouth, Hannah was easily the prettiest of the three of us. Working in a salon, she was always on top of fashion in every degree. She was also the only one of us with a boyfriend. Regardless of the fact that neither of us was looking for a boyfriend, Val and I did not feel that was a coincidence.

"I bet her eyebrows are what helped her snag Andrew's attention," Val helpfully supplied with a grin on her face, referring to Hannah's boyfriend. "You should let her see what she could do for your love life."

"Hard pass." I shook my head. "Nothing you can say will make me let you get near my brows. I'm allergic to your tweezers."

"Oh, for you I'm definitely thinking wax." Hannah smirked as she turned her attention back to Val.

"You'll eat those words, Rachel." Val tilted her head and pursed her lips as she waved at herself to point out the situation she now found herself in.

"Not tonight I won't. Hannah has a hot Valentine's date with her smoochy poo." I got up from the couch and walked toward my bedroom. "I'm off to prep some lesson plans for next week. Better hurry on that haircut so you aren't late." I sent a little wave to them both as I rounded the corner down the hallway to my bedroom.

A few hours later, Val and I put on our annual Valentine's Day movie, *The Notebook*. We were both holding a pint of ice cream in our hands, comfy in our pajama pants and hoodies, hair pulled up, makeup washed off, fluffy Christmas-print socks donned, and a box of tissues handy. I'd even gone the extra step and popped out my contacts. My black-framed glasses were throwbacks to my high school days and seriously out of fashion, but I didn't care enough to buy something new.

Valentine's Day didn't bother me nearly as much as it bothered Val. In fairness, a lot of things bothered Val. Like life. Life definitely bothered her. I sometimes wondered if Val was so grumpy at home because she was so calm at work. My theory was that home was where she vented and fussed so that she could keep it together in the fast-paced, high-stress world of the emergency department at the hospital. Telling myself this kept me from wanting to pinch her sometimes.

"I hate my life," Val muttered around a spoonful of ice cream for the second time that day.

"Yep," I replied around my own mouthful.

"I mean, hate, hate."

"I'm having that engraved on your headstone, by the way," I said. Val just stuck out her tongue at me. "Being single on Valentine's Day is no different than being single every other day of the year." I tried to reason with her, even though I knew it was totally pointless.

"Please. It's totally different, and you know it. We could watch a movie and eat ice cream on any other Saturday night and it wouldn't mean a thing. But do that on Valentine's, and suddenly you're pathetic."

"We're not pathetic. What could a guy give us that we don't have? We have ice cream. We're snuggled up on the couch. We're having a great night," I said cheerfully.

"You know when I go back to work at the hospital they're all going to ask me what I did for Valentine's, and I'm going to have to tell them that my roommate and I snuggled together under my nana's old afghan. They'll give me that 'sad single girl' pity smile. I hate that look!"

She had a point. I hated that she had a point. I hated that I was going to get that look at school on Monday too. So, I said the only thing that popped into my head: "Hate is a big word, too heavy to throw around."

"Thank you, Beverly Stevens, for your wisdom," Val snorted, referring to my mom, who was always dishing up quirky sayings. "Also, that has nothing to do with anything. I can hate a date on the calendar, and I can definitely hate the pity looks. It doesn't mean I'm going to ax murder someone."

"Honestly, Val, I'll be surprised if you *don't* ax murder someone someday," I teased. Val leaned forward and punched me with a pillow, her new bangs flopping over her eyes. I sat up, prepared to fight back, but she grinned and leaned back against the couch.

"I'll start with you," she said as she brushed her hair out of her eyes. I gave her new look a quick once-over again, surprised by how skilled Hannah was. She'd really transformed Val, and the ombré look suited her somehow.

"Quit staring. I look like a circus freak," Val grumped.

"You really don't. It's a great look on you." I smiled and snuggled back down into the cushions.

We'd settled back into the movie for barely a moment when the bang of our apartment door flying open drew our attention. Hannah walked in the door with a huge grin on her face, her arm wrapped around her boyfriend, Andrew. Something was glittering on the hand we could see.

"Oh no. Please no . . . ," Val moaned.

I didn't even have to ask what she meant. It was written all over Hannah's face. I prepared myself for her announcement, feeling both genuinely excited for my friend and a pang of sadness for the changes it would bring. I sucked in a silent breath and let it out slowly, loosening the tightness in my chest.

"We're engaged!" Hannah squealed, face radiant and eyes dancing. She held up her glittery hand and waved it around as she quickly approached the couch.

"Oh no. She said it, didn't she," Val whispered flatly through clenched teeth as she painted on a bright smile for Hannah.

I shrugged off my half of the afghan and jumped up to hug the happy couple. "I can't believe it," I cried. That was a lie. I could believe it. Anyone who had spent any time around Hannah and Andrew in the past six months had known this was coming.

"I know. He totally surprised me!" Hannah returned my hug with the power of a woman twice her size. I glanced at Andrew over her shoulder and gave him a big grin, which he returned.

"Well done, Andrew. Come tell us all about it." I released Hannah and sat next to a silent but smiling Val.

I elbowed her slightly as I sat down and gave her the "get your stuff together, lady" look. Her smile shifted into something a bit more natural, and I figured that was the best I was going to get from her. Val didn't like change and wasn't a huge fan of love. She all but deflated back into the couch and hugged the afghan closer. She was out. It would be up to me to carry on the conversation.

I smiled and nodded at Hannah and Andrew, inviting them to tell us the details; however, in the interest of honesty, I didn't really hear much about how Andrew proposed. I was too busy thinking about how this would officially change everything. The three of us had been sharing one apartment or another for nine years. We'd all come from different towns to the same college and were assigned to the same dorm during our freshman year. We had lived together ever since, eventually graduating and moving out of the dorms into a junky first apartment after being lucky enough to all find work in the same city. Just last year we'd been able to afford this nicer, larger apartment. It had felt like such a huge reward after how hard we'd all worked through school and getting settled into our careers. And now, as exciting as it was, marriage would take one member of our trio. We'd known it would most likely happen at some point, but still . . .

In the middle of that thought was the realization that I was going to be left alone with the grumpy one sitting next to me hugging her afghan and fake smiling. Val was a loyal friend and a hard worker, but the girl was mostly gray skies with occasional sunlight breaking through. I knew she had her good points or we wouldn't have stayed friends for so long. I was just having a hard time remembering them at the moment.

My mind immediately skipped to how my mom and sister would take the news. My mom wanted nothing more than for me to settle down. Why, when she'd been my age, she'd already had my sister, Diana. That sister of mine hadn't helped anything by turning twenty-five and presenting my parents with twin daughters. I'm sure my mom expected me to have triplets by this time. Yet, here I was, two years past that milestone age of twenty-five, and the only thing I was hugging was a pint of ice cream as I watched the clock tick closer and closer to twenty-eight.

Unlike Val, I did believe in love, but I'd given up finding it after a very painful breakup seven years earlier. Even though ending the relationship had been my choice, some part of me had never fully recovered. I'd dated again off and on, but my heart wasn't in it, and I'd given up dating all together about two years ago. I had known that twenty-five was much too young to throw in the towel. I mean, honestly, most people don't marry until their late twenties these days. However, age had nothing to do with the fact that forcing something caused nothing but pain. I hadn't meant to stop trying forever, but my plan to regroup wasn't going as quickly as I'd hoped.

Still, I had a lot going for me. I had a great career teaching second grade at Pine Ridge Elementary. I had good friends and family. I'd been thinking about getting myself a cat. Maybe even two. Two seemed like a better option. I didn't want one to be lonely while I was away working during the day.

Oh no. Oh no, no, no. Did I just think about getting myself a cat? Correction, *two* cats?

". . . and I want you two to be bridesmaids!" Hannah's cheerful squeal drowned out my inner monologue, and I tuned back in. Her face was radiant in a way I hadn't seen before. Andrew looked about the same, as though he couldn't have stopped smiling if he'd wanted to. It lifted my heart.

"Uh . . . ," Val mumbled.

"Awesome!" I smiled, genuinely happy to be in the wedding party of my best friend. It was something we'd talked about many times over the years. It would be fun to see those talks become reality.

Hannah's eyes met mine in a moment of shared celebration and understanding, our memories of those talks flowing between us. But suddenly Hannah's eyes lost their dreamy look, and she zoned in on my face.

"Rach, I'll probably need to do something with your eyebrows before the wedding," she stated.

I was startled by the sudden shift. Val puffed out a low sound of amusement. I had to get the focus off my eyebrows before Hannah tried to make me look like a creepy starlet wannabe, so I blurted out the first thing that came to my mind.

"I was just thinking that maybe I should get a cat," I said a bit too loudly. "Maybe two."

It had the desired effect. I had definitely distracted them away from my eyebrows. The room grew silent. Hannah and Val both opened their mouths and stared. Andrew, poor innocent Andrew, having no idea what that signified, simply looked at me curiously. I had done the impossible and wiped the smiles off their faces. Oops.

"A cat sounds nice," Andrew finally stuttered as he glanced between the three of us. Poor guy—always trying to be kind when confusion reigned.

"Two cats." I couldn't stop the words from coming as the girls continued to stare. "So . . . you know . . . neither one gets lonely while I'm away working."

Andrew smiled and nodded at me in an encouraging way. Val clamped her mouth shut as Hannah turned to her new fiancé.

"Honey, um, I think maybe we should go share our news with your friends before it gets too late. I'll finish telling the girls here all the details later." She stood and pulled Andrew up with her.

"I . . . I'm sorry. I didn't mean to blurt that out," I mumbled as I pushed my glasses back up on my nose. Val patted my arm, and I closed my mouth.

"It's fine. I understand," Hannah stood up. "We have a few more stops. But we *will* talk when I get back!" She inserted a firmness in her voice that let me know she meant business. She'd assumed the mothering role in our trio years ago, so, like a good girl, I nodded. She looked at Val and raised one of her perfectly manicured black eyebrows.

"I got this," Val responded. Hannah nodded and all but dragged Andrew out the door.

After the door closed, the apartment was silent for a few minutes before Val turned to me. "Cats?" she stated, looking right into my eyes. Those almost-black eyes could be intimidating, and when I glanced away, she said, "Why didn't you tell us you'd been thinking about getting a cat?"

"Two cats." I shrugged as I corrected her. Val shook her head and sighed. "She was going for my eyebrows!" I tried to defend myself, but Val wasn't having it. "It's going to be bad when Hannah gets back," I mumbled.

"Oh, yeah." Val chuckled softly and shook her head as she turned back to the TV and hit play on the movie.

I tried to focus on Ryan Gosling and his eternal love, but all I could think about was cats. I had settled on looking for a fluffy white one and a spotted gray one. I spent the next two hours thinking about what to name them and where they'd sleep.

It was almost midnight when Hannah returned from her news-sharing tour. This time she looked a little more tired, though still happy. Her eyes met mine across the room as she took off her black jacket and red patterned scarf and slowly hung them on her hook by the door, all the while staying silent.

Next to me, Val shifted a little and clicked off the late show we were now watching. She knew that the show about to go down in the living room was going to be much more interesting.

Hannah crossed the room and sat in the same chair that she and Andrew had been cuddling in earlier. She tucked her legs under her and seemed to ponder me for a minute. Years of practice sizing people up in a salon mirror had perfected her technique. Her green eyes were both curious and annoyed as she watched me for a moment. I deserved that annoyed look. I'd kind of burst her bubble by making my announcement when I did.

"You want to tweeze my eyebrows?" I teased, trying to lighten the mood.

"I don't care about your personal grooming." Hannah pinched her lips together.

"Since when?" Val poked.

"I gave up on you two apes a long time ago." Some twinkle returned to Hannah's eyes, and I was grateful to Val for the save. "Okay, but seriously, Rachel, two cats?"

"One will be fluffy white, and the other gray with spots." I gave a half smile.

"Names?" Val asked.

"Angel and Princess." I shrugged and held up my hands.

"Oh . . . just . . . no. Not only do they have names, but they have sweet little girly names as well." Val rolled her eyes.

The three of us burst out laughing. I was grateful for the break in their interrogation, assuming it would close that subject and shift the conversation back to Hannah. I was wrong. Hannah, always one step ahead, allowed the smile on her face to naturally relax before she pierced me with a look.

"Rach, here's the thing. I don't have an issue with you wanting cats. I'm more worried about the fact that you have never, in all the years I've known you, talked about wanting a pet. Then *bam*, out of the blue, you blurt it out on Valentine's Day right in the middle of my engagement announcement. This is a day about love and celebration, and instead of joining in, you're throwing fuzzy kitties up as a wall." She paused while my insides squeezed at the truth.

"I mean, owning cats isn't all bad. They're very good pets. Easier maintenance than dogs," I replied softly.

"No one is saying you can't have a cat. I'm simply questioning your timing."

"It makes you look desperate," Val was kind enough to add.

I didn't reply out loud, but I could see their point. My sudden fascination with pet ownership when it had never been on my radar screen before was all but screaming that I had a gaping hole in my life.

Hannah spoke again after a few moments of silence. "I've been thinking about this, and if you really want some cats because that will make you happy, then get a couple of cats. Enjoy having something to care for and love."

"Uh, as the roommate who will be stuck living with the cats, I think I get a vote here," Val inserted.

"She'll need something loving to live with after I'm gone." Hanna smiled sweetly at Val, who stuck out her tongue. Hannah turned back to me. "However, I think this has nothing to do with wanting a cat. I think this is about being scared. So I, Hannah Redmond, soon-to-be Stratton, am giving you, Rachel Stevens, a challenge."

"What kind of a challenge?" I hedged as my self-preservation alert began flashing red.

In the past, Hannah's challenges to Val and me hadn't been exactly fun. Any time our honorary mother decided a change was needed, she'd come up with a challenge for us to complete. Last year, when Hannah discovered that Val's refusal to go to a movie theater with us was the result of her secret fear of dark places, we'd blacked out all our apartment windows and used only strategically placed candles for a solid week. It had been a long week of squinting and stubbing our toes and had officially ended my fascination with all things vampire. Hannah called it a two-for-one win in her book, since she'd never jumped on the vampire bandwagon at all. In college I'd gone through a slightly unsettling fascination with good luck charms, convinced my grades and future success were dependent on a lucky rabbit's foot hanging from my backpack. Hannah had challenged me to wear a second rabbit's foot, as a necklace, to all my finals that quarter. It was humiliating, but my faith in the power of the fluffy little foot was stronger than my embarrassment. Seeing my dedication, and knowing this would require a next-level scheme, Hannah hid my lucky charms the night before my last exam. I was forced to take the test without them, whimpering and trembling the entire time. It was the one final I aced. Hannah's point was made, and I said goodbye to my superstitions.

Yep, Hannah's challenges were the stuff of legend. While I was mature enough to admit that they'd had good results after the pain, I was still childish enough to be stomping my feet on the inside whenever she issued one.

"A dating challenge." Hannah nodded to punctuate her words.

Val groaned. She was a firm believer that women did not *need* a date, or even a man. Women were strong and perfectly capable of taking care of themselves. Because I knew Val had a softer side, I often wondered how much of her talk was bluster and how much was a result of the fact that as a taller, bigger woman, she'd had her share of hurtful experiences. No matter what the true reason, Val had built herself a very high, very strong wall to hide behind. And on top of that wall was a flag of warning, keeping all men at bay.

It was ironic that as a tiny woman, I had also been hurt by thoughtless jabs about my size and lack of femininity. It didn't seem to matter if you were big or small or weren't the perfect five-star average, you'd hear about it. It was a complete stumper to me how Val watched as many chick flicks as she watched. Maybe Val needed a cat too.

"What did you have in mind?" I pulled my mind back to Hannah and her challenge.

"Rach, I love you, but you've put yourself on the shelf for long enough. We all know why, so we haven't pushed. But I think it's time to dust yourself off and get out there. So, I am challenging you to go on two dates a month until my wedding in September."

I quickly did the math in my head. "That's a dozen dates!" I gasped. Hannah nodded. "I can't possibly. I don't even know twelve guys to go out with," I argued.

"I know. But a young, pretty, professional girl like you should have no problem finding people. In fact, I get people at the salon all the time trying to set me up on dates. I'll get you some dates. I'm sure Val could help with people she meets at the hospital." Hannah looked to Val for support.

Val shook her head. "Yep. People at a hospital are definitely great candidates. Just let me get them off the gurney, and they're all yours."

"Ignore her. I'm sure Val will dig something up too." Hannah turned back to face me.

"I don't know about this," I hedged. It seemed like a terrible idea to me. "I think going from zero to a dozen is too big a leap!"

"Rach, we love you, but you've already chosen colors, names, and the number of cats you want to have. We can't let our best friend go down that path!"

"Speak for yourself, Han. I can definitely let her go. I'll enjoy watching." Val grinned.

"I'll set you up on a date too if you don't stuff it," Hannah pretend glared at Val. Val just smiled at her.

"Can I think about this?" I asked.

Hannah smiled at me. "Of course you can. But seriously, Rach, you haven't been the same about relationships since you and—"

"Don't say it," I cut her off in a voice that left no argument. A sudden swell of emotion stabbed me at the mention of my failed relationship. It hurt to even start to think about it. I could hardly bear to hear his name, still, after all this time.

"Fine, I won't bring him up. But it's true. I hate to see you give up on life because of one bad experience." Hannah smiled kindly at me in a way that told me she understood that it had been much more than just a bad experience. "Look, I'll give you a little time to think it over. If you agree, we'll start the challenge on March first."

"When you haven't dated in a few years, it feels like a marathon to date twice in one month," Val said matter-of-factly.

"Oh my gosh," I groaned. "Val is right."

"Val is not right. Val spends all day around the sick and the dying. She can't be trusted with matters of love," Hannah argued.

"For what it's worth, Rach, I really don't think you need to do this. Your life doesn't have to be about whether you have a man or not. Your life is full and happy as it is," Val insisted. Her tone was missing its usual sarcasm, and I saw concern and conviction in her gaze, which only made her statement that much more powerful. She meant it.

I sat in silence, thinking over both Hannah's challenge and Val's assertion. They both had a point. I'd been paralyzed in the love department for a long time now, and in some ways, that meant I was paralyzed in life. Not because I needed a man to move forward, but because it meant I was closed off to new things. I did have a great career and loving relationships, but I had to admit that I'd found a comfort zone and was sitting securely in place regardless of my dating status. I hadn't sought out anything new in a long time. Nothing about my life was challenging.

Should I do it? My mom was always saying that everything worth having took some work. Would it be worth it to go on twelve dates if one of them ended up being Mr. Right?

On the other hand, what if none of them ended up being Mr. Right, and I found myself in this exact same place six months from now? Then I'd be heartbroken and cynical rather than just paralyzed. Not to mention the fact that I wasn't sure I deserved to be happy when I was the reason my heart was broken in the first place. That's what I meant about me being a hypocrite. I had no business feeling lonely when loneliness had been my own choice.

I had tried to put it behind me, to not think of him anymore, but I'd never really taken the time to forgive myself. Was I ready to forgive myself and open my heart to someone else? Was I ready to be more open in general and see where life took me?

Hannah must have realized that I was lost in a pondering mode, so she stood up from her chair and started down the hall to her room. "Just think on it. We can talk more soon. Good night, ladies."

"Han?" I called as she turned the corner into the hallway.

"Yeah?" She turned back to face me.

"I'm sorry about tonight. I didn't mean to ruin your announcement. I'm thrilled for you and Andrew," I stated as earnestly as I could.

Her face relaxed into a smile. "Thanks!"

Val stood up too and lightly tapped my leg with her fuzzy sock-covered toe. "Don't let her get to you. She's high on love right now. You're fine just the way you are."

I half smiled at Val and watched as she too left the room, leaving me alone in the silence. Was I really okay with how I was? Did

I want to only be twenty-seven and have given up on home and family? Was my future going to be lint rolling cat hair off my clothing before work? Hannah had given me a lot to think about. Was I up to the challenge?

The next day was Sunday, and I was happy when the phone rang and it was my mom and sister. Mom tried to talk to each of us weekly. We all lived in the same state but were spread out by a couple of hours. When she hadn't had a chance to get us on our own, she liked to do a Sunday night conference call. I was glad that this week my sister, Diana, would be on the line too. I had a lot to discuss.

I had always looked forward to hearing about Diana and her family, but today it seemed that Diana's update on her twins, Hailey and Heather, and her husband, Jordan, took a million times longer than usual. The twins were ten now and busy with dance classes and music lessons. Apparently, they were showing signs of snagging their place in the popular group at school. It was also apparent that this was something we were supposed to be rooting for.

"It's great they have friends, it really is, but how are they doing with their school work?" I inserted. I could almost see Diana's mouth tighten in annoyance before she answered.

"Fine, just fine. Both girls are doing well," she replied tightly. I smiled to myself.

Diana, being seven years older than I, wasn't always interested in my opinions. I was constantly talking with the girls about good grades, colleges they might be interested in, and careers they might want to have. Diana, however, was always talking with them about hairstyles, fashion trends, and the design of their future home. In spite of our differences, Diana was a good mom, and we both wanted the girls to have happy futures. I simply figured it was the schoolteacher aunt's job to make sure they were getting a little academic encouragement too.

Blind Dates, Bridesmaids, and Other Disasters

"That's great! Just great!" Mom said when Diana had wrapped up her update. I didn't have any idea what Jordan and Diana were up to. Either I'd zoned out or the entire conversation had revolved around the twins. I was fine if it did. I adored being an aunt, but I felt a little guilty for not paying closer attention.

"How are things with you, Rachel?" Mom asked.

"Well, I actually do have something to talk with you two about this week." Even I could hear the tension in my voice.

"Uh-oh," Diana said, laughing.

"I can't wait to hear what this is all about," Mom joined in.

"Hannah and Andrew got engaged last night," I began.

"That's fantastic!" Mom cried. Marriage was, in her mind, the most desired endgame on the planet.

"How great," Diana added. "Now for the fun part. The shopping, the planning, the wedding day, and then—"

"The babies!" Mom interrupted with a cheer.

It was a familiar refrain. Mom would have had a dozen babies herself if the fates had allowed. In the end, she'd only gotten two daughters, and seven years apart at that. She was hoping to make up for it with a million grandchildren. I supposed that was up to me now, since Diana had stopped at two.

We laughed together over Mom's exuberance.

"Yeah. It is really great news," I said. "I'm really happy for her. But then while she was telling me the details, I announced that I thought maybe I'd buy a cat for myself," I continued.

"Oh . . . ," Diana immediately got the cat lady reference.

"A cat?" Mom didn't.

"Two cats actually." I grimaced as I said it.

Diana didn't miss a beat. "Oh, no."

"Yeah," I moaned.

"I still don't—" Mom began, but Diana interrupted her.

"Have you named them?"

"Princess and Angel," I whispered. They were both quiet for a moment, and then Diana chuckled.

"Wait, I didn't know you liked cats," Mom stated in a confused tone.

"It's a new thing," I replied.

"I'm guessing you were on the receiving end of an intervention?" Diana's voice held a tinge of amusement.

"Yep."

"So what did Hannah have to say?" Mom seemed to be catching up.

I told them about Hannah's challenge to have two dates a month until her wedding.

"Praise heaven, my baby is getting married!" Mom hollered into the phone after I'd finished.

"Mom, no!" I snorted at her total predictability.

"Are you going to do it?" Diana asked.

"I don't know," I replied. Then I told them about Val saying my life didn't need a man in it for me to be complete. "What do you guys think?" I asked.

"I think it's pretty obvious how Mom feels," Diana replied with light sarcasm as Mom's end of the phone was muted and we could hear her yelling to Dad, *Rachel is going to start dating again. We're going to get another son-in-law. Did you hear that, Don?*

"Yeah, she's gone. What do you think?" I asked again.

"Well, I guess you need to ask yourself a hard question. Are you okay with how your life is?"

"Well, I thought I was until last night when Hannah got engaged and I realized that life moves along. I understand what Val is saying, but I'm kind of afraid that if I don't try to move along, I'll get left behind."

"You haven't been interested in dating since, you know . . . ," Diana said sympathetically, letting the thought trail off.

I sighed. "Yeah, I know."

Diana was quiet for a minute, and I could tell from a muffled scrape that Mom had stealthily rejoined the conversation as an eavesdropper.

Diana eventually said, "Well, Rachel, that was the past. Now you need to think about what you want for the future. You did college, you've done single girl in the city—what's next? You have a great career and good friends, but is that all you want? If it is, then, well, that's fine."

"Not what you would want though," I kindly interrupted.

"Yes, but we both know you and I are totally different people," Diana teased gently.

"Fact," I agreed.

"You're both wonderful," Mom inserted in yet another familiar refrain. "Every person is a different flower, but together they make a beautiful garden." Diana and I both moaned. "Well, it's true. Keep talking though. Don't let me interrupt."

"That's really all I have to say," Diana stated. "Just think about what you want out of life. If you still have that dream of a family of your own, then this challenge could give you a way to get out and meet people and get back on the path toward that. If you're happy teaching school and spending time with your friends, then pass on the challenge. Of course, you do realize that if you turn it down, that would mean coming home to your two cats and Val for the rest of your life."

"The cats would be good. But Val forever?" I made a funny noise that got a laugh, but I have to admit that I shuddered a bit on the inside at the picture Diana painted.

"Not forever, sweetie. Just until one of those dates introduces you to Mr. Right," Mom replied.

"I appreciate your faith in my power to snag a man, Mom," I said, smiling even though she couldn't see my face.

I was happy to let our conversation flow from there on to Dad's latest aches, Mom's neighborhood gossip cloaked as updates, and how our grandparents were doing. Through it all, I thought about what Diana had said. For all the ways we were different, she had made some good points.

Chapter 2

To get the full value of a joy you must have somebody to divide it with.

~ *Mark Twain* ~

If anyone asked me, I'd say that changing children's lives was the best part of my job as a teacher. I loved teaching, and I loved the children I got to spend my days with. If these things weren't true, I'd have found a new career ages ago.

However, if my closest friends asked me the same question, I'd have to say that the best part of my job was my fellow second-grade teacher Lisa Wilson. I really loved sitting down after the halls cleared and going over the day with Lisa.

Today was no different. Even though it had been a week since Valentine's Day and the bomb drop of Hannah's dating challenge, I was still trying to decide what to do as I walked from the front door of the school, where I'd cheerfully waved off my students, back toward my classroom.

Reminders of Valentine's Day coated the walls, plastered the bulletin boards, and hung from the ceiling. I was truly itching to tear down the cupids that had been dangling over my desk for weeks now. Being single didn't mean I was anti-Valentine's Day, but everyone has limits.

Lisa was in her room next door to mine when I wandered her way. She was sitting behind her desk and holding a paper up to read while supporting her head with the other hand in a weary manner.

"Looks like a good time happening over here," I said, knocking on the doorframe as I entered.

"Yep. Trying to decide how much I really care if my students can spell correctly." She smiled at me as she put the paper down.

Lisa was exactly what you'd picture a second-grade teacher to be: blonde, perky, small enough to get on the floor with her students when needed, but round enough to be soft to hug. Since second graders still accidentally call their teachers "mom" and need a good hug now and again, Lisa was a perfect fit.

"Eh, with spell check I say don't waste your time. Everything will be picture words in ten more years anyhow." I pulled a chair out from a student's desk and sat down. "You surviving?"

"You know the fun never ends," Lisa's mouth tugged in tired amusement. "Today Oliver squirted an entire bottle of glue on his desk while I was working on math with another kid. Savannah raised her hand when I asked a question, and then instead of answering, she announced that she had super star powers and we're all lucky to have her in our classroom. But if anyone was mean to her, she'd zap them. And Brandon's mom wants to know why I have him seated in the back of the classroom when he'd be much happier up front and center." Lisa rolled her eyes.

"Just another day," I said, grinning.

"Just another day," she agreed. "So . . . ?"

"So, what?" I knew exactly what she wanted to know.

"Don't play dumb. You doing Hannah's challenge or not?"

I shrugged. "I honestly can't decide."

"I still say you're stalling," Lisa smiled knowingly.

"I'm not stalling! I'm smart enough to be scared."

"Nothing to be scared of. How bad can it be? Twelve dates is nothing. That's one box of donuts. I went on at least that many before I met my husband," she stated firmly. "Besides, I'm sure there are loads of amazing guys just waiting to meet Miss Fairy."

I shook my head at her joking use of my students' nickname for me. "This from the married girl."

"See, I'm a great example of a dating success story." Lisa gave herself a high five in the air, which made me laugh.

"I don't even know who I would go out with," I hedged.

"Oh, that's the easy part. Paul," Lisa nodded.

"Your brother? The one you've been talking up for like a year now?" A nervous feeling crawled up my throat. I hadn't even decided what I wanted to do yet, and here I was being set up.

After two years, I was totally rusty and a little petrified. It wasn't that I honestly thought that the first guy I went out with was going to be my soul mate. It was that the first date was going to be the first step to being open to falling in love again. And I knew first-hand that the plummet from love left bruises.

"Yep. He's back from teaching English in Asia. He'd be a great first date. He's not a total stranger, so the risk is low."

"He is, in fact, a total stranger, considering I've never met him."

Lisa made a face to let me know what she thought of that argument. "Yes, but someone you know and trust can vouch for him." Lisa was really warming to her subject. "He's great with kids, really active and fun, and handsome too."

"You're creeping me out now with your overselling."

"Just think about it. I love Hannah's challenge, and I think you should do it. If you say yes, let me set you up with Paul as your first date. You'd have a great time. And, hey, maybe it would get you out of eleven other dates if the first one was a ringer."

By now, I was laughing at the look of pure delight on Lisa's angelic face. I had to admit she had a point. I loved Lisa, and if her brother was half as great as she was, maybe I'd get out of this challenge with no war wounds.

I'd thought a lot over the past week about what to do. On one side, I really, really liked my comfy life. Cats were pretty risk free. They might claw my face, but those types of wounds were easily healed. Dating was a minefield. The wounds from that were still throbbing a little in my life.

However, Diana had a strong argument when she'd asked what I wanted out of life. I did want a companion to share it with. I wanted the whole life experience. Families were so important to me, and I wasn't going to get one of my own by hiding away. I wondered how I could both want love and be terrified of it at the same time.

"You know what, Lisa? I think I'll open negotiations with Hannah. Val is making us dinner tonight, so I'll tell her then." I huffed out a breath as the words burst out of me on a wave of nausea.

"And you'll let me set you up with Paul as your first date?" Lisa squealed.

"And I will *think* about letting you set me up with Paul—" I began.

"Oh, you'll let me," Lisa smirked. "Yes, you will."

Hannah, Val, and I relaxed on the couch, our bellies full of homemade chicken fettuccine, salad, and breadsticks. We had bought the ratty old blue-and-green-printed couch and matching chair from a thrift store when we graduated college and moved into our first real unfurnished apartment together. It was torn in places and lumpy in others, but none of us ever suggested an upgrade, even though everything else had improved over the years as we'd settled into our careers. We shared too many memories for that couch and chair to be just thrown away.

"Valerie Allen, that was the best pasta I've ever had," Hannah sighed. "I'm undoing the top button of my jeans. Don't judge."

"If I could walk, I'd be hurrying to my bedroom to tear these jeans right off my body and put on stretchy pants," I agreed. "On a scale of one to ten, how weird would it be to purchase a pair of maternity jeans and call them my Val's Pasta Night Pants?"

"It's ideas like that, Rach, that keep this friendship going." Val gave me a thumb's up.

"I'm not going to fit into my wedding dress." Hannah huffed out another big breath. "And you two better choose something stretchy for your bridesmaid outfits."

"I'm not wearing anything pink," Val stated. "Which brings up another topic. What, exactly, do I have to do for this wedding?"

"Mostly it will involve a lot of tulle and sparkles," Hannah teased. Val stared without cracking, which made Hannah laugh. "Not much. Since I knew you'd be reluctant, I thought I'd ask Rachel to be my maid of honor. She'll help me with all the details."

"Really?" I sat up a bit and smiled at her.

"Really! Who else would I ask?" Hannah said, smiling back. "Val, you only need to wear a dress and smile pretty for the camera."

"How pretty is pretty?" Val's mouth lifted into a mocking shadow of a smile.

"Val!" Hannah and I said together, both of us entertained.

"Fine." She nodded.

"This is so exciting!" I cheered.

Hannah's smile grew. "I honestly still can't believe I'm engaged. I wasn't sure this day would come."

"I wasn't worried about you for a second. Andrew can't take his eyes off you," I replied.

"You're only twenty-seven," Val stated.

"True. But you watch everyone around you finding someone, and you start to worry. And then came Andrew." Hannah's eyes took on a dreamy look.

"She's fallen into the zone again." Val sighed and poked Hannah in the side. "I know what will bring her back to us. Rachel, what have you decided about Hannah's challenge?"

Val was right. Hannah sat up from her slouched position, eyes glittering with interest.

"Well, actually, I did want to talk with you about that—" I began just as the doorbell rang, which was followed closely by a loud thudding knock.

"Rachel, you're the only one whose pants are still buttoned. Can you see who it is?" Hannah motioned toward the door as she leaned back to do up her pants.

"I don't think you get to boss me about everything. Just wedding stuff," I joked as I heaved myself off the couch.

"Val and I need a minute to put our pants back on," Hannah replied with a grimace as she tugged on the zipper.

I unlocked the door and swung it open with a smile on my face, laughing about the idea of stretchy pasta pants. I was slightly distracted, which is why it took a moment for my brain to process the face on the other side. When it did, my heart hit my toes and I could do nothing but stare up at him.

He finally broke the silence. "Hi, Rachel."

Heaven help me, his voice hadn't changed at all. My throat and stomach clenched tightly, and I couldn't help but catalog the changes to his face as I gaped. It had lost the last of its boyishness and looked leaner and more mature somehow. There were lines around his eyes that fanned out attractively, and he seemed taller than I remembered.

While I was struggling to both breathe and form a thought, his green eyes rested calmly on my face. He gave the impression that he was totally cool and in no way affected by seeing me, which made me feel oddly hurt and helped me snap out of it.

"Oh, hey, James," I cleared my throat and replied in as cool a voice as I could muster, despite the fact that my heart was flopping around trying its best to restart. I could feel a tremble in my hands and hurried to tuck them into my pockets. His name kept running through my mind, echoing the past.

"Who is it?" Val asked from behind me.

"Uh, it's James," I replied stiffly, my lips numb from the shock. I swung the door open all the way and turned back toward the room.

"James!" Hannah's eyes gave me a quick worried glance as she jumped up to join us at the door, but she was smiling by the time she reached him. "What a surprise."

As she greeted her older brother, I was seriously tempted to walk straight to my room and close the door. Yet I knew it would only give away my true reaction and create drama where there shouldn't be any, so I took my seat back next to Val on the couch.

Val scooted closer to me so that our legs were touching, lending me her understanding and comfort. My body felt stiff, wooden, and frozen all at the same time. I hadn't set eyes on him in at least five years, not since Hannah, Val, and I had graduated from college. I hadn't heard his voice or seen his face. I had liked it that way. And now, on the very night I was going to tell Hannah I was mostly sure I would accept her challenge, he appeared at the door. The one reason I hadn't allowed myself to try again. The one my heart couldn't quite heal from.

"Come on in." Hannah was cheerfully chatting with him as he entered the apartment carrying two large bags of what appeared to be magazines or books of some sort.

As Hannah and her brother walked toward the kitchen together, I was struck anew by the fact that James was a male version of Hannah. They were both tall and athletic, their brown hair streaked with reddish highlights, high cheekbones, a generous mouth, and eyes that crinkled when they smiled. Their family definitely made a mold, and that mold was as handsome and appealing as it had ever been.

As my mind cleared a bit from the initial shock of seeing him, I remembered hearing Hannah tell Val that James had recently moved to town. I wasn't sure what that would mean for me. I obviously couldn't—and wouldn't—ask Hannah to keep her brother away, but as I sat there, I quickly realized that no amount of time apart was going to make me ready to spend time with him on a regular basis like we had before. That instant familiarity we'd had between us had been replaced by awkwardness and its friend regret.

James raised one side of his mouth in a half smile as his gaze turned to Val. Even though I didn't think he'd seen her in a while, he acted as comfortable with her as if he'd just seen her the week before.

"Hey," His smile grew as their eyes met.

"Stuff it," Val replied in a friendly way.

James chuckled, and the sound of it hit me right between the shoulder blades.

I shifted in my seat, wishing that rather than sitting back down I'd gone to my room after all and let him make of it what he would. Now I was trapped here with him, and I wasn't sure I could do it. Apparently, those sayings about how the heart never forgets were based in truth.

Hannah motioned for James to take the chair she'd been sitting in before joining us on the couch. "What brings you here?" she asked her brother.

"Oh, I got a package from Mom today. It should have come to you, but she got our addresses mixed up. Looks like she bought every single bridal magazine in the city, so I brought them over." He pointed to the large bags he'd left on the kitchen counter.

"And so it begins!" Hannah clapped her hands together.

"I am not looking through those with you," Val groaned.

"It would be awfully hard with those claws you have where hands should be," James inserted. Val rolled her eyes.

"That's fine. I have Rachel for that." Hannah patted my leg and smiled at me.

At the mention of my name, James looked at me, and our gazes caught. His look felt challenging somehow, and I lifted my chin a notch, meeting him head on. I was not about to let him see how his presence was truly affecting me.

I must have passed some test of his, because at my look of determination, he seemed to relax a bit and leaned back into his chair. "What are you three up to tonight?" he asked. It appeared he wasn't in a hurry to leave. He could probably smell the pasta and was hoping for some leftovers.

"Rachel was just about to share some news with us." Val blew her choppy bangs out of her eyes and looked at me. I gave her daggers in return. I couldn't believe she'd bring this up in front of him.

"No, no, we are definitely not waiting for Rachel to say anything." I tried to calmly play it off while my eyes frantically begged her to stuff it.

No way in Hades was I going to let James, who was so self-assured and probably dated all the time, and who knew the real reason I was single, be a part of this conversation.

"Val made her famous pasta tonight," I clumsily said to James. I tried to ignore the fact that the first sentence I said directly to him in eons came out in a shaky voice. "You hungry? I can whip you up a bowl." I untangled my legs from underneath me and got ready to stand as I waited for him to answer.

He shook his head and I sank back down. "My new roommate made dinner, but thanks."

"We could always talk cats," Val pushed. I threw eye switchblades at her, surprised she would actually push me about this in front of him.

James raised his eyebrows at me, a clear invitation to tell him what was going on.

"I'm not saying a word," I stated flatly as I folded my arms across my chest. Something was crawling up my throat and threatening to leave my body.

"Fine. I will then," Val replied.

And she proceeded to do just that. At least she was kind enough to leave out that I was considering becoming a cat lady and that's what had instigated the challenge.

As Val talked, I was intrigued to see James's expression change from curious to something I couldn't name. I had no idea what he was thinking. The fact that I could no longer read his face bothered me more than I'd like to admit.

"I think it's a terrible idea. She doesn't need a guy in her life. She'll only get hurt. There are a lot of total idiots out there," Val finally finished in a gruff voice.

"Not helping," Hannah stage-whispered to Val. Val flashed her an unrepentant grin and shrugged her shoulders.

"Are you going to do it?" James asked me directly. His voice wasn't shaky or clumsy like mine had been, which was totally unfair.

"I think it's a great idea," Hannah jumped in before I could answer, but James continued to hold my gaze.

"It's a terrible idea," Val argued.

"You hate men, so your vote is biased," Hannah responded as I finally let my gaze drop away from his.

"I hate men because they're dumb. My vote is based on fact," Val fought back.

"Stop it," I inserted, tired of my roommates arguing. "It's my choice. I wouldn't be doing it for any of you anyhow."

"Meow," Hannah made a clawing motion both in reference to my statement and my future as a cat lady. It made me laugh and took away the tension of the moment in a perfect way.

"I'm doing it," I sighed as I unfolded my arms and gave up on keeping things out of James's earshot.

"You sound super excited about it too," Val teased. I gave her a look.

"Excellent!" Hannah cheered before I could tell Val how much I didn't appreciate her parading my business around.

"But," I looked at Hannah and held up a hand before her celebration got underway, "there have to be some rules here."

"Okay. What did you have in mind?" Hannah asked.

"You said I have to go on twelve dates?"

"Twelve?" James looked at Hannah and mouthed the word at her as though he was asking if she was out of her mind.

"It's a lot," I said. "Maybe even too much."

"It's definitely too much," Val added decisively.

Hannah sighed. "It was just a jumping off number. What do you propose?"

I nervously cleared my throat. I felt the weight of what I was about to say, knowing it would force me out of my comfort zone. I also deeply appreciated the irony of accepting this challenge in the presence of James. Because, you see, if I'd only left fear behind all those years ago rather than pushing him away, there would never have been any need for this challenge now. He knew it and I knew it, and it made me squirm inside.

"The official challenge will be that I agree to date again with an open mind and I agree to let people set me up. But there is no set number, and I get to decide when I've met my quota." Through my entire speech, I kept my hands clasped firmly together. Having this conversation in front of James was making even the backs of my eyelids sweat. It was mortifying on every level.

Hannah gave one sharp nod as she met my gaze. Her expression said that negotiations were open. "I agree that twelve dates may be too much, and I appreciate that you're willing to date. I think there should be a set minimum number, though, so that you don't become a chicken and stop after just two or three." I rolled my eyes. She smiled at my reaction. "I'm serious. What if we say no less than six dates?"

I studiously avoided looking at James as I thought about it. That was really only one date a month until her wedding. I could do that. Actually, I could probably knock out six dates faster than that if I wanted to. I was a strong, professional, decently groomed, and socially adept woman. There was no reason I shouldn't be dating. Also, I was somewhat motivated by how pathetic this was making me look. The knowledge that I was not, in fact, a pathetic person gave me the strength to nod.

"Great!" Hannah clapped and sat forward in her seat. "Now to get a date lined up." I could see her mind working.

"Actually," I cleared my throat for what felt like the millionth time, "Lisa at work said she'd love to set me up with her brother Paul for my first date."

"Paul, huh? Okay. Let's get some info on this Paul guy and set some things in motion." Hannah jumped up to get a pad of paper and a pencil, which was her go-to for any planning session. She meant business.

When I dared glance at James, he merely smiled slightly at me in a detached way, but Val slapped her hand to her forehead in a dramatic gesture. "And all this time I had you down as the smart one, Rach."

I had a terrible time falling asleep that night. As a reward to myself for surviving my first year teaching, I'd splurged on a down duvet that I called my happy cloud of fluffiness. Tonight, even my ultra-comfortable bed couldn't warm away all the emotions that had rushed back when I'd seen James. I could still picture his face, so serious and cool, as he'd listened to us chat about the challenge. Gone were his easy smiles, his teasing, his casual touches to my hand or my back as we chatted comfortably. It was all gone.

Seeing him again had been a stark reminder of what I'd lost, and while I'd felt somewhat empowered when I'd announced my intention to start dating, I felt slightly hollow now. What if I messed this up like I had before? What if all the good guys were taken? What if no one was interested in dating me? What if I really wasn't the strong, capable woman I wanted to be?

Finally, after tossing and turning for a while, I went into the kitchen looking for a drink. I was surprised to find Hannah sitting at the kitchen table, still looking through one of the bridal magazines James had dropped off. The sight of her in her pink pajamas with her hair pulled up made me smile.

"Hey," I said as I entered the kitchen area and opened a cupboard.

"Hey yourself," she replied. "Can't sleep?"

"Nope." I shrugged and filled a glass with water from the fridge.

Hannah sat up straight in her chair, rolling her shoulders and stretching her arms above her head to loosen her muscles. I wished I could stretch away my worries.

"Listen, Rach. I'm sorry that James got sprung on you today," Hannah said as her eyes met mine over the rim of my cup. "I know it's been a long time."

I did my best to smile at her in a way that would say I was fine. "Don't worry about it. He's your brother and he's moved to town. I knew I'd see him sooner or later."

Surprisingly she bought it and puffed out a breath she'd been holding. "Oh good. I was hoping enough time had passed. He's going to be one of Andrew's groomsmen, and I don't want it to be too awkward. I talked to James too, and he said he's totally over everything, so not to worry about him."

Hearing that made my smile wobble, and I took another sip to cover it up. When I was done drinking, I put my cup in the sink and lightly patted Hannah on the shoulder as I passed by her to go back to bed.

"Night," she said.

I spent more minutes than I would have liked that night rehashing James for the millionth time. Had I been right to break off my engagement with him? As I looked back over the years in between, could I really say I had been better off? Had my fears about marriage at such a young age been justified? I had loved him with my whole heart.

In the end, I decided that if James was over us, I would be too. I would force myself to be cool and casual like he was until it felt natural. I would be brave and give it my best. Bring on the dates!

To solidify my newfound determination, I sent Diana a text the next morning telling her I'd decided to do the challenge.

Don't tell mom though, I typed. *She'll start looking for my wedding china.*

I think it was a good choice.
Thanks.
Keep me posted.
Pray for me.
I always do.

Chapter 3

> Love does not begin and end the
> way we seem to think it does.
> Love is a battle, love is a war;
> love is a growing up.
>
> ~ *James Baldwin* ~

Much to Hannah's endless joy, my first date fell on March 1, the first official day of the challenge. Hannah was convinced that fate was telling us this was a great plan. Lisa was inclined to agree. Val made sure she had a shift at the hospital that night as her way of protesting the entire thing. She wasn't happy that I was letting Paul pick me up at our apartment. According to her, it was blind dating 101 to meet at a neutral location. But I felt safe, because he was Lisa's brother. Besides, I was too nervous about the date itself to worry about knowing all the rules of dating after such a long dry spell.

Paul sounded normal when he called, which helped me decide it was okay for him to know where I lived. He'd made plans and seemed to be on top of things. He even cracked some jokes that were harmlessly amusing. All in all, he had played it cool, which helped me think maybe it *would* be cool. His sister, on the other hand, had sent me about 259 text messages. The last one contained a picture she'd drawn of Paul and me at the altar, with "Mr. and Mrs. Paul Nelson" written on it. I was seriously considering blocking her number until the date was over, and possibly forever after that. Lisa kept saying no pressure, but clearly there was pressure—the type of pressure that Sisyphus, the Greek god of eternal rock pushing, would be familiar with.

I heard the doorbell ring a few minutes before 7:00 p.m., followed quickly by Hannah and Andrew's voices loudly and happily greeting our guest. I was perusing pictures of kittens while hiding in my bathroom attempting to slow down my nerves. I lied. I couldn't actually do this or play it cool. Cats were going to be my new life, and I was happy with that. I gulped and mentally slapped myself. No, I was not okay with that. I was doing something scary but good, and it was go time.

I stood up and looked once more in the mirror. I was wearing a casual green dress with flats and minimal makeup. Paul had told me to dress up a little, and Lisa had hinted at the fact that Paul liked girls who were classically feminine but not too showy. Unsure of exactly what she meant, I was trying to channel my inner Audrey Hepburn even as I told myself I should not be trying to create what Paul wanted me to be. He'd either like me or he wouldn't. Those pep talks had died quickly when the reality of dating hit, and I'd agonized for two days over wardrobe and hair styling ideas, causing the feminist rights activists of the past to cry out from the dust. In the end, my hair did what it always did and hung straight down my back.

Hannah knocked on my door a few seconds later. I was as ready as I'd ever be, so I swung it open with a broad smile and nodded my head. Hannah gave me a quick hug.

"I'm so glad you're doing this. Paul seems nice. Plus, he's in the same career field as you, so you should have plenty to talk about. I'm sure his stories about his time teaching English in Asia will be very interesting. And you already know you love his sister, so there's that . . ." Hannah was rambling big time. "Do you want to borrow a little lipstick?" She dipped her head to look closer at my face.

With a soft chuckle, I held up my hand. "I'm fine, Han. It's going to be just fine."

"Okay." She laughed and snapped back up. "You're right. I'm acting like your nervous mom."

We walked down the hall to the living area, where a tall, heavy-set guy with a bald patch right on his forehead stood waiting. His hands were shoved deep into the pockets of his khakis. His button-down shirt looked ironed, and his sport jacket pressed, so over all, he was a man who gave off a slight professor vibe without the hair standing on end. What hair he did have was the same shade of blond as Lisa's, and as I got closer, I could see some of her in the shape of his eyes and mouth.

I walked up to him and stuck out my hand. "Hi, Paul. So fun to finally meet you," I said with a big smile. This was Lisa's brother, and I was going into it with a hopeful spirit.

He smiled back and shook my hand. "Likewise," he replied in a slightly higher voice than I would have expected out of such a large man. "Lisa has been telling me about you for years now." He gave me an amused look, and I smiled at him. Here we were, bonding over the fact that we'd been the victims of matchmaking hopes.

"You two have fun now." Hannah practically shoved us out the door before anything more was said. I looked back at her to see Andrew standing behind her, giving me a thumb's up and a cheesy grin before the door closed.

I laughed awkwardly. "I guess we're off."

The corners of Paul's mouth lifted, but he said nothing. Instead, he motioned for me to walk alongside him. We were silent as we walked out to the parking lot and climbed into a nice conservative sedan. It was silver. *Boring, boring! . . . I mean*—I caught myself—*steady, steady.*

Paul, with complete dedication to all traffic laws, drove sedately to an Italian restaurant called Francesco's about fifteen minutes away from my apartment. It was a step above my usual haunts, so I felt good about that decision. It was nice to feel he'd tried.

What I didn't love was the silence. I mean, really. I tried a few times, but he finally shook his head and in a condescending way said, "We'll have plenty of time to talk over dinner. No need to waste words now." Huh. Okay. I could be quiet.

Paul had a reservation for 7:30, which meant we were a few minutes early due to Hannah practically kicking us out the door.

He tried to slip the host a twenty-dollar bill to get us a seat right away. The man kindly smiled and informed him that money sadly didn't make tables suddenly appear. Paul had the grace to blush a bit as the host motioned to a set of chairs in the lounge area where we could wait until our table was free.

"So, how do you like being back in the United States?" I asked as we sat in the red leather seats, unsure if we were talking yet or not.

He shrugged and smiled as though genuinely thinking about it. "You know, there are a lot of things I missed about the United States when I lived in Asia. But now that I'm back, there are a lot of things I miss about that place. They do some things better than we do here. And vice versa."

I was impressed with his thoughtful answer and smiled. "Yes, like we don't eat cat, so that's a point for USA."

He lifted his mouth slightly, patiently amused. "Yes. That's true. But they are much more polite, so that's a point for Asia."

I wasn't sure if he meant that as a put down, or if we were exchanging funny banter, so I hedged a bit with a safer topic. "Did you miss American sports?"

He shook his head. "Nope. Don't play any."

"So a point for Asia on that? No Sunday Night football messing up the TV programming?"

He smiled again. "Point for Asia. But American TV is much more relatable. Asian TV can be pretty crazy, so I didn't watch much."

"What's your favorite show now that you're back?"

"I found that I don't need TV in my life, so I haven't bothered to purchase one," he said like it was perfectly normal. Well that was a stumper. He'd just eliminated about 80 percent of my prepared conversational topics.

Luckily for me, we were called to our table at that moment. I was scrambling in my head for topics to discuss over dinner and hoping he'd open up a little. It was hard work dragging conversation out of someone you were supposed to be clicking with.

Paul took the liberty of recommending a dish he thought I'd like after we looked over our menu for a moment. Being a lover of Italian food, I was happy to try something new and told him I'd give it a whirl. His smile in response was pleased, but it left me feeling like a pupil who'd given the right answer.

"You're very small though." He continued with a strange smile. "I'll ask if they have a smaller-size portion. Wouldn't want to waste too much food." He chuckled like he'd made a great joke.

I deflated on the inside, tired of my size being the first thing people noticed and the assumptions that usually follow. He was lucky I'd overlooked his glaring bald spot and given him a shot. I didn't reply but sipped my water and waited for the embarrassing moment that was queuing up.

Sure enough, Paul took it upon himself to order for us, but not in the gentlemanly way that makes a girl feel cared for. Instead, he mentioned his "small companion" and wondered if they had something on the lighter side for my "tiny appetite." He may as well have asked them to bring me a bowl of birdseed with a side of worms.

When it came time to order drinks, I inserted, "A strawberry Italian soda, extra whipped cream please," before Paul could tell them I wanted a water glass with a lid and straw.

Paul nodded at the waiter as if to okay my drink order and then smiled back at me as the waiter walked away from our table to give our order to the kitchen staff.

"Now, Lisa has told me some things about you, but why don't you tell me more?" He said, folding his hands together and leaning back in his seat. The talk window had opened.

"Well, you already know I teach second grade with Lisa," I stated, and he nodded. "I really love it. This is my fifth year. I live with two roommates. One of them just got engaged and I'm going to be her maid of honor."

"That's wonderful. She must be so happy. How long did she and her fiancé date?"

"About seven or eight months."

"Wow, that's a long time. I'm surprised he let her drag it out that long before agreeing to marry him."

I was confused. "Eight months isn't that long." I snickered, hoping he was teasing.

"No, I guess here it's not. I'm still stuck in Asia, I suppose, where parents sometimes still arrange things with the expectation that marriage is going to come from it. It goes pretty quickly, because if you already know you're going to marry a certain person, there's no sense in waiting."

"Yeah, there was probably some culture shock coming back home." I tried to smile and give him the benefit of the doubt, but he was being kind of strange.

Our food arrived after we were awkwardly silent for a few more minutes. I should have asked him about himself, but I was terrified to peel back the layers. The food arriving was a relief, because it gave me something to do with my mouth and hands and made it easy to avoid his eyes.

Things were going well while we ate until he reached over with his fork and took a bite off my plate—my tiny, tiny kiddie-size serving—and helped himself to a chunk. I gripped my fork tightly to keep from either stabbing his thieving hand or returning the favor and taking some of his.

Instead, I looked at him, and our eyes met. He was chewing my food with a smile on his face. "That's delicious. I'm glad I ordered it for you."

"Yes, it is. But there's so little of it, so . . ." I let it hang there.

He didn't pick it up. "Good thing too, or you'd be stuffed," he said, laughing. "Lisa said you were small, but I still can't believe just how small."

I sighed. Either living out of the country for so long had messed him up, or he was already messed up to the core. I didn't know. I was too tired of this date to find out. Too bad he had other plans.

"You know, Rachel, one of the best parts about Asia is the tight-knit families. The reason marriages work so well there is that the man makes all the decisions. He is the head of the household, and everyone is expected to fall in line."

Blind Dates, Bridesmaids, and Other Disasters

At this point, I set down my fork, folded my hands, and leaned back in my chair. This was going to be interesting. I was going to remember every single word he said, because it was only in the thought of being able to entertain my friends with the details of this night that I was able to find something about this date to make it redeemable.

"Really think about it," he continued, warming to his subject. "If only one of you makes all the decisions, why would there ever be arguing or contention? There wouldn't be if both spouses accepted that only one—in our case the husband, given he's the patriarch of the home—made the decisions. It's really the western society culture of women that creates divorce. The women in Asia are dutiful and obedient to their husbands. They have great families and low divorce rates. I think we have a lot to learn from them, wouldn't you agree?" As I opened my mouth to speak, he interrupted with, "Oh, of course you agree, you're a smart little lady. Pretty too." Then he tried to wink at me.

I was speechless—tongue-tied to the rafters. There was just no way. This was not happening. I liked myself too much to even consider dating a man who thought that way.

"How long did you say you've been back in the U.S.?" I asked.

"Oh, about six months now."

"Huh," I said as I nodded my head. "Thinking about going back?"

"I don't know. Why do you ask?"

"Oh, just because I think your wife might be in Asia." I smiled syrupy sweet as I picked up my fork and took my last few bites of food while Paul's expression turned from confused to upset.

Almost the second I put my fork down next to my plate, Paul waved the waiter over and asked for the check, signifying the date was over. I totally agreed. I felt a little satisfaction when I didn't even offer to pick up my part of the tab. If he was so into traditional roles, he could pay for my dinner.

As he was paying, I was tempted to leave the table and ask the host to call a cab for me but decided to try to keep it from ending in a way that we could never come back from. I owed Lisa that.

I should have called the cab. At least the silence on the drive home wouldn't have been so heated and filled with disappointment. I waved him away as he pulled into my parking lot and went to open his own door.

"Thanks for dinner, Paul. I'll walk myself up." I quickly opened the door and stepped out.

"I'll call Lisa," he said flatly.

"Please do." I closed the door and walked quickly away. I heard him peel away from the curb and smiled. Date one down, only five more to go.

I was lounging in bed the next morning, scrolling through cat videos on my phone and waiting for the inevitable call from Lisa, when my door burst open and Hannah leapt onto my bed in a blur of hair and flashing teeth.

"I waited as long as I possibly could. I need details, lady!" She laughed and made herself comfortable, sitting with her legs crossed, facing me.

"You know, I think the best thing about the night was that no one was home to give me the third degree when I got back," I teased. She jabbed my leg.

"Val! She's up. Come in here," Hannah yelled out my door.

I heard Val's groan from her room and smiled. Val was not a morning person. I actually still wasn't sure what time of day Val liked.

"We don't have to wait for her. She'll take forever. Just spill it," Hannah chirped.

I liked mornings too, but Hannah was one level higher than me on the chipper scale. She'd probably been pacing the hall outside my door for an hour before bursting in.

"There's not much to tell. He's a Neanderthal, and I won't be dating him again," I said as I sat up and leaned against my headboard. "Also, did you know the internet is full of videos of cats?" I turned my phone screen so she could see. "They're adorable."

Hannah's face fell as she took it out of my hand and set it down out of my reach. "Yes, I did. Was he really that bad?"

"Shocker," Val grumbled from her place in the doorway. "No such thing as a love match on the first try." Instead of coming in, she leaned her shoulder on the doorframe and crossed her arms. A huge yawn broke across her face, ruining her grumpy look.

"But he looked so nice," Hannah whined.

"Looks are definitely not everything," Val said. "He could have been a male model and it wouldn't have mattered if he's a jerk."

"Well, this guy was actually a jerk." I told them the entire story, from the silence in the car to the tiny portions and men running the family. They were both satisfyingly shocked, making noises at various parts and pulling faces.

"I can't understand how Lisa didn't know this about her brother!" Hannah grumped when I was done with my story.

"Well, he's lived out of the country for years. Besides, do you know how James feels about married relationships or how he treats women on dates?" Val asked.

I felt my nerves prickle at the mention of James and dating. It was an awkward topic, and I wasn't about to remind them that I knew exactly how James treated someone on a date and how marriage to him would be. I could promise that it was a million years away from Paul. The thought made my throat ache, and I swallowed hard to clear it.

Hannah played it cool as she thought for a minute, even though she had begun fidgeting with my comforter. The topic was awkward for her too. "I have doubled with him before and he seemed fine. But, no, I guess it's not something we chat about."

"This is definitely not Lisa's fault. She's basically a cherub," I said sadly.

"Does she know yet?" Hannah asked.

"If not, she'll hear soon. I'm expecting her call. Paul was not pleased with me."

"Now don't you go feeling guilty," Val defended. "I know Lisa is your friend, but who cares if Paul was unhappy with you? You were unhappy with him too."

"I know. But Lisa was so excited," I slumped my shoulders and rubbed my eyes.

Even though Val had just told me not to feel bad, she joined Hannah in making commiserating noises. They knew how bad I felt that it hadn't gone well and how important Lisa's friendship was to me.

"Well, back to the drawing board." Hannah slapped my leg, regaining her cheer as she jumped off my bed. "Speaking of drawing boards . . ." and she disappeared into the hall. I gave Val a questioning look. She shrugged.

Hannah was back in two seconds with an armful of the magazines James had dropped off the week before. "Ta-da! Let's look at bridal magazines and plan me the best wedding ever!" She dropped them haphazardly on my bed.

"I'm out. You said wear a dress and smile pretty." Val turned and walked down the hall. I heard her door shut before I smiled at Hannah.

"This seems a little insensitive after my bad date last night. Maybe my feelings are still tender after that, and you're rubbing salt in the wound," I said.

With a sparkle in her eye, she shook her head. "Nice try, my friend. Here are some sticky notes to put on anything you find of interest."

She plopped down on the bed next to the magazines, and for the next several hours, we had a great time showing each other the good, the bad, and the ugly about weddings. We laughed so hard that I forgot all about Paul.

Chapter 4

If it is right, it happens—the main thing is not to hurry. Nothing good gets away.

~ *John Steinbeck* ~

Lisa was seriously groveling at this point. We'd talked over the weekend, and she'd apologized profusely for her brother's archaic mentality. I thought it was all resolved. Yet, when I saw her face first thing Monday morning, it was immediately clear that she'd been stressing all weekend about it.

Another clue that she'd been stressing was the size of the chocolate cake she was holding out to me when I entered my classroom.

"I made it extra big and extra chocolaty. I can't believe he told you that small people shouldn't get to eat as much. Don't even share this with your roommates!" She rambled as she laid her offering on the desk. I knew her baking skills were off the charts, so I smiled and ran a finger through the frosting, licking it off before covering the cake back up again.

"I'm going to take this because I love your chocolate cake, but you really need to forget about it. I'm fine. Paul is fine. You and I are fine." I laughed as I moved the cake to a shelf behind my desk where my ravenous little student wolves wouldn't catch the scent.

I once again thought we were good, but then she spent the entire hour before our students arrived, popping back into my room, offering various ways that she could be my personal slave for a year. At one point, I think she even offered me her husband. I harbored zero feelings of ill will toward Lisa and was totally ready to blow the whole thing off.

"Lisa, stop it," I said the next time she came into my room. "The bell rings in five minutes, and I still have a lot to do. I am not mad at you."

"I ruined everything. This challenge was supposed to be fun, and I was going to prove to you that dating isn't bad by setting you up with a great first date. Instead you had a horrible date and won't want to keep going," she moaned. At last, we got to the root of her actions.

"Yes, I will. Even if I didn't want to, Hannah would keep after me. In fact, I think she's already working on setting up my next date. Please, stop worrying about it. Just worry about how much hand sanitizer you'll need today and whether or not anyone is going to wet themselves."

Lisa finally cracked a smile and managed to look relieved. "We're really okay?"

I smiled back. "There was never a doubt. And I will keep dating."

Her grin grew, and her natural perkiness flowed back into her. "Okay. I believe you. Let's shove some learning down some throats today."

"Cheers to that." I beamed as she walked out of the room, grateful that things were back to normal.

Five days later, I was standing in the middle of a reception hall with Hannah and Andrew looking up at the domed ceiling and trying to decide exactly what that painted cupid was doing to the angel next to him. I was pretty sure I should be offended, but I couldn't quite define why.

It was our weekend of venue searching. Hannah had already dragged Andrew to four others before he enlisted my help. He wanted to be there to help out, but it was obvious that his version of being helpful was driving Hannah insane. She needed a woman's perspective, and since her mom lived a couple of hours away, the maid of honor was the go-to gal on this one.

"Is that angel in danger, do you think?" I scooted closer to Andrew and whispered out of the side of my mouth while pointing up.

"Huh." Andrew angled his head a few different ways just as I had done. "I have no idea."

"What are you two looking at?" Hannah joined us under the dome and looked up. "Oh. What is . . . I'm just . . . that can't be what I think it is . . . right?"

"Definitely not," I stated firmly, aware that giving Hannah a reason to not like this place was going to make life more difficult for Andrew and me. "It's only a fun little painting. So, what do you think of this one?" I grabbed her arm and redirected.

"It's huge! You could have a hockey game in here." Andrew smiled as he looked around. I gave him a "not helping, this is why you had to call me in the first place, keep your lips zipped" look before smiling at Hannah.

"Andrew's right. It is big. Which means you could definitely fit in all the people you love most. That way your celebration would be full and happy without you worrying about leaving anyone out," I said.

Hannah nodded and chewed on her pencil while she looked around. I caught Andrew's eye and he gave me a lopsided grin. I grinned back as he made the zipping his lips sign.

"You're right. But is it too big? I don't want it to feel impersonal," Hannah finally said.

"Well, you have two choices. You could set up all the tables on one end and have a dancing area on the other. Or, if it's just too much, you could search out smaller venues that will give you that cozy feel."

"That one we saw on Wednesday night was cozier," Andrew added.

Hannah nodded again. "True. But we'd have to whittle down our list quite a bit."

"Is that such a bad thing?" Andrew teased. I gave him another look. He turned around and began looking at the ceiling mural. I had to smile when I saw him pull out his phone and snap a picture.

"I guess it depends on what you want from your wedding. Do you want a huge celebration with everyone you know, or do you want an intimate gathering of your closest friends?" I asked.

I was confident that I already knew the answer. Hannah was the type who wanted to spread her joy far and wide. I was going to do my best to encourage her to go for the big place, but it had to be her decision or she'd second-guess it all the way.

She sighed and flipped through a couple of pages of her notebook before settling on the guest list pages. She mumbled to herself as she read over the names and made some marks. Finally, she looked up.

"At the most, I could eliminate about twenty people who I'm not overly attached to. The rest I would feel too bad about not inviting."

"Twenty people are only like two to three tables," I said.

Hannah nodded. "Probably not enough to make it worth going smaller then."

Andrew was back and grabbed Hannah in a hug. "I think we should go big and throw a huge party. Let's make this a night to remember for everyone," he said, lifting her off the ground and spinning her around. She dropped her notebook and pencil as she wrapped her arms around his neck and squealed. I had to give Andrew credit. He wasn't totally useless here.

"Okay, okay. This will be our number-one choice. I just want to take Rachel to one more before we commit." Hannah smiled as Andrew put her down and bent to retrieve her things for her.

"I think that's smart. Let's cover all our options," I replied with a happy look.

"I'm so glad you came!" Hannah smiled back at me.

The next venue turned out to be the back half of an old secondhand bookstore. The room had once been used as their storage area and had cement everything with high, tiny windows and that cold, musty feeling you expect from an unfinished basement.

Blind Dates, Bridesmaids, and Other Disasters

The three of us stood in the center and turned a full circle while the owner of the building stood silently nearby. It went without saying that this place was not happening, but we couldn't just dash out without at least saying we'd looked.

"You know what would really cheer this place up?" Andrew whispered.

"A mural?" I chuckled quietly.

"Yes. With a naughty cupid and a scared little angel," Hannah giggled.

We all laughed for a moment before we saw the owner's face and quickly got back under control. Hannah politely let the owner know it wasn't quite what she had in mind. We were back in the car within five minutes of exiting it.

"Oh my," Hannah breathed as Andrew drove back toward our apartment. "The sad thing is that someone is going to rent that place."

"There are people who think vampire-themed weddings are fun," I offered.

"Maybe a gothic winter celebration?" Andrew added.

"Could you just picture my grandma in there?" Hannah pulled an amused face. "She'd snag her wig on one piece of metal sticking out of the wall, her slip on another, and end up being bald and naked before she'd even found her table." When the hilarity died down, Hannah was the first to speak. "Oh, hey, Rachel, I almost forgot. I have a date lined up for you. I have been doing this lady's hair for a while now, and all she talks about is her cute son, so I showed her your picture this week, and she is all for setting you up with him. I gave her your number and told her I'd let her know when I'd talked to you. Then she'll give your number to her son."

"Oh, okay. Wait, what picture did you show her?" I asked.

"The one of you in the bounce house at that neighbor boy's birthday party." Hannah smiled as I groaned.

Just great. The one time my size comes to my advantage, and my roomie snaps a picture and shows it to prospective dates. I knew exactly which picture she was talking about. I was wearing shorts, a white T-shirt, and a smile the size of Noah's ark as I flew into the air. My hair was static central and rose above me as I jumped, spreading everywhere.

"You're adorable in that picture, and you know it," she stated.

"I'm not sure that guys who are looking for bounce house party girls are the guys I want to date." I pulled a face. "Do you know anything about him?" I asked.

"His name is Brian. He's about our age. He still lives at home, because he just finished school out of state and is back here looking for a job. But he's not one of those failure-to-launch guys who lives with his mom forever. He's really into motorcycles, and I think he does some racing. He's cute. I've seen his picture."

Well, none of that sounded too bad. And since the ball was already rolling, I supposed I was along for the ride.

"Okay. Sounds good. I'm in." I smiled at Hannah, who had been turning to look at me from the front seat.

"Perfect. I'll let his mom know we've talked. You can expect Brian to call."

Brian did call—about two hours after Hannah told me about him. He seemed friendly, energetic, and eager. The entire time we spoke, I was picturing a cocker spaniel. We set up a date for the following Friday, one week away. He said maybe we could do something active. Active was fine as long as our definitions of active met up. Knowing what I did about his love of motorcycles, I was slightly unsure we'd be on the same page. I promised myself not to worry, and Brian promised to call Friday afternoon to let me know where to meet up with him.

I failed at not worrying—miserably. I must have asked Val and Hannah five times each what their definition of active would be. Val said she wouldn't be surprised if he picked me up on his motorcycle and took me to the racetrack. She didn't seem to think that the fact it was March in the Rocky Mountains would be a deterrent.

"Dress warm," she'd said, laughing.

Hannah said it could be something as simple as miniature golf or an art class. Andrew's face was doubtful as he sat next to her listening in. I trusted Andrew's face more than I trusted Hannah's hopeful thoughts.

In the end, it didn't matter. Brian called as promised, just as school got out on Friday. I was walking through the parking lot toward my car, feeling grateful that a bit of spring sunshine had peaked over the mountains. He sounded a little strange when he told me who he was, and I stood beside my car rather than getting in.

"Brian?" I questioned, doubtful I'd heard him correctly.

"Yesh," he replied in a mumbled tone with a slight lisp.

"I'm so sorry, but I'm having a hard time hearing you." I sat my bag on the roof of my car and used my free hand to plug the ear that wasn't next to the phone, hoping to hear him better.

"That'sh becaush I wash in an ashident Tueshday," he pushed out.

"Oh my goodness. Are you okay? We can totally reschedule!" I mostly felt horrible for him, even if a solid 35 percent of me was completely relieved at the thought of not having to go on a mystery active date.

"No, no. I really want to go out with you. Can we change our plansh?"

I was confused. Why would he still want to go out with me? "Um, okay. What did you have in mind?"

"Here, I'll pash the phone to my mom," he mumbled. My stomach dropped. This was a bad sign, having his mommy set up the date for us. Just what exactly had happened?

"Hi, Rachel?" A woman's cheerful voice came on the line.

"Uh, hi, yes." I didn't even try to keep the uncertainty out of my voice.

"Hi. So Brian was in a pretty serious accident and isn't really mobile right now, but he was so excited about meeting you that he's hoping you'll still be willing to get together tonight." She tittered lightly like this was no big thing. "What would you say to dinner and a movie at our house?"

"Uh, well..." I thought it sounded awful, frankly. I didn't even know this guy. How awkward would it be to sit on his couch while he recuperated and try to make small talk with his mom? I was no good at that kind of thing, even with people I loved. "I'm really fine to reschedule."

"Oh, I won't bother you at all, if that's what you're worried about," his mom laughed again. "I'll leave you two totally alone."

This was not a concern I was having—until she said that. What if she didn't leave us alone and I had to chat with her all evening too? I shuddered inside at the thought. This was not cool. Mystery active date was looking more and more attractive in comparison.

"Oh, no," I hedged. "I'm not worried about you leaving us alone. It's just that—"

"Great. I'll make you dinner, and you can just show up looking beautiful," she cut me off before I could finish my thought. Probably because she knew what my thought would be.

"Um..." I wasn't sure how to reply. Before I fully realized what was happening, I heard traitorous words leaking out of my mouth. "I hate to have you make me dinner. I can bring some take out." I swallowed back a moan. What had I done?

"That would be so thoughtful. Sure. Brian really loves meat. Hamburgers, steaks, that sort of thing. I'm sure whatever you choose will be fine. He said you were planning on seven. Does that time still work?"

This was officially out of my control. I refused to acknowledge that it was my own fault for not standing firm. I usually didn't have a problem with being a pushover, but somehow I was now picking up a steak dinner to take to my incapacitated blind date at his mom's house. The word "blind" stuck in my mind, and I wondered if his accident had involved his eyes and he really was blind now. A sliver of panic rose up, and I cleared my throat.

"Mrs. . . . ?" I had no idea what her last name was, so I tried to glide over that. "Um, look, the more I think about this, I'm not sure tonight is such a good idea." This was a man I'd never met and had no business nursing.

"Oh, nonsense!" his mother said firmly. "I've been a *loyal* client of Hannah's for several years now. If she recommended you, then I'm *sure* everything will be fine." She paused significantly. "So I'll see you at seven?"

The line had officially been drawn, and Hannah had been dragged right through it. The message was clear. If I didn't show, then this lady wasn't going to keep giving Hannah her business. I was angry but felt trapped and used.

"Yep. That will work. Just text me your address, and I'll see you both then."

"Great. And thanks, hon. This will really cheer him up." She clicked off her phone, and I continued staring at mine for a moment.

Well, that had been interesting. There was no way I was going to tell Hannah about this. She'd feel awful and tell me to forget the date. However, with her wedding coming up, I knew money was tight, and I wouldn't ask her to give it up just so I could avoid what was going to be a majorly uncomfortable situation. I was a big girl. I'd handle it.

Just then, Lisa came walking past me to her car. She waved to me, but my mind was wandering a million miles away. Intrigued by the look on my face, she changed course and came over to see what was going on. I told her about the phone call, leaving out the part about basically being blackmailed into the date. I was heartsick enough over it without having Lisa get all fired up too.

"Oh, wow. She didn't say what happened or what his injuries are?" Lisa asked.

"Not a word. I have no idea what I'm dealing with here. He could be in a hospital bed for all I know."

"Maybe he just broke his leg and has to stay off of it," Lisa offered.

"He had a lisp." I pulled a doubtful face at Lisa. Her mouth formed an *O*, but she didn't offer any reply. "I don't see how this night is going to go well," I grumbled.

Lisa tried to rally as she gave me a small smile and a pat on the arm. "The good news is that he won't try to put the moves on you."

"Gee, thanks," I said tongue-in-cheek. "I appreciate the silver-lining moment."

Lisa gave my arm a squeeze and went to her car as I mentally thought over restaurant menus. I could at least make sure my dinner was delicious since the company would most likely be unpleasant.

I pulled up to Brian's mom's house at 7:00 p.m. straight up, with a steaming bag of take-out from Harry's Steakhouse. It smelled so good that my mouth was watering just thinking about digging in.

Unsure if this was really a date, and despite Brian's mother's hint, I hadn't tried overly hard to look my best. I wasn't even sure my "date" could see me. I was in jeans and a flowy top that was all about comfort and less about style.

I took my sweet time exiting the car and making my way to the door. The door was answered before the doorbell had finished dinging by a polished and pressed woman who looked to be in her mid-thirties. I knew she had to be older if Brian was in his mid-twenties, but I could see that Hannah had done an amazing job of keeping this lady perky and relevant. I felt like I'd been bamboozled. There was no way she was going to drop Hannah and risk trying to find someone else who could make her sparkle that brightly.

"Oh, Rachel, you're just as cute as button." She swung the door open and gestured for me to come in. "And that food smells divine. Brian will be so grateful. He's in the basement. Follow me. Do you need plates or silverware or anything?" She turned and started walking toward the back of the house.

"Um, plates and silverware might be good," I said as I tried to talk my clenched muscles into relaxing.

"Great. I'll get you settled with Brian, and then I'll bring you down a couple of things. Just this way, hon," she said over her shoulder as I followed her through the kitchen to the stairs that led down.

For the record, I hate it when people call me "hon."

I followed her into a well-lit basement room. It was clearly a recreational use room since it had a pool table, a ping-pong table, and a huge sectional couch with a big screen TV. Brian was sitting on the couch. He saw us coming and tried to sit up, but it was difficult since he was immobilized by his injuries. Both of his arms were in casts. He wore a neck brace, and there was bandaging around his forehead. My stomach sank so hard that I wasn't sure I'd actually be able to eat. This poor guy was in no condition to be hosting anyone.

"Here she is. Isn't she just as cute as she can be?" his mom said as she pushed me in front of her. I hugged the takeout bag to my midsection and tried to smile.

Brian tried to smile too, but it looked like his teeth were stuck together. Under the bandages, his hair looked to be beach-boy blond. His eyes were blue, his skin tan, and his body showed that he was obviously active. There were several bruises along his jaw, and he had one huge black eye. Even all mangled up he was a great-looking guy. However, the more I saw, the worse I felt for him.

"Hi, Rachel. I'm sho glad you could come," he said.

"Looks like you're pretty banged up," I said, smiling nervously.

"Oh, yes," his mom inserted. "He broke both arms, some ribs, strained his neck, got a nice big gash on his head, and they even had to wire his jaw shut because it broke. Poor guy." His mom helped him prop up on some pillows while she ran off the list of horrors this guy was experiencing.

And I'd brought him steak. On his mother's recommendation. I felt terrible. The situation seemed to decline with every word that came out of someone's mouth.

"Well, I feel silly that I brought steak and potatoes then." I lifted up the bag as I said it. "I'm so sorry."

"Oh, don't be. He loves steak. I'll take care of everything," his mother said. "Why don't you give me the bag, and I'll get it all done." She took the bag from me and turned to go back upstairs. "The movie is in, ready to go. Just hit play. I'll see you in a jiff." Just like that, she was gone, taking all the energy in the room with her.

Brian gestured toward the couch with his knee and I took a seat. "How'd you get hurt?" I asked, because it really needed to be asked.

"Motorcycle crash," he mumbled.

"Must have hurt a lot."

"Oh, yeah."

I supposed that asking for more conversation from a guy with a wired jaw was just rude, so I pointed to the TV. "Want to watch the movie?"

He seemed relieved and nodded. He pointed to the remote with one of the puffy fingers sticking out of his cast, and I picked it up.

"I really would've been happy to reschedule," I insisted one more time, the guilt burning a hole in my throat.

"I know," was all he said. Yet, as his gaze met mine, I was sure his mother had bamboozled us both. Somehow knowing we were on the same side, both thrown into a no-win situation, made the tension drain out.

"So we make the best of it?" I chuckled in relief. He did too.

I hit play. Predictably, it was a movie about motorcycle racers. Normally not my thing, but I was not about to complain. If he could physically suffer through this date, the least I could do was watch a movie of his choice.

It would have been fine if we could have gotten through the movie without more appearances by his mom, but it wasn't to be. She popped down with table settings and then back up. Next, she brought me a throw blanket so I wouldn't get chilly. I wasn't cold—I was hungry. Finally, she brought our meals down. Mine was served artfully on a plate. Brian's was in a large cup full of a lumpy gray substance.

"Thank goodness for blenders, huh?" His mom winked. "He can still have meat. I just pureed it up with the potatoes and some water to make it runnier so he can suck it up the straw. Dinner of champions!"

I almost hurled up my own first bite as I heard him take a slurp of the meat shake. It kept clogging the straw, and he'd have to suck a few times to get it out. Occasional whiffs of it would pass my way and make my stomach churn. Odd how on my plate it all smelled delicious separately, yet glooped together, it smelled awful.

Eventually his mom came down to clear our dishes and bring me a slice of the cake she'd baked. Even though Brian seemed like a decent guy, I was so ready to run screaming from the room at this point that I didn't even bother to thank her.

"Okay, you two. I'll leave you alone now for the rest of the night. But you have to promise me, no hanky-panky down here." She winked at both of us and left.

Honestly, I'd rather he tried to kiss me than having to listen to him sucking steak through a straw. The real grand slam happened when the movie ended and I stood to leave. He heaved himself out of his seat and, once he regained his balance while standing, stiffly bowed at the waist—like a butler in the days of old, or like people had to do when meeting the queen.

"Thank you for coming," he said when he'd straightened slowly back up.

It had to have hurt like crazy to bow like that. His obvious pain on top of the fact that no one had ever, ever bowed to me, made the entire thing hysterical. I managed to keep from laughing, but a huge grin broke on my face.

"I thank you for having me."

I felt laughter—crazy, shocked, disbelieving laughter—trying to claw its way up from my gut. I couldn't bear to hurt this poor guy, so I turned and practically ran out of the room, up the stairs, past his mom in the kitchen and to my car. I made it there before melting into hysterics. I couldn't believe it! Somehow this date had been just as bad as my date with Paul, yet in a completely different way.

Brian seemed okay—meat sucking aside. But I didn't see either of us contacting the other for a second chance. The entire thing was so awkward that I was willing to bet he wanted to pretend it never happened. I was more than fine with that.

Date two, failure two. Only four more to go.

Chapter 5

> It doesn't matter who you are or what you
> look like, so long as somebody loves you.
>
> ~ *Roald Dahl* ~

Time flowed quickly from March into April, and soon I wasn't grimacing when I thought about my dates with Paul and Brian. Hannah kept me busy going over even more magazines and helping finish up her guest list, because Andrew simply could not talk about it anymore. He'd given her his list of guests and would tag back in when the subject matter changed.

April came in with rain and a dreary feeling that took away from the excitement of spring. And, of course, with the rain came my first flat tire in about five years. When I left the school late on a Tuesday night, I was greeted by my car sadly tilting to the right in the drizzly half-light of dusk.

I opened the door and grumpily threw my things into the car before turning back to the tire to take in the damages. I didn't know enough about cars to care about why it was flat. I just knew you couldn't drive on a flat tire. Luckily, my dad, when it was time for me to move away to college and gain some independence, had taught me how to change a flat. I also knew there was no use in crying over something you couldn't undo, so I took a deep breath and popped open the trunk.

"Oh, that can't be good." Lisa's voice surprised me enough that I barely missed knocking my head as I bent over and was fishing around for tools.

I looked up at her, standing warm and dry under her umbrella, with her cute perky blonde curls and big eyes. I shrugged a shoulder and turned back into the trunk.

"Um, can I help you with anything?" she asked timidly.

"No. I know what I'm doing. It's nice of you to offer though," I replied. She really didn't need to stick around. I knew she didn't really want to help but felt compelled to because of our many years of friendship.

"Um, I guess I could call my husband," she offered. At that, I barely managed to keep from snorting out loud. At least she'd lifted my mood.

I popped back out of the trunk, arms loaded with the jack and lug wrench, and grinned at her while some rain ran down my face. "Does he even have a driver's license?" I asked.

"Well, no. He thinks cars are bad for the environment." She smiled back at me.

"Kind of him to let you drive one then," I teased. I turned and walked over to the flat tire, deposited the tools, and came back to get the spare tire.

"He's really great with flat bike tires. Car tires can't be that much different." Lisa followed me back and forth.

"Great. I'll add him to my emergency contact list for days when I'm biking." I lifted the spare out of the trunk and set it down. I rolled it over to the flat and just stared at it for a minute.

"I could hold the umbrella over your head and try to keep you dry while you work," Lisa offered. I nodded. Sounded good to me. I wouldn't mind not being totally soaked when I was done.

I let out a big sigh and looked down at my darling, darling, professionally put together outfit. It was my only actual pantsuit. It was a soft and beautiful dove gray, with a fitted jacket, a pink silk shirt, and the cutest little belt you've ever seen. I wished so bad I had a change of clothes around. I even briefly considered asking Lisa to take me home to change and then come back.

"Today was my annual review with Principal Higgins," I said in reference to my lovelier-than-usual attire.

"Yeah, you looked really cute today." She nodded in understanding, glancing from my clothing to the rain-soaked asphalt.

"I'm going to need a moment to mourn the loss of these pants," I said sadly. "I went two entire months without ordering guacamole and tortilla chips to pay for these."

"Teacher's salaries require sacrifice," Lisa agreed.

We were both quiet for a minute before I finally finished my farewell and knelt down. I then began tugging, pushing, pulling, groaning, lifting, twisting, and all-around sweating as I got busy with changing that flat tire. Sometimes I wished I had Val's muscles and general anger to help get these types of jobs done.

Lisa seemed immune to the effort required and decided this would be the perfect time to chat. Of course, she wanted to talk about my dates, my hopes for the future, my *feelings* about the challenge, and if I had any prospects lined up. I finally gave a loud groan and looked up at her.

"Lisa, I'm kind of busy here."

"Oh, sorry. You're right. I just wondered if you have anyone lined up yet?"

"If I did, I would've made sure to request that he was extra muscly, and then I'd call him over here right now to finish this job for me," I grunted.

"You know, I have an idea for someone—" she began.

I shook my head as I gave a final heave and patted the spare tire before standing up. "Nope. I'm good," I stated firmly.

"Well, okay. It was just an idea anyway. My other brother—"

"No, Lisa. No more brothers." I lifted one side of the flat tire to stand it on end and tried to roll it to my trunk. It was much heavier than the little donut spare had been. Add to it the fact that it had no air in it and I was rolling a big blob of squishy that was totally unwilling to follow any kind of straight line. "In fact, no family members at all," I huffed.

"It's not my brother, silly. I'm smarter than to try that again. It's his roommate. I can't remember his name right now, we're not friends really, but I know he's a good guy and is single. My brother mentioned that he hasn't dated for a while and wondered if I knew anyone."

I finally managed to wrestle the flat into my trunk and glanced down at my clothing. Ruined. I was sadder about the loss of my outfit than I'd been about the loss of a tire. For my birthday this year, I was splurging on Triple A.

I sighed. "I think Hannah is working on something right now, but if things don't pan out, I'll think about the roommate, okay?"

Lisa smiled. "It's a deal. You'll really like him. He has a good job, and he's not too young or too old. My brother says he's the best roommate he's ever had, and he's really picky about who he'll live with."

I slammed my trunk shut. "Thanks for the help, Lisa." I smiled at her and wiped my hands on a towel I found in the trunk. "I think I'm going to call it a night. I'll see you tomorrow?"

"Never underestimate the power of an umbrella and some good conversation," Lisa chirped, fully aware that she'd been absolutely zero help. "Until tomorrow." She waved as she walked to her car.

I drove home using the towel to protect my steering wheel from the grease on my hands and went straight to my bathroom, where I stripped down, threw my poor, ruined, beautiful outfit in the garbage can and got straight into the bathtub.

The best thing Val, Hannah, and I ever did was to make the move a year ago into a three-bedroom, three-bath apartment. It had taken several years out of college with good jobs to make it happen, but I loved my little oasis.

Surrounded by bubbles and finally warm, I allowed thoughts of the day to float from my mind. I'd worry about flat tires and future dates tomorrow.

Four days later, I was in the grips of a head cold, courtesy of the second-grade germ swap that always comes with the change of seasons, compounded by a night spent changing a tire in the rain. Val and Hannah had agreed to clear their Saturday plans and have a chick flick movie night with me. We were all more excited about a girl's night than it warranted, and I knew it was because all of us realized that these days were coming to an end as Hannah's wedding drew nearer.

Since I was sick, I got to choose the movie. I went with a classic: the timeless *Beaches*, starring Bette Midler and Barbara Hershey. Val made chicken noodle soup, and Hannah brought some licorice and our traditional chocolate-covered cinnamon bears. My contribution was in the form of a carton of orange juice and three boxes of tissues. Cold aside, we would need them.

Flopped on the couch in a state of total disarray, we were about three-quarters of the way through the movie, tears already rolling down our faces, the dialogue sometimes drowned out by a sniffle, when there was a knock at the door. All three of us wiped our noses, sniffled together, and looked at the door. A second, louder knock came, and then a muffled voice.

"I know you're in there. I can hear the TV," a voice I really didn't want to recognize said.

My heart constricted a bit as Hannah sighed and heaved herself off the couch. "It's James. I'll get rid of him. Horrible timing!" she grumbled as she went to open the door. She opened it and all but pushed him into the hallway, blocking his view of us with the door. Their mumbled conversation didn't reach us.

I was trying desperately to remember that both James and I were totally over our past history and that it didn't matter why he was there, but I could hear the low timbre of his voice, and with it came emotions best left buried. Suddenly uncomfortable, even though he was standing outside the door, I sat up and tried to pat my hair back into place. It wasn't easy since I was a full twelve hours into crash mode.

Val gave her eyes and nose another wipe and stood up. "May as well get another glass of water while we have a break. You want more orange juice?"

I nodded and reached for my empty cup. "Thanks Val." I coughed into my elbow.

She turned her head away from me and counted to five out loud before looking back toward me. It was her way of trying to keep from inhaling the spores of sickness I'd sent flying her way even though I covered my cough.

She gingerly took my glass from me with two fingers and walked into the kitchen. Hannah and James's voices were still going strong. I could tell by the tone of her voice that she was annoyed, but I couldn't hear what she was saying. I was grateful it was taking a moment, because I'd been able to get over the initial start of knowing it was him and settle back down.

They were still talking when Val came back with our drinks. "Wonder what that's all about." She looked toward the door just as it opened and James strode in behind Hannah.

He was dressed casually in jogger pants and a T-shirt. I berated myself for noticing both how good he still looked after the years that had passed and how he'd matured. The sloughing off of his last bits of boyishness had changed him in a good way.

It was clear from Hannah's face that she was annoyed. "He insists that Mom wanted him to pick up some of the magazines he'd brought over since he's on his way to her house this weekend. No, she apparently simply cannot wait until next weekend when Andrew and I go visit. No, he will not go away. No, he will not wait in the hall." She sent him a look and stomped down the hallway to her room. "No, it doesn't make sense that he has to leave town Saturday night at nine o'clock. It would make more sense to make the drive tomorrow morning." Then she was gone.

James seemed pleased to have both gained entrance and bothered his sister at the same time as he seated himself on the chair. "Looks like I interrupted a real tearjerker," he said as his gaze landed on the tissue pile in the garbage can we'd placed next to the coffee table.

"*Beaches*," Val stated, offering nothing more.

"Ah, haven't seen it. Heard enough about it from girls I've dated to know that it's not my thing," he remarked with a casual shrug.

As soon as he mentioned girls he'd dated, my breath audibly caught a bit. James's gaze swung to me, and I watched his throat work as he swallowed. Even though his expression stayed neutral, it was obvious that I wasn't the only one feeling awkward in the moment.

"You too tough for that kind of movie?" Val asked with a smirk, rescuing us both as his attention moved back to her. "I must say I'm surprised. You strike me as the kind of guy who'd watch a sappy chick flick to score points with a girl."

"I think you have to achieve a certain level of . . . um . . . affection for a girl before you're willing to do stuff like that." He smiled dismissively.

"Let me guess, you've never reached that level of affection," Val said mockingly, knowing well James's and my history. It shocked me as much as his statement had.

James made a face. "Sadly, Valerie, I have not."

Val cracked a smile at his comeback, but all I wanted to do was sob into my pile of tissues. I remembered a time when James would have held me close and watched any movie I'd wanted to watch. To hear him say he hadn't met someone worth watching chick flicks with made my heart pound and my anger rise. I knew it was a lie, and I couldn't decide if the comment had been designed to poke at me or not.

Val appeared to be oblivious to the side play as she cracked up. "I can't say that I'm surprised. A serial dater like you doesn't take the time to really get to know a girl before he moves on."

"Not true." Hannah's voice joined us as she came back with a bag of magazines in her hand. She dumped them into James's lap and sat down on the couch. "James hardly ever dates these days. He's too picky. No one is good enough for him," she teased. Her good humor seemed to have returned to what it normally was with her sibling—annoyed one moment, bantering the next.

"I date," he said in a casual tone.

"You just have to run an FBI background check, have three good references, her income statements, and her religious beliefs before you'll even ask for her number," Hannah went on.

"Again, not true. I'm just against blind dates," he replied. "Not worth the risk."

As I listened to the easy banter between the three of them, I realized I'd overreacted. This wasn't about me and past James. It was about three friends teasing each other. I could join in, or be left out.

"So how do you meet girls then?" I asked, genuinely interested. His gaze flew to me like he was surprised I was there. I was kind of surprised that I'd joined in the conversation myself.

"Let me guess," Val jumped in before he could say anything, "at the gym." Val and Hannah cackled. James's only response was a small, close-mouthed smile, although his eyes crinkled up a little at their teasing.

"He doesn't meet girls—that's the problem," Hannah said. "He's at our mom's house an awful lot on Saturday nights. Pretty suspicious for a self-proclaimed ladies' man."

"Laundry night. Must stay fresh for those ladies," he joked. Even Val laughed at that, and I managed to grin.

"Maybe he'll date more now that he lives away from mommy," Val teased.

"You have to actually be looking to find someone," Hannah added.

"I look," he defended. "You just don't know about it because I do it in person and not through friends or behind a computer screen."

"Huh. Well, if you tried getting set up, you might actually get a date," Hannah smirked. "It's been working for Rachel."

James looked at me and shrugged. "If that's how Rachel wants to go about it, then that's her choice." His tone of voice said he truly didn't care.

I was jealous of how cool he could play it. For all appearances, it looked like it had been the truth when he'd told Hannah he was totally over everything that had gone on between us.

"Gee thanks," I rolled my eyes and muttered, trying to keep it light before coughing again.

Rather than reply, he stood up abruptly and grabbed the bag that Hannah had given him for their mom. "I'll catch you guys later. I have a long drive ahead."

Hannah and Val waved at him as he showed himself out. I didn't bother, because his eyes had never come back my way.

Val, already forgetting about James, hit play before he'd even reached the door. I was worried that I wouldn't be able to get back into the story, but I underestimated the power of the sadness and beauty of this movie about the depths of friendship.

But for me, the tears were more than that. For a long time I'd carried a lot of guilt over breaking James's heart. I listed myself as the reason we were both still single. I thought I'd hurt him in the worst way possible and wondered if he could ever forgive me. But tonight, and the last time I'd seen him, he'd played it totally cool, acting as though I no longer factored in his life. If that was true, then I really was free. I could stop beating myself up and take him at face value when he said he was over it.

When the movie was over and the tissue boxes were as empty as our tear ducts, we sat in silence for a moment before Hannah broke the stillness.

"James is wrong, you know. There is nothing wrong with online dating. I hadn't really thought about it, but we should totally set you up on a singles site," she said, turning to face me. "What do you think?"

"Oh, um, I hadn't really thought about it," I said. It was true. I hadn't. So far being set up by people had worked just fine. However, I could see that pool drying up before my dating challenge was over, so maybe I should consider a dating site.

"I think it's a bad idea. Half those men are married and the other half are weirdos." Val stood up and started clearing the empty glasses.

"Well, there has to be one dating site that isn't bad." Hannah tapped her lips with a perfectly manicured finger and looked at the ceiling while she thought.

"There's one that some of the other nurses at work use," Val stated quietly, almost like she was hoping we wouldn't hear.

Hannah and I both swiveled to face backward on the couch toward where Val was standing in the kitchen. Our faces must have been hysterical, because Val's face expressed her pleasure in surprising us.

"What?" she asked. "Well, if she's going to do it despite my warnings, then as a friend, the least I can do is make sure she gets set up on a decent site!" She threw her hands in the air.

I was so surprised to hear Val say that that I immediately agreed to do it. "Okay, let's do it."

Hannah whooped. "Yes! I'll be right back with my laptop." She was off before I could even think about the mistake I was probably making.

"What's the name of the site, Val?" Hannah asked before her body had even made it back to the living room.

"I think it's The Setup dot com," Val answered as she sat next to us on the couch.

Hannah started typing and scrolling, busily doing things we couldn't see, her face alive with excitement. "This is going to be so great. I just know we'll find someone for you, Rach. The men are going to be beating down our door as soon as they get one look at you."

"I don't see how the internet will magically make that happen. I've been walking around for twenty-seven years with this same face and nothing like that has happened." I laughed and then sneezed into a tissue.

"That's because you weren't wearing a sign listing all of your great qualities. We put your face on the internet, along with a sales sheet, and the guys will love you," Hannah said over the clicking of her keys. "Okay, I found it. It looks legit. We need to set up your account. What do you want your username to be?"

"Oh, um, can't it just be my name?" I asked.

"Really? Rachel Stevens?" Hannah gave me a look. "No one will even click on that. It has to be something cute and catchy."

"How about fairy teacher?" I asked.

Val and Hannah busted up. "If you don't see anything wrong with that, then you really are spending too much time in second grade," Val said between breaths.

I blushed as I realized how simpleminded it had sounded. My mistake. "Fine then. I have no idea what to use."

We all sat for a moment thinking on it.

"Okay, here are the things we know about you. You're talented, educated, cute, and fun with a great sense of humor," Hannah said. That made me sound pretty great.

"How about fun educator?" I said. Val and Hannah shook their heads.

"Honestly, Rach," Val cleared her throat as her lips twitched, "I don't think you can help us with this. Your ideas are way too . . . um . . . naive."

I sighed, aware she was right. "Fine, it's not my fault I live my life with crayons." I stood up to get more tissues for my runny nose.

"That's it! That's perfect." Hannah clapped her hands.

"What?" I stopped walking and turned to look at them.

"We'll call you Life In Color." Hannah smiled and began typing again.

And that's how the user LifeInColor, with a profile picture of a tiny fairy lady in the bounce house, came to the online world looking for love. I wasn't sure if it would attract anyone. More than that, I wasn't sure if I wanted the type of person it would attract. But that ship had sailed, and now I was just along for the voyage.

Chapter 6

> I have learned not to worry about love;
> but to honor its coming with all my heart.
>
> ~ *Alice Walker* ~

As luck would have it, despite my reservations, I had a surprising amount of interest shown on my online dating profile. Hannah, Val, and I spent an hour or so looking through the five guys I thought I'd be willing to go out with and finally narrowed it down to one named Justin. Correction: I agonized while Hannah and Val perused the guys and gave their opinions. How on earth was I supposed to choose someone based on what could have been totally made-up information? At least I had someone vouching for them when I was set up on a blind date. Then again, vouching hadn't exactly gone well so far.

If Justin had a last name, I didn't know it. His username seemed normal, and there were no pictures of him wearing an eye patch or snuggling a pet parrot, so he appeared to be safe. We set up a date for the first Friday of the month. Val advised me to stop watching the news for a few days leading up to the date in order to keep from stressing too much about being kidnapped. It was not helpful in the least. I pretended to be annoyed by her comment, but in the privacy of my bed at night, I prayed my heart out that I would come back alive.

Justin called the night before the date and asked me which movie I'd prefer to see out of a few currently playing and if I had any food allergies. I'd never been asked about food allergies before, but I was somewhat impressed by him thinking to ask. I'd given him my choices, and he said he'd take care of the rest.

Not wanting a total stranger to know where I lived, I arranged to have him pick me up in a grocery store parking lot a few blocks from my apartment. He told me to park in a certain area and that his car was red and I'd "never miss it." Val, deciding it would be her duty to get a first look at who this Justin person was, insisted on following me to the meet up.

Promptly at six o'clock on Friday night, a bright, cherry-red muscle car with two white stripes going across the hood toward the windshield screeched into the parking lot and came to an abrupt stop near my car. It had to be Justin. He was right; I'd never have missed this car.

Val, who had parked next to me, stepped out of her car before I could get out of mine. She walked around to meet him, wearing a huge frown on her face. It probably came as a shock to Justin to be expecting the girl whose picture he'd seen but instead be met by an angry-looking, almost-six-foot-tall woman wearing scrubs. I gave him points for never batting an eye. Val gave him a clear once-over before nodding back at me as I came around to stand near them.

My first impression of Justin was that he seemed a little slick. His dark hair was combed straight back from his face with some sort of gel, his jacket was a really shiny faux leather, his pants were something other than denim, and his smile was bright enough to blind you. But hey, he was clean and smiling. I was certain I could work with that.

"Rachel, you're as pretty as a princess." He smiled as he reached out and shook my hand. I returned the smile in acknowledgment of the compliment. I felt as pretty as a princess in my flirty purple tunic, black leggings, and knee-high boots. Another choice I'd agonized over.

"Thank you," I replied.

"Are you ready to go? Make sure you have everything you need for a long night of fun." He smiled that huge smile again.

"I'm good," I replied as I lifted the jacket I had slung over my arm and put my purse over my shoulder.

I turned to Val and gave her a weak smile. I was nervous to be going out with a total stranger. I'd been less nervous about moving away to attend college with no one I knew. At least with my first two dates someone had been connected to them in some way. Val gave me a big smile and nodded her head.

Justin and I walked up to the fully restored muscle car. It was old enough to be something my dad would have driven as a teenager. I could tell he loved it, because it was shiny enough to see my reflection in it, and there wasn't a dent or ding in sight.

"Isn't she pretty?" Justin rubbed his hand along the hood as we got near the car.

"Yes, I love the color." I nodded.

"I've given my lifeblood to bring her back." Justin opened my door. "She's a 1971 Chevy Chevelle SS Custom fourspeed." He stood holding the door, listing all the details long after I'd sat down in the car. Oh boy.

I smiled and nodded, maybe even patted the dashboard a time or two, until he finally closed the door, walked around to the driver's side, and got in. The engine revved loudly as he started it up. He looked at me and grinned as he pushed the gas pedal a few more times for me to hear it again. I wasn't sure what he was hoping I'd do. It sounded good to me. I mean, it was running, and none of the tires were flat. So, yeah.

He all but laid a strip of rubber getting out of the parking lot, and we made our way into traffic. Then, rather than turn toward the downtown area of the city like I'd expected, he looked at me and smiled again.

"I hope you're okay, but I decided to surprise you with a plan change."

My stomach sank a bit. "No dinner and movie then?" I asked.

He smiled even bigger. "No dinner and movie. I think you're really going to like what I have planned though." He reached over and squeezed my hand before I gently tugged it back. "You game?"

I was, in all honesty, not feeling game at all. I was seriously considering asking him to take me back to my car. Who knows what this guy had planned? I took a few deep breaths and reminded myself that I was stepping out of my comfort zone and trying to be open to new people. I supposed I should make the best of it. Having made my decision, I nodded my head and settled back into the seat.

"Awesome!" He pumped his fist into the air and hit the gas pedal again, flying down the street like lightning. Before I realized where we were going, he was making good time up the freeway onramp.

"Hope you're okay with this, but I brought along some road tunes for the drive," he said over the load hum of his engine. He waved a tape in my face—yes, a cassette tape—but I wasn't able to see what it was before he happily put it into the tape deck and hit play.

Disney songs burst out of the speakers loudly enough that they drowned out the engine rumble and road noise and made me jump in my seat. Not just any old Disney tunes, but Disney love songs. It was rather jarring to hear Jasmine and Aladdin belting out *"I can show you the world"* as we sped down the freeway. Even more jarring, and slightly alarming, was that he insisted on singing along just as loudly. Everything about this moment in my life was loud—loud engine, loud song, loud singing, and my heart beating loudly in my ears.

"You can relax," Justin shouted my way. "I'm not taking you somewhere to murder you or anything." He wiggled his eyebrows and grinned. When I did nothing more than smile weakly back at him he added, "Feel free to sing along. I'll bet you won't find anything else that makes you feel as good as a Disney song."

I tried to play it off by shaking my head and smiling at him. Instead of letting me be, he kept reaching for my hand and trying to swing it along between us to the time of the music. I'd tug it away after a ridiculous moment, and then when the next song came on, he'd reach for it again.

The tape had two sides, which meant I was blessed with a thirty-second reprieve when he popped it out and switched sides. I bought myself an extra thirty seconds by asking if he was thirsty. I couldn't believe that his voice hadn't given out with how loudly he was singing along. I was sitting on my hand by now, but he'd still try to snake his hand under my leg and snatch me back, all the while singing and smiling. It was the longest hour of my life. Yes, we drove for an entire hour.

We finally ended up in a small town called Easton. It was nothing but potato fields and small houses. I suspected we'd crossed over the state border at that point. We were definitely nowhere near Pine Ridge. He'd said he wasn't taking me away to murder me, but I couldn't imagine any other reason he'd have brought me here.

Justin kept belting out the songs until we pulled up to a tiny city park, and he finally turned off the engine.

"We made it. What a ride, huh?" He smiled as he jumped out of his door and came around to open mine.

I agreed that it had been quite a ride. The sun was getting lower in the sky, and my stomach was screaming at me. I jumped out of the car, careful to keep my hand away from his, and surveyed the area. It was a grassy field with a baseball diamond on one side and a forlorn-looking children's playground on the other. I didn't see any bathrooms, which was a concern, because I knew I had another hour-long drive ahead of me to get home, and my bladder was about as big as you'd expect in someone my size.

"I hope you're hungry. I packed us a picnic." Justin smiled again. He was awfully smiley.

"Oh, great. I'm starving." I was genuinely grateful we'd be eating.

He walked around to the trunk, popped it, and pulled out a huge basket with a lid and a large handle. "Follow me." He gestured toward the park, and I walked alongside him to the middle of the grassy area.

He set down the huge basket and opened the lid. On top of everything was a blue-and-white checkered picnic blanket, which he pulled out and flapped a few times before setting it down. He gestured for me to sit, which I did, hoping there was something delicious in the basket.

He knelt and pulled out a decent-looking picnic. I was incredibly relieved. There were sandwiches, soft drinks, chips, and some fruit in cups. I may end up dead later, but at least it wouldn't be from hunger.

"Hope the sandwiches are still okay. I forgot how long of a drive it is to get here," he said as he handed me one. "Egg salad is my favorite, but it doesn't travel well."

Oh, dear heaven. I took back my earlier happy thought. I was going to die, but it would be in this city park from food poisoning, not from being murdered. I was hungry enough that I opened my sandwich and sniffed it. I wasn't sure if I should eat it or not, so I set it aside while I gave it some thought. I picked up a bag of potato chips and tore it open.

Justin smiled around a big bite of sandwich. I took a deep breath and did my best to smile back before putting a few chips in my mouth.

The only sounds for a few minutes were the crunching of my potato chips and him making satisfied sounds as he chewed his sandwich. Guess he really did love egg salad. He loved it so much that he ate my sandwich too when he saw it still sitting there. I didn't try to stop him, even though I'd almost talked myself into eating it. I hoped his car wasn't a stick shift, because if he got sick, I wasn't driving us home.

I helped myself to the cup of fruit and enjoyed the silence. The sound of him thoroughly enjoying egg salad was better than the operatic Disney performance I'd endured. In fact, now that we were sitting there and my stomach wasn't rumbling quite so loudly, I was able to appreciate the millions of stars that were beginning to pop up in the dusky sky. As I relaxed a little, I started to find Justin's singing more amusing than mentally imbalanced. Until . . .

"Do you like stories?" Justin asked, interrupting my ponderings.

I found the question odd since he knew I was a second-grade teacher. Not to mention the wording of it. Adults ask if people read or if someone likes books. Not if people like stories.

"I do. I read stories a lot to my class," I responded.

"Great. I brought a few I thought you might like. Lay your head on my lap and look at the stars, and I'll tell you some stories." He patted his lap.

Um . . . (a) no, and (b) eww. I was seriously considering standing up and walking home.

I shook my head. "You know what? I'm good right here. But you are welcome to read if you'd like," I stated.

He patted his lap again and tilted his head. He most likely thought he was being charming. "Are you sure? I'm very comfy," he coaxed.

"I'm good." I smiled a bit and cracked open my bottle of soda. "Hard to drink lying down."

"Okay. Well, at least look up at the stars while I read," he said as he opened the first book.

I looked up and almost burst out laughing at the return of the absurdity. I did not mention that this was crazy but instead listened politely while I sipped my root beer and daydreamed about picking out my new kittens.

The books were good ones. I'd read all three of them to my class at one point or another. I was no longer invested in this date, so I didn't feel the need for conversation. I was gazing at the stars, sipping some soda, and enduring.

I'd zoned out enough that I wasn't prepared when Justin reached for my hand for the millionth time, and he was able to make the grab. I quickly looked at him. He rubbed the back of my hand with his thumb as he contemplated me.

"Rachel, how did you feel about those stories?" he asked in an oddly gentle way.

"I really like them. I've read them before." I half smiled, trying to tug my hand away.

"Wonderful. I'd love to hear your thoughts on them."

"What do you mean?" I succeeded in pulling away my hand, but now his hand was on my knee. I shifted.

"I mean, what do you think the deeper meaning is behind those books I read you? Nothing is as simple as it seems at first glance." He smiled and shifted my way a bit.

"The raccoon is scared to go to school, so his mom kisses his hand." I raised my eyebrows and clamped down hard on the sarcastic tone that was begging for release.

"What do you think the mother's kiss and the raccoon's fear represent?" he pressed as he leaned further into me.

I couldn't help it. At this I did laugh. "A kiss and a scared little boy?" I shook my head.

Justin sat up straight and gazed away, his jaw moving around a bit. Apparently, I'd hurt his feelings or something. I wasn't sure. Then, like a lightning strike, he turned back to face me and came in for a kiss.

I squeaked and backed away as fast as I could, but he grazed my cheek a bit. "What are you doing?" I exclaimed.

He shrugged and smiled again before reaching into the basket. He acted as if he'd just waved a fly away, not tried to kiss me. "If you don't want to talk books, I have another thing planned," he said cheerfully.

I was completely uninterested in what he was going to pull out of that basket next.

He pulled out a deck of cards and started shuffling them. Okay, cards. I could do cards. It was getting late, and I was getting cold, but cards I could live with if at the end of the game I got to leave.

"How do you feel about strip poker?" He looked at me and wiggled his eyebrows a bit. "I never lose."

Nope. I jumped up. "Sorry, with how long the drive was, I think we'd better head back." I quickly put my garbage in the basket and began tugging on the blanket to get him off it.

"Well you're no fun tonight," he stated. "It's not even that late."

I didn't reply. Newsflash, he was no fun either.

I had the picnic basket packed in record time and we were on the road again. I had to go to the bathroom, but I wasn't about to make this trip home take any longer than it absolutely had to be.

"Do you have any road tunes for the drive back?" I asked, hoping to avoid talking to him at all. Every time he opened his mouth, it just got worse.

He smiled, clearly delighted that I'd asked. "All I brought was my Disney, but I'd love to listen again," he said.

"Sure. That's great." I tried to smile back.

We left Easton behind in the fumes of American muscle and with the echoes of Snow White telling us how sure she was that someday her prince would come. And you'd better believe that the first thing I did when I got home was deactivate my online dating profile. No thanks, strange world. I'd be sticking with setups and snagging my own dates from then on.

A week later, on a Saturday afternoon, I officially found out how I was going to die. It was going to be suffocation at the hands of a gerbera daisy and its partner in crime, calla lily. The entire living area of the apartment was full of flowers. I hadn't counted, but I was guessing somewhere around thirty arrangements of varying sizes covered every available space. The smell had gone from pleasant, to overpowering, to needing a gas mask in a matter of minutes.

"You've got to be kidding me," I groaned as I opened what felt like the hundredth knock at the door to be greeted once again by Andrew's dark hair peeking over the top of some flowers. "Maybe stop shutting the door all the way when you run out to get more flowers."

"Good tip," he replied from somewhere inside the bouquets. "Where should I put these?"

"Wherever you can find a space." I gestured around the room even though I knew he couldn't see me.

"Think you could take a couple?" he asked. I reached for one that I thought would most likely free up his vision. I guessed right and was rewarded by his smile. "Thanks."

I leaned the door closed behind him, figuring Hannah would be coming with an armload as well, as he walked around finding places to set his bouquets. Hannah had taken flower selection to the next level.

"Are there any flowers left in Pine Ridge?" I asked Andrew's back.

He shook his head and chuckled lightly. "It wouldn't surprise me to hear we've cleared out every florist in a twenty-mile radius."

"She can't look at pictures?" I teased. I wanted to be grumpy, but the more flowers Andrew brought in, the more amusing this endeavor became.

"She did. And then she bought the ones she liked best to make sure they really are what they seem to be." Andrew stopped and cocked his head. "Or, something like that."

Hannah burst through the front door, her reddish-brown hair in a fluffy halo around her, holding a copy paper box full of papers. One glance told me that they were invitation samples. I knew who would be looking through all this with her, and her name was spelled R-A-C-H-E-L.

"Did you get all the flowers, babe?" she happily asked Andrew as she kicked the door closed behind her. At least she was being cheerful about the whole thing. She was doing things on an epic scale, but she wasn't acting like a diva.

"I did." Andrew took the box from her, and Hannah smiled up at him.

"This is so exciting. I'm loving actually seeing all these flowers. I feel like I can really make the best choice now," she chirped.

Andrew smiled softly at her and leaned down for a quick kiss before she began perusing the room. He carried the box into the kitchen and set it down under the kitchen table, which was the only free place where someone wouldn't trip over it.

"Uh, Han? Don't you think this is a little overboard bordering on crazy?" I asked as I gestured around the room.

"I get how it looks that way. Pictures just weren't doing them justice, you know?" She leaned in to sniff something pink.

"Okay. How on earth did you pay for all this?" This question seemed very pertinent to me, especially considering she had rent to pay.

"I got creative." She smiled and picked up something yellow. "Some of it was with money. But I'll also be giving a lot of free haircuts, manicures, pedicures, waxing . . ." She let it trail off as she rubbed a yellow flower against her face.

"You just let her do this?" I whispered to Andrew as he came to stand next to me.

"I love her," he said, shrugging.

He had a point. Darn it, I loved her too. She was my best friend and had been for many years. I guess I could support her in her flower strangeness. It's not like it would be the first foray into Crazy Town for us. I smiled as I watched her happily surrounded by flowers. The picture of joyfulness she made helped me shift my mindset from observing to participating, and I began following her around, sniffing and touching petals too. I had no idea what exactly we were looking for, but I was going to help her find it . . . and then she was going to buy me some Benadryl for my efforts.

"What in the name of Mother Nature . . . ," Val's voice entered the conversation as she popped in through the front door. "Did the Garden of Eden return to the earth and claim our apartment?" She stood still, just looking around and soaking it all in.

"Yep. Careful where you look. We're wearing nothing but strategically placed leaves!" I cracked from behind a bouquet. Hannah and Andrew were in stitches.

"I feel like I fell into a potpourri sachet and someone sewed it shut with me inside. I'm going to be sick. I could smell it all the way down the hall," Val pronounced.

We laughed harder as she strode over to a window and opened it. She went to the kitchen to open the sliding glass door, mumbling about Hannah losing her mind and Andrew being so smitten he couldn't see the nose on his face.

"I'm choosing flowers. Come help." Hannah's eyes were bright with excitement.

Val shook her head. "Oh, no. Pretty dress. Big smile. Nothing said about flowers." Val pulled a kitchen chair out to sit down and stubbed her toe on the invitation sample box.

The three of us lost it at the look on her face. I'd thought Hannah and Andrew were crazy, but seeing them through Val's eyes made everything that much more hysterical.

"Do I even want to know what I just banged my toe on?" Val tilted her head down to look under the table.

"Probably not," Andrew said with a smile.

"This entire house is being taken over by this wedding!" Val complained, but I knew it was half-hearted and hoped Hannah did too.

"It'll go faster if you come help sniff," I said to Val. "Seriously. A honker like yours could be a real asset," I teased.

Val finally huffed out an amused breath and shook her head. "I don't know why I ever thought living with you two would be a good idea."

Even though she refused to move from her seat at the table and actually sniff or touch anything, Val was surprisingly helpful. She said it was because of her time at the hospital and seeing which flowers held up well, which made the room stink, and which were the most popular choices. Hannah, Andrew, and I weren't about to question her reasoning. We were just happy to have her helping.

Over the next hour, we managed to whittle the thirty bouquets down to ten. It was slow going, but it was progress. I shuddered just thinking about the task waiting for us in that box under the table.

Lucky for me, just about the time my nose couldn't sniff one more time, my cell rang. It was my sister, Diana, and I took the opportunity to escape for a minute.

"Hey, Diana." I let myself out onto our balcony and deeply inhaled the fresh air.

"Hey. You been exercising? You sound winded."

"Nope. I've sniffed about thirty bouquets of flowers about a hundred times. I'm trying desperately to get some fresh air into my lungs."

"Well, that's . . . different," Diana said slowly.

"Not much really surprises me these days," I said, laughing.

"Wedding planning?"

"Exactly. What are you up to today?" I asked.

"Well, I wanted an update on the dating challenge, but I didn't think you were telling Mom about it."

I giggled. "You're right. I'm afraid she'd start monogramming towels with our initials before I'd even gotten home from the date."

Diana made a sound of agreement . "I hate to admit this, but you're smarter than I was when I was dating. I told her every detail.

It ended up being a big circus some days. So, spill it. What's been going on?"

I told her about Paul, Brian, and Justin. She was the perfect audience as she gasped and threw out a "No way!," "You're kidding!," and "Oh *my* gosh!" a few times before I wrapped it up.

"Jeez, I remember dating being kind of a pain, but I didn't go through anything like that," Diana said when I was done with my tale telling.

"Imagine what Hailey and Heather will have to face if dating gets any worse," I teased. Diana made a gagging noise that made me laugh.

"So what are you going to do now?" she asked.

"I don't know. My last date was the worst. I'm not sure I'm brave enough to go out with any more guys right now. I'm not even sure I'll ever be able to watch a Disney movie again."

"Can't say that I blame you," Diana agreed. "Are you going to beg off?"

"Believe me, I've thought about begging off. It's probably all I've thought about in the week since my date."

"But . . . ?" Diana prompted when I grew quiet.

"But James moved to town," I admitted.

Diana made a sympathetic noise. She knew my story, and I was grateful that she immediately understood that having him around again would change some things for me and probably motivate me in ways I otherwise would have ignored.

"Just seeing him again, and seeing how he's over everything, well, I think Hannah was right to challenge me, and I don't think I want to give up yet." I was mildly surprised to hear those words come out of my mouth directly after I'd finished telling her about such awful dates.

"Even if the next three are all that bad?" Her question was serious, but I could hear the teasing tone in Diana's voice.

"The thought did occur to me. I keep thinking about how you asked me what I wanted out of life. I'm still not there, and I can't say after three dates that I really gave it my all. Unless it keeps getting worse, I'm going to keep trying."

"Well, good for you. I think you should."

"I think I have to. I can't stay stuck in the past anymore."

"So, who's next?"

"Well, actually, Lisa has someone she's been wanting to set me up with." I told her about Lisa's idea, and Diana agreed it would be better than someone online again. We chatted a few more minutes and then said goodbye. I was glad she'd called.

When I hung up the phone with Diana, and before I could lose my nerve, I shot off a text to Lisa.

You have the green light to set me up with your brother's roommate.

Lisa's reply was almost instant.

Sorry your last date was so bad. But yay!

I hoped I would feel *yay* myself when it was all said and done.

Chapter 7

Love is of all passions the strongest, for it attacks simultaneously the head, the heart, and the senses.

~ Lao Tzu ~

It took a bit of time for Lisa to get the arrangements made for my setup with her brother's roomie. Turns out said roommate wasn't too fond of blind dates. I'm not sure what swayed him, but I certainly understood his worry about agreeing to it and in no way took it personally.

During the waiting period, Lisa had done nothing but talk this guy up. He was, according to her, the best looking, the funniest, the kindest, the most selfless, compassionate, witty, charming man to walk the earth. He was so good with children, the elderly, and the downtrodden that I was surprised he hadn't been called back to heaven. The strange part was that I wasn't sure she'd actually met him personally.

Regardless of whether she had actual knowledge of him or not, her constant chatter did the opposite of making me excited to meet him. Instead, I was beginning to despair. I didn't think of myself as bad looking, but I certainly wasn't in the league of angelic volunteer super models, which is what this guy sounded like he needed to be dating. I began to rethink my idea of ditching the dating site. There was something to be said for going out with a total stranger. Lisa's buildup was seriously wigging me out.

In an effort to make things more comfortable for me this time around, Hannah and Andrew had offered to come along and make it a double. I quickly agreed. We decided bowling and dinner afterward would be a great way to go. It would keep us busy with an activity, with the added bonus that we could play one game if it was awful, two games if it was going well. Andrew would drive, which would prevent me from being held hostage in a car again. Our plan seemed faultless.

In honor of the occasion—and the fact that I couldn't risk being blah—I'd gone shopping and bought some cute new jeans and a top. I let Hannah style my hair and do some heavier makeup than I typically wore. She even put on some super heavy-duty lipstick that was supposedly going to stay there until the day I died, or until I washed it off with a special soap. It was all the rage in Hollywood, so I puckered up.

As I looked in the mirror one last time before we left, I was pleased with what I saw. I felt a little different than my usual self. My long black hair had some wave to it, and the darker eye makeup she'd used really made my blue eyes stand out. I decided the new look was good, because I wasn't sure typical Rachel was going to pull it off with this guy.

As Andrew drove, Hannah distracted me by going over a few wedding details. It didn't keep my hands from gripping each other tightly, or my nerves from jumping around in my stomach, but it helped.

Flowers and invitations had been chosen. We'd spent another day or two shopping around for just the right florist to pull off the vision. We'd picked a photographer after perusing about a bazillion websites each night after work and then interviewing three. The busy days had passed so quickly that it surprised me to realize that today was the last Saturday in April. Time was flying!

With a photographer chosen and a date set for the engagement photos to be taken, we were on to discussing shoot locations. I'd been voting for city hall. It sounded tacky, but in Pine Ridge, the city hall was a beautiful gray rock building with a white domed roof from the 1800s. I loved its history and charm. Andrew wanted to do the botanical gardens in neighboring Paradise—aptly named. Hannah was thinking up the canyon near a local lake.

We had just settled on the botanical gardens—time to throw Andrew a bone—when Andrew parked the car and pointed to a red brick townhouse a couple of doors down. Hannah and I had been so busy going back and forth between the options, her facing slightly backward, that we hadn't paid much attention to where we were going. In fact, I'd typed my mystery date's address into Andrew's phone and let him do the driving so Hannah and I could chat.

"We're here." Andrew put the car in park and turned off the engine.

"Really? Already?" I looked away from Hannah and out my window. It was a nice, well-cared-for townhome community, but nothing I was familiar with.

Hannah faced back forward and looked out the windshield. After a brief silence, she made a funny noise. "This can't be right."

"It is, babe. Look at the address if you want." Andrew passed her his phone so she could check the address.

"No way. This definitely can't be right." She sounded a little dazed as she mumbled under her breath.

"What's going on?" I asked, her reaction making me nervous.

"You know what? I'm sure it's nothing. This is a big community, and a lot of people live here. Plus, I think most of these are three bedroom, so there could be a lot of, you know, roommates in the same townhome." She turned to face me in the back seat and gave me a thumbs-up sign.

"I am not getting out of this car until you—" I started to say.

"Oh my gosh! I just realized—" Andrew interrupted me. His eyes were getting large, and Hannah gave a quick shake of her head before he could finish up.

"Go on, Rach. We'll be waiting right here." She smiled at me again, but it felt forced and made my heart beat harder. She knew something, or at least was worried that she knew something.

What I knew was that Hannah was going to be really stubborn about this, so I let out a dramatic sigh, kicked open my door, and stomped up the sidewalk to the unit marked 718. My stomach was in knots. I was about to meet the most perfect guy alive according to Lisa, and back in the car my best friend and her fiancé were stressing over some mystery while they watched me closely. I had a bad feeling about this.

I reached up a shaking hand and knocked on the door. I heard some footsteps and then the door swung open to reveal a fairly handsome guy who looked to be about my age. I was instantly relieved. He looked normal.

"Hey there, you must be Rachel." He reached out a hand and we shook. Immediately a smile broke out on my face. I was going to be okay. I had no idea what Hannah had been freaking out about.

"Yeah, I am. It's nice to meet you. Are you ready to go?" I asked.

"Oh, no. I'm Lisa's brother, Chad. It's my roommate you're here to meet. Although I have to say that if I didn't have a girlfriend already, I'd be pretty jealous of him tonight." His compliment was harmless and kind as he smiled again and swung the door wider.

As he called to his roommate, I had a chance to quickly glance over him. If I'd done that when he first opened the door, I would have known he was Lisa's brother. He had the same curly blond hair and smile as Lisa. Drat. I was still in waiting mode. All I could do was try not to lose my cool as the nerves returned.

Just as I finished letting out a slow, deep breath, I glanced up and forgot my resolve to be calm. I was definitely about to lose it in a bad way. Coming down the stairs was a familiar face. He was looking down, watching his step, but I knew he was handsome all right. I also knew he was kind and considerate and, really, most of those things Lisa had said.

"Hey there—" he looked up with a smile on his face right as he hit the bottom landing, but his greeting and smile were cut short when he saw me standing there. He'd been holding a jacket over his shoulder, and it dropped along with his hand as his expression turned to one of shock. His head tilted a bit to the side as if he didn't trust what he was seeing.

My date was none other than James Redmond, brother to Hannah, my former boyfriend. No, it was worse than that—my former fiancé.

Luckily, I'd had a short second to put it together before he saw me. I'd used that blip of time to try to shake off the surprise. However, I could hardly make my voice work around the sudden dryness in my throat. "It looks like you're my date?" I asked—no, stated—in a stilted voice.

The shock on his face was quickly replaced by a look that caught me off guard for a few seconds; a look that was impossible for me to read. One thing I did know was that he was as surprised as I was, and it wasn't necessarily a happy surprise for either of us. A new worry entered my mind. Would he humiliate me by slamming the door? I didn't know how I wanted him to react or what I wanted him to say. This was an ultimate no-win situation.

"You?" James said in barely more than a whisper.

"Who?" roomie Chad asked.

"I thought you didn't do blind dates," I said with a shaky giggle, ignoring Chad and trying to figure out how this happened.

"I was bullied into it," James replied with a slight lift of the corner of his mouth.

"That's just what a lady wants to hear when she picks up her date for the evening." I tried to crack a joke, hoping it would help me relax at least a little. It made James smile fully, but it didn't reach his eyes. The tension was still there.

"How do you two know each other?" Chad inserted.

"We've known each other for years." James still had his eyes on me as he answered, almost as if he couldn't quite believe I was standing there.

I couldn't tear my eyes away from him either. I wasn't sure what he was seeing as he looked at me, but it seemed that my eyes couldn't get enough of this unexpected chance to really study him. Between the time passing and how much Hannah had done me up, I was sure he saw me as a stranger. Who was I kidding? We'd broken up a little over seven years ago. I practically was a stranger to him.

"I look weird, don't I?" I felt the words tumbling out uninvited. It was a statement more than a question, and I felt embarrassed to have said it. He just shook his head but offered no comment.

"Hannah and Andrew are in the car waiting," I interjected into the silence. It was too uncomfortable. I had to say something.

He glanced over my head toward the parking lot, his expression changing to bemusement. "This night couldn't get any stranger," he mumbled.

"Tell me about it."

It was the craziest, most heartbreaking twist of fate, and we just kept standing there, unsure of what to do. It felt like the universe had thrown us full circle, but with so much history, we were paralyzed with feelings that we couldn't possibly make sense of.

"Well, you can't cancel the date," Chad said, reminding me that he was still standing there too. "Not after all this planning and prodding." He sounded concerned.

James's expression snapped back to coolly detached, and he shrugged casually as he looked back down at me. "With Hannah and Andrew coming along, I'm still up for bowling and dinner if you are," he said to me. I read his tone like a challenge and figured I wouldn't show my weakness if he didn't.

"Why not?" I replied rising to the bait as I grandly gestured out the door toward the car. Hey, two old friends could enjoy a night out with other friends. This didn't have to be as big of a deal as I was making it.

James pushed his arms quickly into the sleeves of his jacket as he stepped out onto the porch next to me and said goodbye to a still somewhat confused Chad. The look on Chad's face as he closed the door made me chuckle.

We didn't really have a chance to say anything else to each other before Hannah jumped out of the front seat of the car and met us on the sidewalk. She looked hesitant and concerned, but as she came closer her face relaxed into a smile, her eyes dancing. She was clearly relieved that James hadn't sent me packing and that we both looked relatively okay with things. I couldn't focus on what Hannah was saying to James as I tried to take a few deep breaths without anyone noticing.

James opened both the front and back doors of the car for Hannah and me to get in and then walked slowly around to let himself in the other side. So slowly, in fact, that I couldn't help but think he wasn't as relaxed about this evening as he appeared to be. When he got in, he reached forward and gave Andrew a handshake over the back of the seat.

"Hey man. How crazy is this?" Andrew smiled at James.

James looked at me, and his eyes were unsure for the first time. "Small world, I guess. I had no idea that Lisa knew Rachel."

"We teach together. She's my best friend at work," I explained. "I had no idea she knew you. She couldn't even remember your name."

"All Chad told me is that I was meeting Rebecca, or Rachelle, or Ra- something." He shook his head and chuckled lightly. The sound of his amusement caused a tingle in my chest that was very unwelcome. I didn't want to remember his laugh.

"We don't have to do this if you'd rather not," I suddenly said, turning to face him. "I know it's weird."

Hannah and Andrew remained silent while James looked at me. His cool look slid quickly back into place. "I have no reason to feel weird about this."

It hurt more than it should have.

I gave a quick nod. "Okay," was all I managed to say before I turned and faced forward.

James looked away from me and began talking animatedly with Hannah and Andrew while we drove to the bowling alley. Everyone else seemed so relaxed, but I was having such a difficult time releasing the tension that I sat back in the seat and gazed out the window as we drove.

I could not believe my blind date was James. Given my dating struggles these past weeks, I wasn't that surprised to find out my setup wasn't turning out how I'd planned. I just wasn't sure yet if this twist was a welcome one. I was feeling relieved that he wasn't a crazy person, but I also knew that this date had the power to hurt me a lot more than the others had. The others had been harmless because my heart hadn't been involved.

Hannah, Andrew, and James kept up a comfortable stream of chatter on the drive to the bowling alley, for which I was grateful.

When we arrived, James and Andrew were quick to step up and pay for the games, for which I was not grateful. It was bad enough that we'd been thrown together. I didn't want him to have to pay one cent for me.

"We can go dutch tonight," I said to James as he was reaching into his wallet.

He looked down at me and time froze as old memories crashed down around us. I could see them playing across his mind too. He had always, from day one, insisted on paying for me. And I'd always, from day one, insisted I could pay too, even though I had secretly loved his desire to take care of me. This was a conversation we'd had a million times, in a million places, but never with tension and awkwardness between us. I held out the money I'd pulled out of my pants pocket, but he shook his head and turned to the cashier.

"We'll need a size six shoe for her and a twelve for me," he said as he handed over some money.

It brought a bittersweet feeling to know he still remembered my shoe size. Guess we weren't total strangers after all. I thanked him as he handed my shoes to me.

By the time we'd changed our shoes, James had apparently shaken off our shared memories moment and was prepared to make the best of this night.

"I get to choose everyone's names," he said as he finished tying the shoelaces. He shrugged off his jacket and draped it over the back of the bench we were using as he stepped up to the computer screen.

"Um, veto!" Hannah retorted as she went to stand next to him and pulled a face. "You always come up with the worst names." James just pulled up one side of his mouth in a half grin and started typing.

I moved to stand behind Hannah, and Andrew came to stand next to me. Hannah quickly scanned what James had entered so far. "So am I Flopsy, Mopsy, or Cottontail?" she asked.

I looked at the screen to make sure I'd heard correctly. The names he'd chosen were actually really clever. I heard Andrew chuckle next to me. When I turned to see what he found so funny, my eyes crashed into James's. He had also turned at the sound of Andrew's mirth. I smiled without even thinking about it.

"Let me guess. You're going to be Mr. McGregor?" I said to James, referring to the farmer who tried to capture and eat the rabbits in the children's book.

"You got it!" James turned back and finished typing in the last name.

"Nice," Andrew said.

"Because you're expecting to kill us all?" Hannah made a face that said she thought he was being particularly lame. Typical sibling stuff.

"Basically." James gave her a competitive look. "Hannah and Andrew are Flopsy and Mopsy. Rachel, you get to be Cottontail."

Andrew and Hannah playfully groaned as they walked away to pick balls. I chuckled as I followed along.

The first game was close. Flopsy and Mopsy were holding their own against Mr. McGregor. I, on the other hand, was lagging seriously behind. I had no skills at bowling. The balls were always too heavy, they never actually rolled where I aimed them, and I couldn't stop thinking about how there had been a study done showing that a lot of nasty things had been found in the holes of bowling balls.

Losing and bowling ball germs aside, we were having a better time than I'd believed possible. Andrew and Hannah were both competitive, and although I remembered that James typically wasn't, I knew that when it came to letting Hannah beat him, he couldn't help but try to win. It went against the way of all big brothers to let their little sisters beat them.

Having something to focus on instead of each other helped keep the tension down. By the time the first game drew to a close, James and I had finally managed to relax a bit, and we agreed to play a second game.

James started telling a few jokes and teasing Hannah and Andrew. While he was more cautious with me and I knew nothing was suddenly fixed, I began to hope that we could find a way to be around each other. With the wedding coming up and the fact that James was now living in town, we wouldn't be able to avoid it.

Hannah and Andrew tried to include me by chanting, "We need a bowler, not a lame-o roller," after my ball went straight to the gutter. I appreciated the efforts and snickered along with them. I was sure that despite Hannah's cheerful actions, she knew how awkward this was.

We were on frame eight out of ten, with me standing next to the ball return lining up my shot, when the lights suddenly dimmed and a loud voice came over the speaker announcing that it was now 8:00 p.m. and disco bowling would start. A mirror ball dropped from the ceiling, followed by black lights. Funky disco music suddenly blared from the speakers. The four of us looked at each other and started laughing. Andrew whistled, and Hannah cheered.

James's amusement turned into more of a choking sound after a second, and he pointed at me while looking at Hannah. Hannah and Andrew both looked at me. Andrew smiled as Hannah let out a loud whoop and came to my side.

"Um, you know what happens when black lights hit something white?" she asked, giggling breathlessly.

"Oh, you mean like my pale skin?" I surmised sarcastically.

"No, I mean like your white bra glowing through your shirt." She gestured in the general direction of my chest, and I looked down. The new shirt I'd bought was a dark maroon color. Apparently, the fabric was more breathable than I'd thought, because glowing eerily through it in all its glory was my bright white bra.

I laughed as a blush crawled up my face. "Oh, this is just great," I said.

I looked up at James, not knowing what to expect. His face had returned to its cool detached expression, and he was walking toward me with his jacket in his hands.

Somehow, him wanting to cover me up rather than joke along with us made me blush harder than I had in a long time. He draped his jacket across my shoulders, careful to keep a distance between us.

"Want to keep a little mystery, right?" he said in a casual tone close to my ear, causing goose flesh to rise.

I was grateful for the darker lighting as I slid my arms into his jacket and pulled it tight around me. His smell hadn't changed one bit in all those long years. The heaviness and size of his jacket wrapped around me was at once familiar and strange. I wanted to close my eyes and breath it in, but I held back. I knew I would regret it when daylight came. No use traveling down that path.

In the end, Hannah won, which she crowed about on the drive to the restaurant, all through salads, all through her main course, and while she ordered dessert. James suggested that married life might be harder on Andrew than he'd originally suspected.

Dinner was good but more stilted than bowling had been. Fortunately, Andrew and Hannah mainly held up the conversation. I was quiet, having nothing to distract me from the myriad emotions running through my mind and heart. How I wished I didn't know that he ate with his left hand even though for everything else he was right-handed, or that he preferred to drink lemonade instead of anything carbonated. Even the sound of his chewing felt familiar.

On the drive back to James's townhouse, I replayed the date in my mind. I decided to look on the bright side. After seven years of not seeing each other more than twice, James and I had managed to be thrown together a couple of times and had survived. We'd now spent several hours together, free from the horrors of the first few dates I'd gone on. In fact, I'd even managed to laugh.

While Lisa would be disappointed to find out she'd been foiled again, it had been good to spend an entertaining evening with friends and restore my hope for new beginnings.

Chapter 8

We love the things we love for what they are.

~ Robert Frost ~

Fridays in May are honestly the worst for teachers. It's the last month of school and the last day of the week. In Pine Ridge, the weather starts to warm up and the anticipation for summer vacation shoots in rainbow arcs straight out of the classroom windows.

This particular Friday had been seriously tedious. The kids did not want to learn, and I was having a hard time focusing myself. I was as eager for summer break as they were. It didn't help that I'd forgotten to fully silence my phone. It was buzzing in my desk enough that one of my students suggested it was an emergency and I might need to check it.

I sighed and asked the kids to work quietly on their math for a moment while I went to turn off my phone. I wasn't intending to actually check my messages then. I did have a job to do after all, but I did get enough of a glimpse to know they were from Hannah and contained pictures of possible bridesmaid dresses. I ignored them and turned off the phone, already dreading the hours I knew I would spend that evening at a dress shop. The flowers had been a frightening glimpse into what I could expect.

The afternoon dragged, and the moment the bell rang for school to get out, the students burst from my room like a pack of wild dogs after a steak. I waved at them as best I could and wished them all a happy weekend.

Five minutes later, Lisa was lying next to me on the reading rug as we stared up at the ceiling of my classroom.

"Are we too old to be lying here like this?" she asked.

"No, you're only too old if you're doing this on accident and you can't get back up without any help. I don't think we're there yet," I replied.

"I will definitely be there by the time this school year ends." She punctuated her sentence with a groan.

"True."

It was a scientific fact that teachers' bodies started breaking down on the first day of school and were almost obsolete by the last day of school. Luckily our brains and hearts continued to function. You had to really love this job to keep doing it.

"What are your weekend plans?" Lisa asked.

"Dress shopping for bridesmaid dresses with Hannah and Val."

"Sounds fun!" Lisa enthused.

"Do you remember the flower selection process?" I reminded her with a giggle. Lisa made a little noise of sympathy. "I'm expecting to be zipped into at least fifty dresses before Hannah decides which one she prefers."

"Maybe she'll find one she likes at the start."

"That will never happen," I stated. "My only hope is that none of my skin accidentally gets zipped in during the manic changing session. Besides, the likelihood of Val and me agreeing to wear the first dress Hannah suggests is almost zero."

"So? Pretend you like what she likes and just live with it for one day." Lisa turned to me and smiled. "Does it matter?"

She had a good point. It didn't really matter. It was Hannah's day. I'd seen the movie *27 Dresses*. I knew Hannah had good taste. I relaxed a bit.

"You're a smarty pants." I smiled back at Lisa.

"I am. I should go into the world and share my knowledge," she stated firmly. We both cracked up.

"What are your weekend plans?" I asked when we were quiet again.

"Double date with my brother Chad and his girlfriend." Lisa rolled onto her side facing me. "Speaking of Chad, have you heard any more from James?"

"Uh, James? Why would I have?"

"I guess he told Chad he had a good time." Lisa wiggled her eyebrows playfully.

"That doesn't mean anything." I shook my head and smiled at her hopeful look. "I already told you that we've known each other for years. He's Hannah's brother. It was funny how it worked out like that though. I mean, what are the odds?" Lisa chuckled lightly in agreement. "I'll just have to keep looking." I kept my voice casual and light.

I had never told Lisa that James was my one great heartbreak. She would have felt worse about setting me up with him than she had about setting me up with her brother Paul. However, not telling her the truth about James had felt like I was lying to her somehow. I tried to avoid the topic as much as possible.

Lisa pulled a sad face and rolled onto her back again. "Any other dates lined up yet?" she asked after a few minutes of comfortable silence.

"Not yet. I have time though. I've already done four of the six required. First I have to get myself hooked up with a nice little navy blue number for the wedding before I can worry about a guy," I replied.

"Navy blue, huh? It'll look great with your coloring. Lucky for you that Hannah didn't choose yellow or orange."

"What are you trying to say? I can pull off those colors!" I gasped in mock insult.

"Oh sweetie, you really can't," Lisa said, laughing.

I swatted at her, but she quickly rolled away and stood up. "Happy Friday, Rachel. Now, I have some papers to grade, some concerned parents to email, and some caffeine to drink. See you Monday." She waved one last time as she rounded the doorway and disappeared from my view.

Two hours later, Hannah, Val, and I walked through the door of Elite Bridal. Hannah took the lead, beaming from ear to ear, at ease in her element. I walked in next, clutching a mug of cola in my hand, needing my fuel, and feeling no shame about it. Val sulked in behind me.

Val had been told she wouldn't have to do anything other than wear a dress and smile. She'd agreed to enter this shop under protest. While we mostly kept her out of the planning loop—well, aside from turning our living room into a greenhouse—it had taken Hannah some serious talking to help Val understand that part of wearing the pretty dress was to try on several pretty dresses.

I was impressed with our surroundings. The store was designed with the idea of wooing brides in mind. The colors were whites and beiges, the furniture comfortable, the gowns sparkling, and the employees impressively flawless. The place oozed a feeling of glamorous confidence. They were here to make dreams come true. Well, that and to dazzle lovebirds into opening their wallets.

The attendant—not to be confused with a simple employee—greeted us with a huge smile and lots of bling. The lady was beautiful. She was immaculately styled from tip to toe in a way I couldn't even begin to want to try. I was exhausted for her. But it worked for her, so bravo.

"Miss Redmond!" the attendant lady chirped as she extended her hands and quickly hurried to our little group.

She grabbed Hannah's hands when she reached us and gave them a squeeze before looking behind Hannah to where we stood. The little lambs. I had to give the attendant major credit for keeping that smile in place and not giving away a hint of how she really felt at the prospect of dressing us. Val and I had both changed from our work clothes into T-shirts and comfy jeans. I felt terribly underdressed standing in that sparkle palace. It was a good thing my clothes would be spending the majority of the evening plopped in a dressing room out of sight.

"Hi ladies. You must be Rachel." She looked at me first, and I nodded. "And Valerie." She looked at Val, who just shrugged.

"Wonderful. My name is Gloria. I'm so excited to work with you today." She gestured for us to follow her to a seating area of spotless white upholstered chairs arranged around a glass table where delicate little snacks and drinks were laid out for us.

I became hyperaware of my giant blue mug of cola as we made our way to the chairs, and I felt like a buffoon when I set it on the tabletop. It looked like a giant plastic thorn among the roses. I made a face of apology to Gloria as it clunked down. She didn't appear ruffled and smiled happily back at me. I got the feeling that I could slap my stinky bare feet up on that glass table and she'd take it like a champ. Working at a bridal shop probably gave you a stiff upper lip.

"Now, Hannah and I have already met and discussed colors and styles that would suit both her wedding ideals and the two of you," Gloria said, smiling. I was kind of relieved that some of the legwork had already been done. "But, of course, as Hannah knows, you never can decide until you see it on." Gloria shared a smile with Hannah.

It was obvious that they were two little peas in a pod. I felt my spirits sink a bit. It was going to be hard enough to keep Hannah reigned in without her being whipped into a fabric frenzy by Gloria.

"I wasn't sure that we could find matching dresses that would look good on both of you, but Gloria says we can do it, so that's our goal today." Hannah smiled adoringly at Gloria before looking at Val and me.

Val and I shared a look. Matching dresses? For us? Our body types and styles were so incredibly different. It would take a miracle.

"We specialize in miracles and making dreams come true." Gloria must have read our look.

"You do realize that Rachel is five foot two and I'm five foot eleven, right?" Val looked at Hannah. Hannah's smile faded a bit as she nodded. "Add to that the fact that Rachel is built like a bird and I'm built more like a 1930s pin-up girl, and, well, good luck making this dream come true."

Hannah's smile died totally, and she looked at Gloria. Gloria was still smiling, but now it was more the way your mom smiles at you in public when you're about to die but she has to wait until you're in private to make it happen.

I jumped in. "Let's just see what they have, Val. I think we can find something that will work for us." I reached out and gave Hannah's hand a squeeze. "That's what fittings are for, right?" I added.

"Exactly." Gloria gave one succinct nod. "Would you like me to get out the book of dresses first or bring out what I've put on the rack for you to look through?" Gloria's smile had relaxed again.

"Let's just dive right in. Can you bring out the rack?" Hannah wisely replied.

"Of course. I'll be back in a moment." Gloria stood up and quick-stepped out of view behind a curtain.

Hannah looked at Val and me and raised one of her perfectly sculpted eyebrows while pursing her lips. Val stared right back at her. I nudged Val and held up a finger to Hannah to keep her from launching into her pep talk. For once, I had one of my own to give.

I turned to Val. "This is one day. One. It's not our day. It's Hannah's. It's one tiny day in our entire lives, but it's one major day in Hannah's. We can find a dress that we can both live with for one day, okay?" I pleaded with Val.

Val's eyes softened, and she huffed out a breath. Hannah grabbed our hands, and we sat that way for a minute until Val nodded and squeezed our hands tight in her own.

"We're going to outshine the bride, you know," Val offered with a slight smile.

"It's true," I said, laughing in relief. Val sometimes left us wondering, but she always came through for our little trio in the end.

"It's a curse having two hotties as friends," Hannah agreed before we released our hands and the tension we'd been feeling.

"So what kind of food do you think that is?" I asked, pointing to the tiny canapés.

"The kind that's going in my belly." Hannah grabbed one and popped it into her mouth.

"Eat up." Val smiled. "I have a feeling it's going to be a long night."

Long didn't even begin to describe it. Extensive, lengthy, time-consuming, prolonged—those words scratched at it, but it was soul killing for someone like me who never even tried on clothes before buying them. Val and I did our best to keep a smile on our faces. It was made possible by sharing that giant mug of cola between the two of us. At one point, Gloria even had a staff member go get us a refill. The cola made for a slew of necessary bathroom breaks, but that ended up being a blessing, since it gave us a five-minute break every hour.

Gloria, bless her perfectly coifed heart, kept us going with a steady supply of determined cheer. Hannah was so blissful at the thought of finally getting to play dress up with us that she was totally immune to the fatigue we were experiencing.

The shop eventually had to close. We walked out right at 10:00 p.m. to the sound of the door locking behind us. I wasn't even sure they normally stayed open that late. We'd arrived at 4:00 p.m. There wasn't enough chocolate in the world to make up for what we'd been through. On the bright side, we had narrowed it down to two dresses.

Val and I had firmly and unanimously voted for Hannah to make the final decision between the two. We were fine with whatever she chose at that point. We'd go back the next month for fittings, measurements, and adjustments.

"No offense, but I'm going straight inside to my bathtub, and I don't want to see either of you until at least noon tomorrow," Val said as we climbed the stairs to our apartment.

"No offense, but I don't want to ever see anything navy blue again," I announced.

"Or ever be zipped into a dress again," Val added.

"The sound of a zipper has now become the sound of my nightmares," I agreed.

Hannah chuckled. "You guys were great tonight."

"I hope you know this has helped me make some decisions about my future wedding," Val said as we headed to our rooms.

"Oh yeah?" Hannah sounded surprised. Probably because Val had told us she never planned on getting married.

"Yep. I've decided after watching all of this that if I ever get hit on the head hard enough to want marriage, I'm going to elope."

Her plan sounded perfectly perfect to me.

Chapter 9

*You don't love because: you love despite; not
for the virtues, but despite the faults.*

~ William Faulkner ~

It didn't matter how long I'd known Val or how well I thought I knew her, she still had the ability to completely shock my eyes right out of my head. This time she did it by being the one to set me up on my next date.

She'd come home one night a week or so after our evening at the dress shop and told us a gruesome story about a guy who had gone hiking, slipped over the edge of a ravine, and tumbled down several yards before being able to stop himself on a boulder. He'd sliced up his hands pretty good climbing back up and had a gash on his head, along with a lot of bumps and bruises. Val had helped stitch him back together.

"We talked while the doctor stitched, and I thought he seemed like your type," Val stated nonchalantly as she popped the last of her dinner into her mouth.

"Because . . . ?" I asked. "I fall a lot?"

I wasn't sure what exactly she saw in him that suggested he might be a match. I certainly wasn't spending my free time hiking. I also wasn't sure how she was still eating. I'd pushed my plate away when she started discussing his injuries. I have a huge problem when people are talking about getting hurt. I imagine how it must've looked and immediately become nauseated. Val knew this. She kept telling me stories anyway.

"I don't know. He acted nice and not stupid. He said he was single. So, I showed him your picture and gave him your number." Val stood and took her plate to the sink.

I laughed at her strict parameters for someone who would be "my type." Nice, not stupid, and single. "Thanks for your high standards." I smiled.

"Wait, are you saying you set Rachel up?" Hannah looked up from painting her toenails and blinked a few times at Val. "I thought you were totally against her dating."

Val shrugged as she leaned against the counter and folded her arms. "It doesn't matter what I think. She's determined to do this challenge of yours. So, since I'm totally against her going out with freaks, then I can at least try to help by setting her up with a non-weirdo," she clarified.

With Val, a person had to learn to listen less to the words she used and more to the thought behind them. I was touched by her show of concern.

"That's so sweet," I said, smiling at her.

"Yeah." She brushed it off as she unfolded her arms and pushed away from the counter. "Anyhow, his name is Doug, and he should be calling in the next little while. He'll have bandaged hands for a few days, so don't expect anything immediate." Then she strode off to her room.

I shared a glance with Hannah, not knowing what to say. She shook her head back at me. We were both speechless. Val had a way of doing that to us—dropping bombs like she was telling us the weather. It certainly made life with her interesting.

I cleared my half-eaten food from the table and wandered over to sit on the couch near Hannah. She smiled at me as I sat down. She'd taken her contacts out and was wearing her vintage glasses. Unlike my glasses that were from my high school years, hers were actually the cool vintage that people wanted to wear. She said she saw better through them and needed the extra zoom while painting her nails.

"You ready to go on another date?" she asked.

I pursed my lips and made a face. "Yeah, I guess."

"I never told you that I'm sorry you ended up having a date with James," she said softly while keeping her eyes focused on her toes.

I could tell she was hesitant to bring it up, and I didn't blame her. When the relationship between James and I had first exploded, I hadn't been able to talk about it with Hannah. She was too close to the situation with me being her best friend and James being her brother. In some ways, she was almost as hurt as I was. It had been a source of tension between us, and once she forgave me, it became the norm to just ignore it.

"It's okay. James told you he's over everything, right?" I replied.

"Yeah." She hesitated for a moment and looked at me before deciding to plunge ahead. "I'm really glad he is. He was really heartbroken." Then she gave me a soft smile. "You both were."

I realized too late that I didn't want to have this conversation after all, so I played it cool. "Yeah, it was hard, but that was a long time ago."

"That's what James said too."

"He's right. We've moved on. That's what this dating challenge is about. So, yes, I'm ready to go out again." I stood and faked a yawn. "I'm off to my room to work on some things for class tomorrow. Good night." I smiled at her and headed out.

"Night," she replied as I hurried away.

It took Val's setup, Doug, a little over a week to call. I didn't let it faze me. Calling a stranger for a date is never easy, no matter who you are. He probably wondered what kind of friend Val would have, and I couldn't blame him. She was pretty intense. I'd kept busy with teaching and secretly talking Hannah into choosing the bridesmaid dress that I preferred, so I hadn't minded the wait.

Okay, in all honesty, in spite of the fact that I'd played it off with Hannah, I really was anxious about going out again. I was secretly glad it had taken him a week to call. Knowing I needed to move forward was the only thing forcing me to strap into my big girl pants; however, knowing how crazy dating could be kept me quaking in those pants.

Doug invited me to join him on a fishing trip the following Saturday. We negotiated a 6:00 a.m. pickup time after he'd initially suggested 4:30. I only agreed because I hadn't been fishing for probably fifteen years. I figured we could be done by noon and I'd have the rest of my day free. I also thought that fishing would be a great way to be able to visit and really get to know someone without too much distraction—assuming he turned out to be a little more normal than my other dates had been.

Val had insisted that Doug wasn't a creeper, so I gave him the apartment complex address and met him in the parking lot before the birds had even started chirping. He could know the complex where I lived, but I wasn't quite up to giving him the actual apartment number yet.

My first reaction upon seeing Doug was that he seemed like a cool and confident guy without being cocky. He looked like an outdoorsman, with smile lines around his eyes and mouth, tanned skin, and somewhat messy light brown hair poking out from under a ball cap. Dressed in jeans, a T-shirt, and an open flannel shirt, he looked casually comfortable.

Unfortunately, I wasn't sure he was going to get a great first impression of me. I'd stayed up way too late obsessing over what kind of outfit would work for fishing. I figured it needed to both keep me warm in the early morning air and dry quickly since there was always a possibility of a dunking. Aside from my lack of sleep, with it being so early, my face had revolted against make-up, and there was no stinking way I was getting up before the sun to really do my hair. I was hoping he was good with a more natural look.

He was smiling and cheerful. He chatted with me on the drive up. He was a big outdoor enthusiast, which I could get behind even though I spent most of my time indoors. He had a job as a manager of a sporting goods store and was thinking about breeding hunting dogs on the side.

"I've heard a lot of talk about how there are already so many dogs in shelters and being euthanized that need good homes," I said thoughtfully. "Wouldn't it be better to rescue some of them and train them to hunt rather than breed more dogs?" I asked.

Not being a pet owner myself—or having one as a child—I was genuinely asking a question, hoping to start a discussion. It must not have come out that way, because he glanced at me with a confused look on his face.

"I would make sure my pups went to good forever homes before I'd let them leave."

"But, do you really ever know? I mean, things change in people's lives, and they may have to give up the dog. Wouldn't it be better to search shelters first? Plus, getting an older dog might save you from bathroom accidents, excessive chewing, and other puppy things," I said musingly.

"Have you ever owned a dog?"

"No. My mother was allergic."

He nodded like that answered that and he didn't think I knew what I was talking about. I didn't have enough vested in the topic to care, so I was game to move on to something else. He told me about some of his favorite places to hike and about government forces trying to close some of those areas off.

"I don't pay a ton of attention, but aren't they trying to preserve the land from overuse by closing it off?" I asked.

"That's what they'd like us to believe, but all they're really doing is taking away our freedom to explore and discover the beauty of what God created," he huffed. "Those Washington bureaucrats know nothing about life here. They sit behind a desk and listen but don't ever see with their own eyes."

For the most part, I agreed with him that government could be out of touch, but having been raised to do my best to see both sides of a situation, I couldn't help but say, "You're right. They don't actually live here, and that probably makes their jobs even harder, don't you think? They have to listen to so many arguments and so much propaganda and then try to make the right choice. I wouldn't want to be them and have that responsibility."

"I think money is what makes their choices," he replied sarcastically.

I nodded. "Sadly, you're probably right more often than we'd like to believe."

We were quiet for the rest of the drive up, both of us seemingly lost in our own thoughts—until the Lysol incident. I made the terrible mistake of sneezing. Before I even pulled my face back up out of my elbow—I had covered it, after all—Doug was holding a can of spray Lysol, which he shot directly at my hands until they were coated, and then sprayed it into the air around me.

I tried not to choke on the fumes as I wiped my now-soaked hands on my pant legs to dry them off. He saw me wiping my hands on my legs and sprayed them too. Now my jeans were a little damp, and everything smelled like lemon-coated chemicals.

"What on earth?" I said, glancing at him in confusion.

"I can't afford to get sick. I'm going to Peru to hike Machu Picchu in a couple of weeks."

"Okaaaay." I elongated the word to show my annoyance. "I teach second grade, and I don't douse my students with Lysol," I replied uncomfortably.

"You teach little kids all day?" He looked at me like I'd grown a second head as he tucked the Lysol into his cup holder.

"Yes, I love it."

"Are you wearing clean clothes this morning?" he asked.

"What?" I was totally confused.

"Like, are you wearing anything right now that you wore to teach in?" His eyes ran quickly over my clothing before going back to the road.

"I don't think so," I replied. "Teachers don't usually wear jeans, T-shirts, and tennis shoes to school."

"Good." He nodded. "Very good."

"For the record, spraying people with Lysol isn't exactly FDA approved."

"Oh, I take it you're green then?" He quirked a smile.

"Green? As in a lover of mother earth?" I asked. He nodded. "Because I don't want to be sprayed with Lysol? That's not being *green*. That's wanting to stay out of the hospital."

"I'm guessing you're one of those trying to save our planet from aerosol sprays and global warming." He chuckled.

"Aren't you?" I would think someone as outdoorsy as him would have been punching his card with nature lovers everywhere.

"Sure I am. I'm also a lover of antibacterial everything. Nothing worse than a cold while you're traveling," he said. I just stayed silent.

He was so confusing to me. He seemed like a decent guy, but he was full of contradictions. I was curious to see how our time on the lake would go. Either we'd find common ground, or we'd have a long, awkward time ahead.

The lake we'd be fishing on came into view just a few minutes later. Doug got the truck and boat into position and put the truck in park for a moment while he pulled on a pair of waders. Then he backed down the ramp into the lake and we both got out. I walked around the front of the truck while he waded into the water to unhook the small fishing boat. He came back out to where I was standing, and after asking my permission, he lifted me into his arms and carried me to the boat so that I wouldn't get wet. It was nice of him, until I saw him pull out some hand sanitizer after he set me down and quickly scrub his hands.

"I'll be right back. Going to park the truck." He jogged up to his truck and pulled it away, leaving me floating in the boat with no knowledge of what to do with it.

Luckily, I was in pretty much the same spot when Doug splashed into the water and jumped in. He dug around underneath the bench and pulled out a brown hat with a floppy brim all the way around it. He leaned over and dropped it on my head, saying something about me not getting burned out on the lake. It didn't smell like roses, but it was another nice gesture, and I left it on.

He started up the little trolling motor and we headed out into the lake. While we bumped along, he gave me instructions about the fishing gear and how everything worked. Then he finished up with this gem:

"When I fish, I think it helps to do it in silence. Too much talking scares them away. So, at least while we're in the middle of the lake, let's just keep it quiet and enjoy the peace." His face was dead serious, and I had no choice but to nod my assent and hope we'd make it a quick trip.

Gone were my daydreams of sharing our thoughts while floating lazily on a lake. Also—could the fish really hear us?

The next three hours—yes, *three*—were the longest in history. I made lesson plans in my head that would finish out the last weeks of school before summer break. I created plans for my dream home. I began a list of places I'd most like to travel to. I came up with creative and painful ways to kill my rotten skunk of a roommate, Valerie Allen, without ever being caught. I promised myself that when this was over, I was going to put a snake in her bed so she'd know what I thought of her little setup.

Doug, my dreamboat of a date, wasn't fazed in the least by any of it. He hummed a little, shared a snack of some crackers and cheese he'd brought, and seemed all around happy with how his morning was going. I almost told him that humming was considered noise, but in the end, I let it go.

As we floated lazily, I tried hard to focus on how beautiful our surroundings were. At this higher elevation, the pine trees were majestic, and occasional whiffs of their scent blew to us across the water. The lake sparkled in the sun, and the birds soaring in unhurried circles high above us were postcard perfect. Still, even basking in the lovely mountain air didn't erase the agony of enforced silence—or the smell of my floppy hat.

When it was finally time to leave, I'd caught absolutely nothing. Doug had caught four good-sized fish, which he spent the ride back to the boat launch talking about. They were going to be delicious. Too bad I wouldn't be there to eat them. As far as I was concerned, catching one fish per hour was a waste of time. I could have marched down to the store and bought four salmon filets in twenty minutes, and they would've had the added bonus of not tasting like trout.

When we got back to the boat launch, he grabbed the hat back off my head and again carried me in his arms as we got out of the boat. This time, though, before he'd let me get in the truck, he asked me to sanitize my hands and sing the ABCs while I did so. That way he'd know I'd gotten all the germs from fishing off me before getting in the truck. I started singing in my head, but he requested that I do it out loud. I did so through such tightly clenched teeth that I could hear my dentist groaning.

On the drive back down the canyon to Pine Ridge, Doug was all jovial again. He'd had such a great time, and it was so nice to be out on the water. I was pretty quiet.

"Did you not have fun?" he finally asked.

I tried very hard to be diplomatic in my answer. "You know, sitting for that long without talking isn't the best way to get to know someone new," I finally said.

He seemed to think about that for a second. "Well, that's your opinion, I guess. I think it was great. I found out that you have a lot of those . . . opinions . . . I mean . . . I think it's cool that you're so smart and stuff, but I prefer a woman who is a little more agreeable. Have you ever thought about, like, not having so many opinions?"

I couldn't stop a surprised burst of laughter from coming out as I turned to see that he was completely serious. I snorted as I tried to suppress it.

"You know what, Doug? I have never thought of myself as being opinionated." I giggled.

He scowled. "Well, you are."

"Well, that's your *opinion*, I suppose," I threw back at him.

He didn't even react to my joke. He was seriously annoyed. I'll admit that I loved it after the four hours he'd put me through. I was tempted to fake sneeze into my hand to get under his skin some more, but it wasn't worth getting coated in Lysol again. Besides, he wasn't exactly a jerk. He just wanted someone who didn't have my particular character traits, and that was the only thing we'd agreed on all day.

Sometimes when your morning date goes crummy and you smell like fish and Lysol, it helps to know that there is something ahead of you that will make up for it. It was just my luck that the very night of fishy date was cake-tasting night at our apartment. I'd daydreamed quite a bit while floating on a piney breeze about walking into my apartment and seeing cakes on every available surface. In my mind it would be like flower arrangement day all over again, only with fluffy, sugary cake. Yum!

Sadly, another dream lay dead at my feet when I came out from my shower into the kitchen that afternoon with my hair still damp and wrapped in a towel. Hannah had a serving platter on the table with ten measly slices of cake on it.

"Well, this will just about make up for my day," I joked as I pulled out a chair and sat down, glad I'd worn old stretchy sweat pants. "Where are *your* samples?"

"These are all the samples. We're sharing," Hannah replied, too busy writing in her wedding notebook to pick up on the humor. She had her hair slicked back into a ponytail and not an ounce of make up on. She was in serious work mode here.

"Uh, but on flower day there were like 100 million flowers in here," I replied in confusion.

"True. I needed to smell, touch, and see how they all looked together."

"But, I need to smell, touch, and taste a lot of cake tonight," I whined. I knew I was whining, but I didn't care.

Hannah finally looked up. "What's happened?"

"Three hours of silence on a lake after getting sprayed from head to toe with Lysol. I'm going to kill Val." I huffed as I glanced lovingly at those ten slices of beautiful cake.

"You'll have your chance soon. She's joining us." Hannah went back to her writing.

"Wait? There are three of us are sharing these?" I sagged a little in my chair. *Of course* this would be the one part of wedding planning that Val would willingly participate in. Eating cake. She was a double rotten snake.

"Four. Andrew is coming too," Hannah replied matter-of-factly, clearly not listening to my needy pleadings.

"Four?" I cried. "I thought you loved me. I really did," I mumbled as I let my head fall to the table. My towel turban unwrapped, and I felt Hannah reach out and pat my head. I knew it was only fair for Andrew to have a say in his wedding cake, but still!

"That bad, huh?" she said kindly.

"Did I mention the three hours of total and unconditional silence?"

"Oh, yikes," Hannah replied.

I sat back up, happy to have her attention. "He sprayed me with Lysol," I whined again as I pushed my hair out of my face and gathered up the towel to drape it over an empty seat back.

Hannah cracked a smile despite her best effort. I heard Val enter the room from behind me. Hannah looked at Val. "That Doug guy sprayed her with Lysol."

Val started laughing as she neared the table. "That's funny," she said.

I glared at Val as she pulled out a chair and sat down. "It's not funny. As a nurse, you should know that I could have been poisoned. He said I have too many opinions, and then he acted like I'm a germ machine."

Val pulled a face. "Huh. He seemed so nice."

"Probably because when you met him he was high on pain medication," I grumped.

Val shrugged. "Oh well. No harm, I guess." She slid the serving dish over closer to her to have a peek. I was a little put out by her lack of reaction.

"I'll show you no harm," I muttered as I stood up and went to the cupboard under the sink. I wasn't exactly angry, but I really owed Val a little discomfort. I finally found the Lysol spray and went back to the table.

"Hannah, could you slide those cakes out of the way for a second?" I asked sweetly from behind Val. Hannah looked up and quickly snagged the serving platter with a look of horror on her face.

Her look cued Val in, and just as she turned around, I sprayed a stream of Lysol at her bare legs. She squealed and jumped up. "What are you doing?" she yelled.

"Oh . . . huh. Did you just get sprayed with Lysol? No harm." I smirked as I threw her words back at her. "Just giving you a taste of my day." A giggle burst out as I dodged her attempts to grab the Lysol from me.

"The cake!" Hannah screamed and jumped up with the platter still in hand as she moved out of the kitchen into the living area.

At this point, Val and I were essentially wrestling over the Lysol can, both of us in hysterical fits, my long, wet hair occasionally whipping one of us in the face. Val had me on size, for sure, but I had her on speed and was able to dodge her grabs for a while as I kept spritzing the air around her and ran into the living area.

Obviously, this was when Andrew walked in. Hannah was holding the cake platter in the hallway now, poking her head around the corner every few seconds and screaming at us to stop. Val was yelling and lunging with a grin on her face. I was standing on the back of the couch, holding the can above her head, and spritzing whenever she'd get near, my sides nearly splitting as my eyes watered.

"Never a dull moment." I heard Andrew's voice before I saw him.

His voice had the effect of a freeze ray gun on our antics. The sudden silence was deafening as we stood frozen in place. Even though we'd seen a lot of Andrew over the course of the past year, Val and I weren't exactly engaged in public behavior at that moment. We typically tried to use our manners when he was around.

"Well, thank goodness you came when you did." Hannah poked her head out of the hallway and made a face at me.

"Do I want to know?" Andrew was glancing back and forth at Val and me, who were breathing heavily with big smiles on our faces.

"Bad date." Val's smile drooped as she pointed at me and then shook her head as if she had no explanation for why I was doing what I was doing.

Andrew's eyes moved to mine. I still had a huge, silly, and now somewhat embarrassed grin on my face. My wet hair was hanging over one side of my face, and my sweatpants had hitched up strangely so that the ankles were now around my knees.

I dropped my Lysol-holding arm to my side but couldn't keep from laughing when I said, "Val set me up, so I was teaching her a lesson." I jumped off the couch and pushed my hair out of my face.

Andrew nodded and chuckled in amusement. "Sorry I interrupted," he said as his eyes followed Hannah into the kitchen with the cake platter.

"On the bright side, our house is germ free." I smiled and bent down to pull my sweatpants back into place.

"And fresh smelling too," Val inserted with a grin.

"Come sit." Hannah was back with the cake and motioned for us to gather around the table. She sat first, and Andrew bent to kiss her before he sat next to her. "So, we have ten options here." Hannah pointed around the serving platter.

"Only ten?" Val quipped, pulling a face at me. She'd obviously heard my whining earlier.

"I'll eat your share." I smiled at her with my best innocent face. "Bad date. Your fault. Need cake."

"Listen, we need to eat before they dry out." Hannah tapped the table with her pencil, calling us back to order. "So, I put a number by each of the slices and made you each a tasting sheet with corresponding numbers. Taste them all and then rate them. Let's get this done. We have the music playlist to get to tonight also."

"Music playlist?" Val asked.

"Yes. For the dancing at the reception." Hannah nodded and took her first bite of cake.

"I was only told about cake, not making playlists," Val said quietly.

"What happened to only wearing a dress and smiling pretty?" I replied.

"Cake happened," Val gestured at the platter with her fork.

"Well, you don't get to only do the fun jobs," I replied. "If you taste cake, then you have to help with music too."

Val looked like she was deeply considering if she should stick around or leave now before we dragged her in too deep. In the end, she picked up her fork. Cake makes up for a lot of things.

"I like cake, but what's my job here?" Andrew asked as he took a bite of the cake in front of him.

"You get to be the guy," I replied since Hannah's mouth was full. "You have to keep us from ordering only lavender- and rose-flavored icing."

"Oh, good. I'm pretty good at being a guy," Andrew said around his bite, his teeth flashing in a smile. "But really, does that mean I just smile and nod at whatever you three decide? Or do I actually vote here?" Andrew grinned. Hannah playfully swatted at him.

"Do whatever you're told to do," I said.

"I can do that." He grabbed another bite of cake and began writing.

We were all quiet for the rest of the cake tasting. It was really making up for my terrible morning. I was in heaven with varieties of chocolate, lemon, red velvet, carrot, and white cakes swirling around in my mouth. Fillings of fruit, mousse, and curd were delicious. This was the kind of silence I could enjoy.

Sadly, it didn't take too long for the four of us to taste all the cake options. I felt a little sick to my stomach, but I was tough enough to keep from complaining about it. Hannah passed out glasses of milk and collected the voting sheets.

"Andrew, did you copy all my answers?" Hannah huffed in amused annoyance as she looked the sheets over.

"I'm happy if you're happy," he said, shrugging one shoulder.

Val snorted at his reply. Hannah smiled a little and leaned over to give him a kiss.

As Hannah sipped more milk and read over our responses, Andrew gave Val and me a smile, letting us know he knew exactly what he was doing. It made me choke a bit on my drink as I smothered my merriment. Hannah finally nodded once, satisfied that we'd taken our jobs seriously, and tucked the sheets away in her file folder.

"Next order of business—music." She grabbed a bag that I hadn't seen from under the table and pulled out an iPod and speakers. "I've gathered a list that I'd like to play through and see what you guys think."

"Couldn't we have done this while we were eating cake?" Val asked.

"I need you to focus on one thing at a time," Hannah responded as she fired up the music. "Now, I'm thinking it should start with something sweet like 'All of Me' by John Legend."

I nodded. It seemed a good choice. Val disagreed.

"Too sappy," she said.

"It's a wedding," I reminded her. "Expect some sap."

"How about 'Uptown Funk' by Bruno Mars?" Andrew said with a straight face. I have no idea how he kept it straight, but the man held it while we all looked at him.

"'Hey Ya!' by OutKast?" Val added.

Andrew pretended to think it over while Hannah sat and watched, waiting for us to get it out of our systems.

"I've got it. 'Thriller' by Michael Jackson," I added with a grin. Andrew laughed out loud, and I was surprised by the sound of it. I was trying to remember if I'd ever heard him laugh like that. He was always nice but maintained a certain level of politeness around us.

"That's the one. I think it will really set the mood." Val chuckled and reached over to give me a high five.

"Are you three done?" Hannah asked. We kept smiling but nodded at Hannah. "Good. Let's do this."

It was surprisingly entertaining to pick music for the wedding and reception. It fell apart halfway through, and Hannah rolled with it, playing whatever she had that we called out. My only request was no Disney songs. I never wanted to hear a Disney love song again as long as I lived.

At the end of the night, we ordered pizza and threw on a movie. Andrew was invited to stay, which he did in spite of the fact that I figured he was due to reset his testosterone levels.

The night had made up for my horrible morning, and I was glad once again for good friends to help keep me looking forward instead of back.

Chapter 10

Love is the answer to everything.
It's the only reason to do anything.

~ Ray Bradbury ~

Sunday night I was lounging in the comfy over-stuffed chair in the corner of my room, flipping through an old copy of *Pride and Prejudice* that I'd read a few times. It was peaceful for a change, and I was enjoying imagining Elizabeth and Mr. Darcy growing to love each other.

My phone rang with the jaunty tune that meant it was my mom. I quickly snatched it up from my nightstand, happy to hear it. I figured Diana would also be on the line, and I was looking forward to catching up with them.

Diana went first, entertaining us with stories about the twins and what her family was up to. Mom went next, telling us about a house project her and Dad were planning. With my life having recently become unusually chaotic between dating and wedding plans, it was comforting to listen to the chitchat and normalcy of their lives.

When it was my turn, I had them in stitches as I told about cake tasting, picking songs, and reading the story of the three little pigs to my second graders the previous week. After I'd read the story, I thought it would be fun to do a hands-on project. The students were supposed to build houses out of marshmallows and clay before trying to blow them down. It had ended up in marshmallow warfare and clay in hair and carpet, and I'd been completely wiped out by the end of the day. I'd even had to wash two stray marshmallows out of my hair that I hadn't known were there until I'd gotten home and Hannah had laughingly pointed them out.

While I was debating saying anything about dating, Mom popped in and asked how it was going.

"Diana! You promised!" I accused.

"Diana didn't say anything. I just know these things," Mom replied before Diana could defend herself.

"How?" I asked.

Mom chuckled. "I didn't. I just thought I'd ask and see how you reacted. Now I know you decided to do the challenge. So, how's it going?"

"Fooled again," I said, laughing. I was too amused by my mother's manipulation skills to be mad.

"It's a gift we mothers have," Mom replied.

"It's true. The twins are always busting themselves just by the look on their faces or by me asking the right question," Diana agreed happily.

"It's been . . . interesting," I began. I gave them some date highlights. They reacted the way any sane person would, by being shocked that those kinds of things were actually happening to innocent people.

I made sure to leave any mention of my accidental setup with James out of the conversation. My mother had loved him almost as much as I'd loved him. When I'd called it off, I was actually as worried about Mom forgiving me as I'd been about James forgiving me. I knew that if she heard James had moved to town, she would start her candle burning again with hopes of a reconciliation. I didn't have the strength to have that conversation with her, and I was terribly grateful to Diana for not mentioning it either.

"What are you going to do now?" Mom asked when I was done.

I paused for a moment. "I know I should say that I'll keep trying, but it's been a big letdown."

"Anything worth having takes work," Mom replied with one of her typical sayings. It made me smile to myself even if it didn't convince me.

"Well, this has definitely been work." I chuckled.

"Keep trying," Diana encouraged. "The first date I went on with Jordan was a total disaster. When he asked me out again, I was very hesitant, but I'm so glad I went."

"I appreciate the thought, Diana, but none of these guys are second-date material," I responded.

"Sadly, I agree," Mom sighed. Her dreams of a summer wedding had just tanked.

"What about your online dating profile?" Diana asked.

"You're online dating?" Mom sounded appalled. Oops. She wasn't supposed to find out about that. To people of her generation, only girls of a certain reputation would look online for love, and the men who went looking there weren't much better. "Nice girls don't have to sell themselves that way. Plus, that's where all the loons go to find dates, honey." Mom was not pleased. "Finding a good guy online is like finding a needle in a haystack."

"Well, Mom, if you have any other suggestions, I'm open," I said, laughing.

"I'm sure I could find someone—" Mom began.

"No. No. I'll be okay," I jumped in.

"I just want you to be safe and happy, dear," Mom replied. I knew she did, and I loved her for it. "Don't give up yet."

"There's no rush though, Rach," Diana inserted. "You have time. Use it."

It was probably the most helpful thing anyone had said to me about dating recently. I was surprised it came from my traditional marriage-minded sister. It said more about her love for me than she could have imagined.

After we hung up, I thought over Mom's dire predictions of online dating, and I was afraid she was right. I'd certainly had very little luck so far. Still, when hope is all we have, we cling to it.

Oddly enough, the next morning after talking with my mom and Diana, I decided to reactivate my online dating profile. I only had to go on one more date before I would officially complete Hannah's six-date challenge, and I wanted to get it behind me so I could be more laid back about dating.

Ironically, by Thursday night, I had two dates lined up. To my annoyance, however, that meant I would be pulling a double header on Saturday. I wasn't sure I was up to it. With that Friday being the last day of school, I'd been expecting to crawl into my bed directly after school and stay there until Sunday morning.

However, Andrew had come back from a weeklong work conference. He said he'd miraculously bumped into an old high school friend there who was moving to a close neighboring town. He'd given him my number. This guy's name was Rob. According to Andrew, he was going to be the one to make my dreams come true.

While Rob was deciding if he wanted to call me or not, I was contacted by Nick through my online dating profile. He seemed decent, so we set up a date for Saturday evening. Rob finally called on Thursday and was only free on Saturday, so he suggested we do lunch. I hesitantly agreed.

Lying in bed Saturday morning, staring at my ceiling and wishing this day were already over, I listed my mistakes of past dates. Evidently, I was too opinionated and closed-minded. Today I would try to be open-minded and go with the flow. Maybe being open to new experiences would help me. Although I didn't think of myself as inflexible, maybe I had been too quick to judge my past dates. Who knew? It was an impossible web to navigate.

When I only had an hour left to go before date number one arrived, I pulled myself out of bed and into the shower. Andrew's friend Rob had said we'd go to a short, casual lunch and just get to know each other before we set up a longer date. It sounded reasonable to me, and it helped keep me from putting too much pressure on things. In the spirit of that, I spent a short, casual amount of time on my look. Wearing a small amount of makeup, a cute top, shorts, and sandals, I was ready when he arrived right on time.

Rob was clean-cut and smiling when Val let him in. He looked like he was close to our age, which made sense if he was Andrew's friend. He was of average height, with black curly hair and smiling hazel eyes. He seemed friendly and polite. Maybe Andrew was going to win this game.

However, ten minutes later, when Rob pulled into the Tasty Taco parking lot, I began to have my doubts. I'd never been taken there on a first date. Okay, any date. Usually guys tried a little harder, at least in my age group. But he'd said casual, and I wasn't against tacos, so I smiled and hopped out of the car to follow him in.

We walked up to the counter and stood there quietly looking over our menu options for a minute. I reminded myself to be more open-minded and try to enjoy the date. The conversation on the drive over had flowed comfortably, and I was feeling hopeful that we could hit it off regardless of where we were dining.

He finally broke the silence by looking at me and saying, "Hey, I'm kind of strapped for cash, going through a divorce and stuff. Do you mind choosing something off the kid's menu?"

I was too surprised to say anything, so I just nodded. Andrew hadn't mentioned a divorce. Not that it was a deal killer. It was just that I thought it would've been worth mentioning. I stood silently while Rob ordered us both kid's meals.

In my surprise and slight discomfort, I didn't even think to just pay for myself and get a full meal so that he could do the same. Instead, I smiled at the teenage employee when he handed me the smallest cup known to man, and while Rob paid, I went to fill my drink at the soda fountain. After a three-second fill-up, I chose a booth close to the fountain. I had a feeling I'd be making a few return trips.

Rob waited at the counter for our food and joined me a couple of minutes later, the plastic seat squeaking as he slid into place.

"So, uh, Andrew tells me you're in the market for a relationship," Rob said as he settled in across from me and passed me my brightly colored children's bag.

Thanks a million, Andrew. "Well, that's not embarrassing at all." I formed a smile while inside I promised myself retribution. "I wouldn't say I'm looking for a relationship exactly. Mostly just trying to get back into the dating world and see where it goes from there." *Salvage, salvage, salvage* was my mantra as I made a hasty explanation.

Rob laughed, understanding my embarrassment. "No worries. We're old friends, so he was just being honest with me. He knows I've had a rough patch and wanted to make sure I knew what I was getting into if I asked you out."

I wrinkled my forehead in confusion. "What do you mean, getting into?"

Luckily—or not—Rob's cell rang at that moment, and he looked at the screen. "Dang it. Just a second," he grumbled as he picked it up. "What do you want?" he said into the phone.

From there I could only hear his side, but it sounded like he had a child and the child had done something naughty, or else Rob was in trouble, and he didn't have time to babysit right now because he was on a date. It was terribly confusing and even more embarrassing to listen in on. At one point, I got up and basically trickle filled my soda cup to try to give him some privacy. It took a measly ten seconds.

When I came back, Rob had hung up. He smiled at me as I sat down. "Sorry. That was my ex. She won't bother us again."

He asked me a few questions about myself, and the conversation was flowing nicely. I was able to relax and put the discomfort of the phone call behind me as we talked. He had a great sense of humor, and he was cute. For the first time in a long while, I was really engaged in the conversation. We were actually hitting it off! I was feeling some warm fuzzies when the phone rang again.

He sighed. "Sorry, have to take it."

It was the ex again, or possibly now the ex's mother? Either way it was an argument. I sat quietly eating my food while all the good vibes I'd been feeling drained away. I wished like nobody's business that I'd be either swallowed up by the booth or magically transported back to my bed only to find it had been a bad dream. When he finally hung up again, he looked apologetic.

"Sounds like your life is pretty crazy right now," I said to fill the awkward silence.

He simply shrugged. "You have no idea."

"I'm not trying to be rude, but are you ready to date yet?" I asked, trying not to be too disappointed that the only guy I'd had a chance of hitting it off with so far was in no place to hit it off with me.

He looked me over for a minute, almost like taking stock of me before deciding if I'd be worth the hassle. While he was giving me the once-over, his phone rang again. He looked down at it and back at me.

"I think that's your answer." I smiled kindly and stood up. "I'll call myself a ride home," I offered.

"No, no. I can talk and drive. I'll take you." He stood up with me, and I gathered up the garbage as he began talking into the phone.

On the drive home, I tuned out his conversation while listing the positives. While Rob wasn't potential relationship material right now, I'd found that there were some nice guys out there, and I was capable of hitting it off with someone. All hope was not lost. I'd gotten a free $4 lunch today. I wasn't going to have to harm Andrew in any way. He'd been right. Rob was a nice guy—pulled in too many directions, mired down in some messy stuff right now, but a decent guy.

Round two kicked off at seven o'clock that night. With Rob I had known we were going casual, but I wasn't sure what Nick had planned. He'd told me we'd do dinner and then see how things went from there before making other plans. I'd readily agreed. No point in committing to an entire night together if you couldn't even make it through appetizers. But he'd given me no clue on dress code. After trying to talk to Val about my wardrobe struggles, and her telling me to get a grip, I'd finally decided to change into something a little nicer.

I was pretty excited about the cute new "school's out for summer" flowing embroidered shirt I'd bought and thought I looked pretty nice when I left to meet Nick in the parking lot of our apartment complex. I wasn't comfortable with him knowing exactly where I lived, so I'd walked through the large complex to the manager's office at the front of the property and waited for him there.

Nick was considerate enough to actually park his car and get out to greet me. He even complimented me on my outfit, which was a total bonus. He looked as different from Rob as possible. Tall, skinny, blond, and sort of struggling with acne, he appeared much younger than his profile stated. I felt a little hesitant about how young he looked but reminded myself to not judge a book by its cover. It wasn't like I never got a zit here and there . . . weekly.

We chatted comfortably while we drove. He said he was taking me to one of his favorite restaurants, and I was glad I'd dressed up. I was less happy about dressing up when Nick pulled into the Tasty Taco parking lot. I began wondering if I was being pranked, but no, Nick turned off the car and got out. I had no choice but to follow as I fought down laughter that was threatening to burst out. At least I was familiar with the kid's menu if I needed to use it again.

Nick and I walked to the counter, and he began looking at the menu. When I accidentally made eye contact with the employee, he gave me a confused look. I smiled and nodded at him. *Your eyes aren't playing tricks on you, buddy. It's me again.* He must have gotten my message, because he smiled back.

Nick ordered first and then pulled out his wallet to pay before I'd ordered. Thankfully my brain picked up what was happening before I opened my mouth. It appeared I'd be paying for myself, so I stepped to the side a little. I was totally fine paying and wasn't fazed. The employee, however, paused and looked at me. Nick finally picked up the hint and looked at me too.

"Oh, you'll need to get yours," he said nonchalantly and handed the employee his debit card.

The employee gave me a little look out of the corner of his eye. I nodded at him to go ahead. I'd get my own. It's not like I wasn't able to pay for myself, and it really was unfair to assume the man would pay. It was no big deal to buy my own food. At least that way I could comfortably order anything that looked good.

I opened my purse and stepped up to order, but my wallet was gone. I searched a second time and even set my purse on the counter so I could rifle through it better. Nothing. Where on earth could it have gone?

"You don't have any money?" Nick asked.

"I guess not. I have no idea where my wallet could be." I was still looking through my purse and coming up empty. I remembered getting it out to pay Hannah back for some shampoo she'd brought home from her salon. I guess I'd forgotten to put it away. How frustrating!

"Bummer, man. Guess I'm the only one eating then. You can keep me company," he stated matter-of-factly. My head shot up to see if he was kidding. He wasn't. He grabbed his cup off the counter and went to the soda fountain to fill it.

I stood frozen with my hands in my purse, watching as he walked away. Then I looked at the employee, who seemed to be as surprised as I was. "Uh, is this a date?" he asked uncomfortably.

"I thought it was," I replied self-consciously. He smiled a little as I picked up my purse and chose a booth to sit in.

It had to be one of the more mortifying experiences of my life. I wasn't mad that he didn't pay, but I *was* mad that he was so rude. He didn't care that he'd be eating alone or that I was going without. I didn't need money, but I did need some respect and basic human caring.

"So, your profile says you teach school?" Nick slid into the seat across from me and took a big sip of his drink. Before I could reply, he said, "Oh, hey, they'd probably give you a water cup for free if you're thirsty." He suddenly seemed to notice I might want something.

"It's fine." I shook my head and tried to play it cool. No way was I going back up there to embarrass myself by asking for water.

"Suit yourself. So, you teach?" he asked again.

I nodded. "Second grade."

"Cool. They're probably still kind of snotty and gross at that age though, right?" he said, laughing.

"Sometimes." I was so not in the mood to make conversation, which was unfortunate, because that was whole point of this entire fiasco. It was discouraging, to say the least.

"Ma'am?" I heard a voice at my elbow and looked up to see the kid who had taken our order. Well, Nick's order and my side of humiliation.

"Is that my food, man?" Nick looked at the tray.

"No." He sat it down in front of me, meeting my questioning look with a smile, before looking back toward Nick. His smile turned into a scowl as he said, "No girl should go without food on a date." Then he looked at me again. "I got this. Don't worry about it. I hope it's something you like." Then he turned and walked away.

I was shocked. It was probably one of the nicest things a stranger had ever done for me. This teenage kid was working here for minimum wage and was giving up some of his small earnings to right a wrong. My entire insides turned to happy, happy mush.

Nick looked a little baffled. I picked up my taco or burrito or whatever it was and took a huge bite, enjoying watching him watch me eat while he had to wait on his food. It was petty. I did not care. Then I slurped my soda while he leaned forward, watching to see if his food was coming. Karma was my friend in that moment, along with a teenager who smiled at me again when I looked his way.

Nick seemed to realize, as I did, that this date was not a date and wasn't going to lead anywhere. We ate mostly in silence with stilted conversation. When we were both done eating, he said he was sorry that he had other plans that night and he'd take me home. I hoped his other plans involved developing the ability to care about another person's needs.

Nick parked strangely crooked in the parking lot, so when I got out, I had to walk around the front corner of his car to get to the sidewalk. He gunned it to back out, but I guess he didn't realize it was in drive, and he nailed my leg just above my knee, dropping me to the ground in a burst of pain and shock.

"Oh my gosh!" I heard him scream from inside the car, followed by a door slamming and him huffing around to where I was lying on the sidewalk.

"Are you okay?" he asked as he crouched down next to me.

My leg wasn't broken, but it hurt like the devil, and I largely hated him at that moment. I should have never reactivated my online profile. I should have stayed inside my apartment and bought myself two cats. Cats don't drive cars into your legs!

"I think I'm okay," I moaned, holding my leg. I wiggled my toes and bent my knee. It shot more pain up my leg into my hip, but all the parts appeared to be working.

"Here, let me help you up," he said, and then he scooped me too quickly off the ground and set me firmly on my feet. Another zap of pain zoomed up my leg, and I cringed.

"Just give me a minute, okay?" I snapped at him, causing him to back off a bit.

I tentatively took a step forward. It hurt really bad, but I was still standing. I looked back at him and tried hard to smile, but I'm sure it came out as a frightening grimace.

"I'm okay. You go ahead and take off. I'll go on in myself," I stated firmly.

He finally got the message and backed away to his car, apologizing the whole way. He slowly backed out of where he was oddly parked on the sidewalk and drove away with a wave.

As soon as he was out of sight, I sat back down on the sidewalk and rubbed my leg, letting some tears of pain, frustration, and anger well up. I wasn't much for crying, but man I was having a seriously bad day, not to mention that being hit by a car is the best excuse ever for some wallowing.

I was the equivalent of a block away from my apartment and wasn't sure I could hobble back under my own power. I called Val, who I knew had the night off and would be home.

"Yep?" She answered in her typical way.

"I got hit by a car. I'm sitting on the sidewalk by the manager's office and can't really walk. Can you come help me?" I pushed out gloomily.

"Holy Jupiter! On my way." She disconnected the call. Sometimes Val's lack of chattiness was a blessing.

It wasn't long before her car pulled up next to the curb where I was sitting, still rubbing my leg and pushing back the tears.

"Are you okay?" she asked as she jumped out, all concerned.

I explained what had happened and that I was fairly confident it wasn't broken but that putting pressure on it hurt and I needed an arm to lean on.

She gently helped me up and made the best crutch ever as she helped me into the passenger seat before driving the short distance back to her parking space. We eventually made it up the stairs and onto the couch. I was buoyed up from all the nasty things she said about Nick during our slow journey.

"Let me see your leg," she instructed, laying me on the couch.

She pushed the hem of my shorts up a little higher and pressed gently as she looked around a bit. It still hurt, but I thought something broken would hurt a lot more. She agreed with me.

"It's not broken, but you're going to have one heck of a bruise there. Probably limp for a couple of days too."

I sighed. "Today has been one for the record books."

She brought me some ice and ibuprofen. "Anything else I can do to help?" she asked as I got situated on the couch.

"Yes. I'm going to need some Tums. I ate at Tasty Taco twice today," I moped. She groaned in my behalf and went to do as I'd asked.

At times like this, living with a nurse came in quite handy.

The rest of my evening was spent scrolling through pictures of adoptable cats at the local Humane Society and perusing more cat videos. Those fuzzy faces were making me feel a lot happier than my dates had.

Chapter 11

A loving heart is the truest wisdom.

~ *Charles Dickens* ~

Normally at this point in the year, I'd be celebrating the end of school and the official start of summer. I loved teaching school, but I also loved my summers free to do all the things I didn't have time for in the teaching months. I knew I was spoiled that way with my career, but I felt I'd earned it by surviving nine months of student shenanigans. This year, however, my first week of summer vacation had been spent lounging around trying to recover from my last date's car attack. As predicted, my leg had gotten a deep bruise and become stiff and sore. I was limping—or hopping—but not able to fully use the leg for a couple of days.

On the bright side, I was totally caught up on all the latest pop culture news. On the downside, I was considering taking up knitting. I'd be horrible at knitting. I couldn't even braid my own hair. It was clear that I was bored out of my mind.

My leg finally healed, and in celebration of my ability to leave the apartment without wincing, Val and Hannah both arranged to take a day off. We were hitting the mall like a bunch of teenagers. I couldn't remember the last time the three of us had walked through the mall together. The smell of pretzels baking and scented candles burning brought a wave of nostalgia. We'd window-shopped an awful lot during the cold winter months of college.

Of course, during wedding planning season, no outing was to be wasted. Hannah announced as we entered the mall that she had the tiniest errand to run and that if Val and I were good girls who cooperated cheerfully in her little errand, she'd buy us an Orange Julius.

Hannah's mission was to select a wedding ring for Andrew. I found it amusing that she'd tried to pass that off as the "tiniest little errand." Val wasn't buying it either, but the promise of an Orange Julius convinced her to join us at the jewelry store rather than going to buy some pants and meet up with us later.

Unlike many other couples I knew, Hannah and Andrew had decided to surprise each other with rings. Andrew had given Hannah a simple band with a diamond on it when he proposed, but he was busily selecting the setting it would be moved into for their wedding day.

The hot topic of the morning was whether to engrave or not. Hannah was for, Val was—big shock—against, and I was—yet another shocker—the girl stuck in the middle. I'd fully supported whatever style of ring Hannah liked, having no skin in that game. She had gone for a traditional gold band with no frills. I thought it would be perfect. Val said it was too wide and she should choose something thinner. When Hannah said she'd chosen a wide one so she could have it engraved, Val's reaction put her in danger of losing her promised Orange Julius reward.

"Engraving is so dumb. No one ever sees it. What's the point?" Val pulled a face.

"It's private and special between two people. Everyone who sees the ring will know he's married, but what's written on the inside will be ours alone," Hannah argued back. "I think it's so romantic!"

"Plus, if it ever got lost, it would be easier for people to find its rightful owners," I helpfully added. It earned me a smile from Hannah and an eye roll from Val.

"What if he doesn't engrave yours?" Val pointed out.

"I don't care. That's his choice." Hannah seemed genuine about that. I was wondering if I should secretly let Andrew know that Hannah found engraving romantic. That felt like the kind of thing a maid of honor would do.

"What would you even have engraved on it?" Val flipped her choppy bangs away from her eyes with an impatient hand.

"I've been doing some research on that." Hannah opened her notebook and began flipping pages.

Val gave me a comical look over Hannah's head and whispered, "Of course she has," which made me stifle a laugh.

"Okay." Hannah found her page. "Here are my favorites. My top one is 'Our love is eternal.'" Val groaned and made a gagging sign. I swatted her arm and gave her a stern look. Hannah simply raised an eyebrow and continued. "I also like something simple like 'H loves A,' 'A and H forever,' or 'You are my soul mate.'"

"How about 'Do Not Remove'?" Val cracked. "Or 'Property of Hannah'?"

"I have no idea why I even bring you along," Hannah said, sighing. She smiled in spite of herself and put her notebook back in her huge bag.

"I don't either. It's your fault. I told you I'd wear the dress and smile for the pictures. All this other stuff I should be left out of," Val agreed, cheerfully acknowledging her faults.

"What about engraving it with your wedding date?" I asked Hannah.

She thought about it for a minute. "I'll add that to my list." She smiled and gave me a quick one-armed hug. "It's good to have some support." She playfully glared at Val. Val just shrugged. "I'm going to wrap it up with the salesperson. I'll meet you guys in a minute."

"Let's look around while we wait," I suggested to Val, figuring she'd tease me, but she surprised me by being up for it.

We walked to the other side of the store, where women's jewelry was, and started looking. I was surprised by how styles had both changed and stayed constant. A few years back, I'd come into a store like this and chosen a ring I liked—no, loved. When the breakup had come, I'd refused to think about weddings at all for a while. Now it was fun to have the past mostly behind me and be girly for a minute.

"See anything you like?" a voice said quietly from behind me. I jumped nearly out of my skin and let out a little squeak as I spun around. James was there, and my entire body turned to both fire and lead.

"You scared the cookies right out of me." I pressed a hand to my chest and managed to talk around the memories floating to the surface as a lump formed in my throat.

I swore I could see those same memories float across his eyes—us looking through jewelry cases with his hand on the small of my back, his lips near my ear, his warm laughter filling the space. James had been over the moon about us becoming engaged. I had been pretty over the moon myself, until the worries and doubts had crept in. Not doubts about James. Doubts about marriage, the future, my age, and . . .

I shook my head to dislodge that train of thought and asked, "What are you doing here?" I glanced around desperately, only to see that Val was several yards away from me. I guess I'd been caught up in my head and hadn't noticed her move along.

He snapped out of whatever he'd been thinking and visibly straightened his shoulders. "I'm trying to find a gift for a work friend who's getting married. I think I heard someone say they're registered at the Bed Bath & Beyond." He shrugged like he wasn't sure what he was doing. His demeanor was cool and aloof, and I wondered why he'd even bothered to stop.

"I don't think people usually call it *the* Bed Bath & Beyond," I managed to say in a lightly teasing tone. I wanted to be aloof too, but it was virtually impossible to escape the memories.

"Ah, thanks for the tip." His expression stayed the same, but his eyes crinkled up a bit.

"James?" Hannah joined us and gave her brother a quick hug. "What are you doing?"

"Shopping," he stated, apparently not wanting to waste words by repeating what he'd already told me. Hannah just shook her head.

"Obviously." She pinched her lips in fake sibling annoyance. "This is actually good timing. You can help us settle something. To engrave or not to engrave?" Hannah asked him.

At this point, Val had wandered back over and was watching James closely to see what he'd say. I took the opportunity to move slightly out of the circle and gather myself again. I'd never asked what James had done with my ring when I'd given it back to him. Standing in a jewelry store with him now felt like a cruel twist of fate.

"What are we engraving?" he asked.

Hannah sighed the put-out sigh of misunderstood brides everywhere. "Andrew's wedding band."

He raised his eyebrows a bit and looked at the three of us. "I'm not sure I want to be in the middle of this. Do what you want," he replied.

"Smart man." Val grinned. I simply nodded when he looked at me. Hannah pulled a face.

"He's right, Han," I soothed. "Just do what you want. This is your wedding and your man. Engrave the heck out of it."

"What would you have engraved?" James wondered in a way that said he'd honestly never thought about engraving anything.

"Aha!" Val pounced. "I'm sure he speaks for men everywhere. Andrew won't care."

"The question is why do *you* care?" Hannah speared Val with a look, and Val seemed to deflate a bit.

"I don't," Val finally replied.

"Good. Then you can stop arguing with me." Hannah turned and started walking out of the shop. "And you can sit and watch while Rach and I get some Orange Julius," she shot over her shoulder as we followed her.

"We're getting Orange Julius?" James immediately stepped into formation with us as we followed Hannah. I chuckled at his pleased expression.

"Everyone but Val," Hannah said.

"I wasn't a good girl," Val explained to James as she pushed out her lower lip in a teasing pout.

"Don't worry, Crabby, she didn't ever expect you to be. She'll probably buy you one anyway," James replied.

Hannah smiled at James's comment as she turned and waited for us to catch up.

"Val will be lucky if I let her have a sip of mine," she joked. "I think for her punishment I'll make her go help James with his shopping."

"But I've been a good boy," James quipped, and once again I admired him for moving on in a way that I didn't seem to be able to.

Chapter 12

There is no remedy for love but to love more.

~ Henry David Thoreau ~

Through the shiny window of Elite Bridal, I could see Hannah and Gloria—bridal attendant extraordinaire—with huge smiles on their faces. Andrew stood next to Hannah with his arm casually around her waist, and Val was sitting slouched on one of the pristine white chairs near another man I didn't know. It was probably Garrett, Andrew's cousin and best man. I'd been told about him and that we'd be matched up at the wedding itself, but I hadn't met him yet. Between meeting my "partner" and having to try on a dress again, I wasn't sure I wanted to go in there. Last time had been brutal, and this time I hadn't been able to bring caffeinated products with me. I needed a minute to psych myself up.

"I take it I'm not the only one who would rather be somewhere else?" a voice behind me interrupted my thoughts, and I spun to find James standing casually near, looking over my shoulder at the same scene I'd been taking in.

That was the second time he'd sneaked up behind me in the past month. His nearness caused my pulse to pick up, and suddenly going in didn't seem like such a bad idea.

"I should stop being a pansy and just go in. It can't be as bad as I'm building it up to be," I stated as I stepped back from the window and turned to go in. James reached around me and grabbed the door handle to open it for me before I could to do it myself. I offered him a smile as thanks for his kindness.

"Care to place a wager on that?" he asked in a quiet voice as I walked past him into the door. I knew he was whispering to keep Hannah from hearing, but his soft voice close to my ear caused a tingle to dance down my spine.

"Nope. Not even a little one," I retorted over my shoulder. "You know I always lose."

Hannah heard us come in and clapped her hands together before James could reply. She hurried over to give both of us hugs and then turned back to the group.

"They're here. Let's get started! Andrew, Garrett, and James, you can go over there with Elaine." She pointed to a pretty blonde woman waiting near a set of curtains. "Oh, wait, you haven't all met Garrett. Let me introduce you." Hannah grabbed both James and me by the arms and steered us over to where the man I'd seen was standing up out of his chair.

Garrett turned to face us, and I was immediately struck by how handsome he was. He was of average height, and it was obvious he was into physical fitness. His dark blond hair was spiky, and his bright eyes radiated good humor. When he smiled at us, I felt a pleasant tingle of awareness. Suddenly I was just fine with being partners for the wedding.

He stepped forward and held out his hand to me first, eyes dancing. "Hey there. You must be Rachel."

I took his hand and smiled back. My eyes were probably dancing a little too. "I am. I'm so happy to meet you."

"I'm James Redmond." James stepped forward and shook his hand as soon as Garrett dropped mine. "Hannah's brother."

"Well, great, man. Good to meet you." Garrett smiled, and then his gaze swung back my direction. "So I hear we're partners for the wedding. Maid of honor, right?"

I smiled, praying that charming dimples would suddenly appear on my face. "That's right."

He gave me an obvious pass over and smiled again. "Looks to me like it's going to be a great night."

Oh, my heck! Even my ninety-year-old blind great-aunt would have recognized the flirting in that statement. I blushed so hard it probably looked like I was sunburned. The embarrassment of knowing I was blushing made it even worse. I heard James clear his throat and Val make a scoffing noise as I smiled back at him.

"Okay you two," Hannah giggled as she came up to us. I could see how pleased she was that we were hitting it off. "Save that for later. Let's get everyone suited up."

Hannah grabbed my arm again and walked me to the other side of the shop where we went behind a curtain that matched the same one the guys disappeared behind.

"Oh, I think you're going to be thanking me." Hannah smiled knowingly.

I nodded, not even pretending I didn't know what she was talking about. Garrett would be a great wedding sidekick.

"You might be right." I couldn't help but giggle as I said it.

Val was already standing in front of a three-way mirror, being zipped into her dress as I began changing. She looked so feminine in the navy blue flowing material, even if the slight frown on her face detracted from the overall effect.

"Val, you look so pretty." I smiled at her as our eyes met in the mirror.

She turned from side to side and then glanced back at me. "I don't know how this is possible, but I kind of like this dress on me." She continued to frown, but now I realized it was in confusion, not frustration.

"Gloria said she was a miracle worker," I teased as I stepped into my own dress with Hannah's help.

"Not to mention that the bride has impeccable taste." Gloria herself entered the conversation as she came into the room with a stack of shoeboxes in her arms.

Hannah zipped me up, and I walked over and stood next to Val. I was as surprised as Val. We were wearing the same dress—navy blue, floor length, with a scooped neck that hit right at the top of our collarbones, a navy lace-covered bodice, capped sleeves, and a high waistline cinched in with a ribbon belt. We looked elegant. Val's curves were enhanced in just the right way, and somehow the dress made me look like I actually had some.

"I'm completely—" I said as I looked at myself.

"Speechless?" Hannah jumped in between us, throwing an arm around both of us and smiling. "I knew we could do it. You both look amazing!"

"Hannah, you made the perfect choice for these two. But there will need to be some adjustments." Gloria joined us and began pulling, tugging, and pinching at the dresses here and there, getting a preliminary idea of what alterations would be needed.

After another moment, Gloria handed us each a box and told us to put on our shoes. They were flirty, navy-blue strappy heels, and I loved them. I was probably three inches taller.

"Is this what the world looks like up here?" I laughed as I stood up straight and looked around. Hannah gave me a grin.

After both Val and I were strapped in and standing up, Gloria looked us over to see how the dresses fell with the addition of the shoes. Then she directed us to go out into the open area to meet up with the men. A tailor was ready to make official notes and take measurements. Also, Hannah and Andrew needed to make sure they were happy with how we all matched.

The men were already in the main room. Andrew stood on a stool of some sort, while a small woman was tucking the hems on his tux and the pretty blonde, Elaine, was pulling on the cuffs of his jacket. James and Garrett were standing nearby watching silently.

Gloria motioned for us ladies to have a seat, and she went to where the three men were standing to start making notes on her tablet. "Hannah, will you join me? I need your opinion here," Gloria said as her nails clicked on the screen.

James and Garrett both turned at the sound of Gloria's voice, and I couldn't help but admire how they looked in their tuxes. When they saw Val and me sit down, they came to join us. Garrett sat next to me and faced me with a whistle.

"Wow, hard to believe, but you look even prettier in that gown than you did when you first walked in," he said, grinning.

I smiled, totally willing to flirt with this guy, and complimented him back. "Not looking too bad yourself."

"If you're not careful, you may outshine the bride." He nudged my shoulder playfully with his closest elbow, and it made my stomach tingle again. It was fun to tingle a little when I'd been tingle-free for so long.

I glanced to where James and Val were sitting watching us. Val looked like she'd smelled something bad, and I couldn't read James's look. I didn't have time to really try to read his expression before he turned to Val.

"You look great too," he said to her.

Val shocked me by smiling at him. "I do, don't I? I didn't think she'd pull it off, but that Gloria doesn't mess around." She looked down at her dress again like she couldn't quite believe it.

Her happiness made me happy. She really did look stunning. Val thought she was too big, but the rest of us saw her differently. She was curvy and confident. It was great for her to get a glimpse of that for herself.

"Crabby?" Garrett leaned close and whispered in my ear.

"Don't ask. They're being nice right now," I whispered back. He nodded and zipped his lips, which made me chuckle.

"So, Rachel, tell me, what does a pretty lady like you do for fun?" Garrett sat back in his chair and crossed one leg so that his stocking foot rested on his knee.

"I plan weddings, try to keep my roommates from killing each other, and teach school," I replied with a grin. "What about you?"

"I don't know if I can measure up. Let's see. I fight fires, occasionally help with the family business, and I try to keep my dog from having accidents in the house." Garrett smiled and gave me a barely perceptible wink when he finished.

"You're a fireman?" James asked.

Garrett spared him a glance and nodded. "I am. And a trained EMT. I love it." James nodded with a thoughtful look on his face.

"I'm a nurse at St. Joseph's. Maybe I'll see you sometime when you bring in a patient," Val joined in.

"Maybe." Garrett smiled kindly at her. Then he turned back to me. "What grade do you teach?"

"Second. It's an adventure every day."

"So do you do another job during the summer, or are you off?" he asked.

"I'm off."

Garrett smiled and leaned closer again, opening his mouth to whisper in my ear when—

"Rachel, you're up," Hannah interrupted from across the room. Andrew was stepping off the stool, and Hannah was waving to me.

I waved back and started to stand, but Garrett jumped up and reached down his hands to help me up. As he gripped my hands in his, he gently tugged me toward him and smiled down at me.

"Hurry back," he said quietly.

I couldn't say anything over the fluttering feeling in my chest, so I just smiled and nodded. I was blushing so hard that I thought my face would blow up. But hey, if it had, there was a fireman in the house.

Later that night, I gushed to Diana about Garrett when she called to ask me about the annual Fourth of July party my parents hosted. She laughed when I told her about him telling me to hurry back.

"Wow, he's a major flirt!" she said.

I giggled like a teenage girl. "It was so fun! I can't remember the last time I flirted with someone that way."

"Maybe you two could go out," Diana suggested.

"He'd really be better than the last one. Andrew set me up with an old friend of his, and then a guy from online contacted me and . . ." I filled her in on the horrors of the Rob and Nick fiasco.

"You got hit by a car?" Diana was as shocked and as angry as I'd been. "Sounds to me like you may need a break from dating."

"I'm with you on that. Although," I said with a giggle, "Garrett was delicious enough to make me change my mind. I wonder if Andrew gave him my number."

"Well, I admire your willingness to try again for the cute firefighter," she teased. "Speaking of delicious, are you going to make it to the Fourth of July party this year?"

"Of course. Wouldn't miss it," I said. I loved my parents' annual party. "I invited Val, Hannah, and Andrew to come too," I added.

"Great. There's definitely room for everyone at mom's house if you want to sleep over."

"I'll plan on it and let them know. So, what's our official business tonight?"

"How to keep Dad from blowing up the house," Diana joked.

We talked for a few more minutes about plans for the holiday, how we really thought our parents were doing, and, of course, my cute twin nieces.

"You know, you could send me some of the online dating profiles you've been looking through," Diana said as we wound up our chat.

"I'm pretty sure we just decided I was never looking online again."

"Come on! It would be fun. I could find you a match with my great wisdom."

"You're going to be underwhelmed," I made a noise.

"Probably. But at least I'll get a laugh out of it." She agreed in such a straight way that it made me chuckle.

"Fine. Don't say that I didn't warn you. And tell Jordan he can thank me later," I teased, referring to her husband.

"For what?"

"For reminding you of what a stellar husband you have."

Chapter 13

Love is a serious mental disease.

~ Plato ~

As June rolled to a sunny close, I was thrilled to get a phone call from Garrett. Thrilled with a capital T! I'd been hoping and waiting. I knew I could ask Andrew for his number, but after everyone had watched us flirting so heavily at the dress fitting, I was embarrassed and didn't want to get everyone's hopes up. Okay, my hopes up. I was afraid that it had meant more to me than it had to Garrett.

As more time passed, I'd started to wonder if I'd imagined the whole thing. Doubt paralyzed me for a few days, until I finally realized that I didn't have to sit around and wait. I decided that if I hadn't heard from him by the Fourth of July holiday, I would talk to Andrew about getting his contact info.

When he did call, he was as flirty and cheerful as before, and my relief was palpable. His schedule was crazy with fire season being in full swing, so it was hard to make plans. He was due for a day off on the coming Saturday, and if I was willing to keep my schedule open, he'd call me when he knew what time we could meet up. Since this was Andrew's cousin and my partner in the wedding party, I gave him my address and agreed to keep my Saturday open.

Sure enough, on Saturday afternoon, he shot me a text saying he would be out my way in about twenty minutes. He could pick me up then if I didn't mind running a quick errand with him. His family had extra work in the business he'd mentioned when we met, and he'd agreed to pitch in. After the errand, he'd take me for *"the best pancakes I've ever had."*

I'd been cleaning my bathroom and doing laundry, but I figured I could slap myself together in twenty minutes and meet up with him. The more I thought about it, the more I was feeling hopeful about Garrett. In my opinion, a good-looking, cheerful firefighter who helped with the family business was nothing to scoff at. I was downright giddy over this date.

I texted him back that I would be ready in twenty. I put my hair up in a cap so that it would stay dry while I took a speed shower. Then I put on some light makeup and ran a straightener over my long locks before slapping on some jeans and a cute top. I was proud of myself for not overthinking it.

By my calculation, it had been 19.5 minutes—a record for me. In almost exactly twenty minutes, there was a knock on the door. I was home alone, so I quickly answered it, anxious and nauseated at the thought of seeing him again. What if he wasn't as great as I'd remembered?

Garrett was as great at second glance as he'd been at first. His smile lit up his entire face as he stepped forward and gave me a hug in greeting. I happily hugged him back.

"Thanks for being willing to come on such short notice," he said as I locked the door behind me and we started down the stairs to the parking lot. He pointed to his dirty work clothes and pulled a face. "Sorry I'm a mess. We'll stop by my house so I can change after we run this errand."

"No problem. You saved me from the horrors of housework." I smiled and he smiled back.

Garrett took me to a big red lifted truck with a giant blue tarp covering whatever was in the bed. He politely opened the door for me, and I climbed in, grateful for stretchy jeans, my flexibility, and a handhold near the dash. The truck was messy on the inside. A box of plastic gloves was spilling out, and there were soda cans on the floor of the passenger side.

Garrett climbed in his door and smiled apologetically at me. "Sorry about the mess. I really have been working all week and just sneaking in meals on the run. I didn't have a chance to clean it up."

"It's fine. So tell me about your family business." I smiled at him, hoping to appear relaxed even though the messy truck was disgusting. I was not going to come off like that germophobe Doug with his Lysol cans at the ready.

"Actually, you're in luck. You'll get to see it firsthand. I need to stop by three different vet clinics before we grab those pancakes."

"Okay, sounds good," I said happily.

Garrett was relaxed and an easy conversationalist as we drove to our first stop. He shared funny stories from the fire station, I shared funny stories from second grade, and we agreed that maybe firefighters weren't that different from young children.

Garrett had grown up in the area and still worked with his mother in the family business on weekends here and there. His dad wasn't around anymore, and I was impressed by Garrett's efforts to help his mom keep things going. Happily, my immediate initial attraction to Garrett was still going strong.

We arrived at the first clinic, and Garrett invited me to come in with him. I was excited to join him, thoughts of cute animals dancing through my head. He walked me around back and knocked on an employee entrance door. A vet tech let us in, and I followed Garrett into a big room full of boxes and equipment but no animals.

Garrett put on a pair of those plastic gloves that had been sitting in his truck, walked to a freezer against the back wall, and opened the lid. Then, to my horror, he began pulling out frozen animals in clear plastic bags. I couldn't stop from staring in surprise and no small amount of disgust.

"Only three today?" Garrett called to the vet tech standing near me.

"Yep. Their information is all there and ready to go," the tech replied.

Garrett nodded and closed the lid of the freezer before walking back to where I stood feeling as frozen as the three animals he was holding. He smiled at me, obviously completely unaware that I was freaking out in my head.

"That's it for here. Let's get moving." He motioned toward the door with one of the animals. It made my stomach flip, but not in the way you want it to flip on a date. Definitely not the way it had been flipping thus far.

I hurriedly led the way back out the door and around to the truck. Garrett lifted one corner of the blue tarp and gently set the animals underneath. Then he pulled off the plastic gloves he'd been wearing and threw them in as well before closing the tarp again and coming around to open my door.

"Surprised?" he said, laughing as he swung the door open and offered me a hand up.

"You could say that." I hesitated to take his hand but ended up accepting his help into the truck. He grinned at my reply, shut the door, and walked quickly around to the driver's side.

"So, you've probably guessed by now what the family business is," he said as the truck roared to life and he steered it back onto the road.

I, in fact, had no idea what the family business was. What type of business involved picking up dead, frozen animals from vet clinics? I just shook my head, which he saw out of the corner of his eye as he drove.

"Cremation," he stated. "After a pet dies, or is euthanized, we pick them up and take them to our shop where my mom cremates them. Depending on the situation, we either keep the ashes and put them in a nice urn for the family or dispose of them. We do it all." He was enthusiastic about this topic and turned with a smile on his face, mistakenly assuming I would be as excited too.

"Sounds interesting," was the best I could come up with. While I appreciated that pets were like family to some people and having their ashes would be a comfort, I wasn't super excited about the process behind it.

"Yeah, it's kind of different, but business is steady, and it keeps food on the table." Garrett laughed as he realized I was feeling squeamish.

"Bills have to be paid," I said, trying to stay positive.

"Exactly. But I'm guessing this means you want me to do the rest alone?"

"If you're hoping I'll want to eat later, that might be best," I tried to tease, but I meant it wholeheartedly.

Garrett winked at me. "That works for me."

Garrett kept a steady flow of conversation going as we drove to the remaining clinics. I stayed in the truck as he ran in and made the pickups. Not having to actually see the animals, combined with Garrett's casual chitchat and obvious flirting, eventually helped me relax again. Garrett wasn't bad at all. His job was the pits, but at least he was normal and friendly and this was only a side gig. I could move past it. Heaven knew I wasn't perfect either.

Eventually we picked up all the animals and made a quick last stop at his family's shop to drop them off. Garrett scored points with me by running in and changing his clothing before we left to go get dinner. His hair was wet when he came back, and I was comforted by the thought that he'd washed up too.

By this time, it was still only 4:00 p.m. Looked like we'd be dining with the oldies tonight. It was fine. I had no idea if he had anything planned for after we ate, but I could easily fill up my Saturday night if he didn't.

Garrett took me to a pancake place I'd never heard of called Granny's. It felt like walking into a truck stop, which in my experience typically meant the service would be sassy and the food would be greasy but delicious.

The green linoleum in the booth squeaked as we slid into place and picked up our menus. Our waitress filled our water cups, suggested the special—an omelet—and hurried away to help other diners.

"Order whatever you like, but their pancakes really are the best," Garrett said. "And I'm paying."

He had no way of knowing how much I appreciated him just laying that out there. I smiled genuinely across the table. He was pretty cute.

I took his advice and ordered the pancakes. They were, hands down, the most amazing pancakes I'd ever had. After my first bite, I looked up at his expectant face and just nodded with my mouth full of light and fluffy goodness. Garrett laughed and reached across the table to squeeze my hand. I felt a little sad when he let go.

The pancakes were so good, I almost didn't want to talk, but we easily kept up the conversation until our plates were empty. I appreciated him not commenting on the fact that I'd all but licked my plate clean.

"So, listen. It's still early. You up for some fun?" He glanced at his watch as he patted his stomach.

At this point, the date had been one of my better ones—ever. I had nothing pressing at home and wasn't anxious to get away from him, so I decided to go with it.

"Sure. What did you have in mind?" I asked. He gestured for me to lead the way out the door, and as we reached his truck, he opened my door, giving me a hand up before walking around to get in.

"Ever been up to Cedar Grove?" he asked as he started up his truck.

"Heard of it. Isn't it just up the canyon a bit? I think there's a pond and some campsites?" I hesitantly replied. Why would he be taking me there? I mean, I knew we'd been flirting shamelessly all afternoon, but I was not going parking with this guy up the canyon.

"Yep. Close to it is a little dirt road that takes you around the front of the mountain where you can see down into the city. It's really pretty when it gets dark." He pulled onto the road and headed toward the hills.

"Um, I hate to have to say this, but I'm not the type of girl who goes parking, you know?" I said as firmly as I could. "In fact, the only reason I'm even entertaining the idea of going up the mountain is because Andrew is your cousin and would know where to find you if I disappeared."

He laughed. "Good. I don't date that kind of girl. This is all innocent and fun, I promise. Besides, I can't make you totally fall in love with me on one date. I'm going to need to spend a lot of time wooing you." He winked and reached over to take my hand in his. Again. "You cool?"

I let my hand open to hold his back. It felt nice. Still, I couldn't help the little bit of worry that crept in. "It's not going to be dark for a while. It's only five," I hedged. It was the end of June. Dark was not for another few hours or so.

"We can just explore the hills in the truck until then," he said, smiling. "Maybe hike a bit. I try to get up there a few times a month to blow off some steam. Come on. Let's have some fun." He was pretty convincing with his smile and his excitement.

Sadly, his version of fun and mine split paths about an hour later. I had no idea how he'd done it, but he found literally the one mud puddle left in the entire state at this point in the year and gotten stuck right in the middle of it. We seesawed back and forth for a long time before he finally admitted he was stuck.

"We'll need to put it in four-wheel drive," he said sadly.

"You mean we weren't in four-wheel drive before you tried to drive through this thing?" I said in a slightly short tone. "You had no idea how deep it even was before you zoomed on in?" I was feeling super irritated after rough-riding over what felt like every bump in the road before ending up lodged in this muck.

"Hey, half the fun is not knowing what's going to happen," he said, grinning at me. Funny, he was looking less cute than before. "Do you know how to lock a hub?"

"A what? Don't you have push-button four-wheel drive?" I was a little surprised here. His truck didn't look that old, but then again, what did I know about it?

"A hub," he said. Then he painstakingly explained the procedure to me before saying, "You get the passenger side, and I'll do the driver side, okay?"

"How exactly am I supposed to get to it? It's under the water." I felt this was an incredibly valid point.

"You should be able to reach it from the doorway if you hang onto the door and lean out a little."

I still wasn't capturing his vision, but I wanted to get out of the puddle, so without really watching what he did, I opened my door and leaned out. You'd think a smart person like me wouldn't be so stupid sometimes. All I succeeded in doing was falling out of the truck. Luckily, I had been hanging onto the door and was able to catch myself and land on my feet, but I was almost up to my crotch in mud and water. I could feel it oozing into my sneakers, and I prayed my underwear wouldn't get wet too, because wet, muddy underwear was where I drew the line.

Garrett laughed from the cab of the truck. "Oops. My side is done. Since you're already muddy and out there, just walk over and twist the—" I held up a hand to stop him from talking as I sloshed over and did what he'd asked.

Then I sloshed back to the truck and lifted a leg to climb back in. I could see the expression on his face telling me loud and clear that he wasn't excited about having a muddy passenger. My eyes dared him to say a word. He didn't.

He fired up the engine and revved it as soon as I was back in and the doors were closed. I expected to fly right out of there, but we still spun out with no traction. My right elbow banged into the door as we bounced a little, but still nothing budged.

"Why aren't we moving?" I asked as I rubbed at my arm. Garrett tried again, turning the wheel back and forth and then slamming it into reverse and drive. Nothing.

Finally, he cut the engine and looked at me. "Sorry, Rachel. We're really stuck. I think we're going to have to call someone for help."

I took a deep breath and let it out slowly. "Okay. Go ahead," I said.

"Um, my cell phone is still at home. I accidentally left it in my pants pocket when I changed." He at least had the decency to look embarrassed.

"Okay. We can use mine." I pulled mine out of my purse and held it out to him.

He shook his head. "I don't memorize numbers anymore, because they're all in my phone."

"Not even your mom?" I asked in disbelief.

"She's out of town. That's why I had to pick up the animals today."

"None of your fire buddies?"

"Sorry." He shrugged and winked at me again. This guy was a winker, and the more he did it, the less it made me sparkle inside.

I took another deep breath. "Okay. I'll see who I can get ahold of."

I angled away from him and started thinking. I had no idea who to call. None of my friends drove trucks, and my family lived hours away. I didn't exactly have towing coverage on my auto insurance for stuff like this.

I finally just called Hannah. She was kind of my second mom. I knew she'd know what to do. When she answered, I succinctly told her what had happened and asked if Andrew had access to a truck.

She had the audacity to laugh before she got around to replying. "Wow, Rach. You have the worst luck."

"I know," I sighed. Garrett had been so cute, and I'd been having such a good time. Now it was like a balloon that had been pricked by a pin. The good feelings were leaking out slowly.

"Okay, I'm sorry. Let me think. You need a truck to try to tow you out?" Hannah said.

"That's what I hear," I responded.

"Oh, James drives a truck. I think it would be big enough to do the job. Do you have his number?"

"Nope." I figured it was a moot point, because even if I did have his number, he was the last person on earth I was going to call to rescue me on a date. "Isn't there anyone else?"

"Why? I thought you and James were cool."

"We are. I just don't want to call him out to join me on my *date*!" It came out harsher than I'd meant it to. I did not want to have James around as much as James seemed to be around lately. It was one thing to pretend I was okay with him around when it happened, but it was another to seek out his company. I just wasn't there yet.

"Okay, okay," Hannah pacified me. "I get it—it's weird. The thing is, Rach, there's no one else I know."

I sighed and thought for a long moment. "Text me his number. We'll call him if we can't figure anything else out."

"Will do. Good luck," she said.

"Thanks, Han. Fingers crossed," I replied.

I hung up and looked over at Garrett. The hesitation must have shown on my face because he jumped in before I could say anything. "I don't know who your friend told you to call or why you don't want to call them, but we're really stuck."

"We could walk to the road and try to flag someone down," I offered.

"What if we can't find anyone? A walk back to town would take a really long time," Garrett said. "If you want to give me your phone, I'll make the call." He held out his hand, completely serious about calling a stranger for help.

"What about a tow truck? Do you have coverage?" I crossed my fingers.

"Nope. And even if I did, they'd charge a huge premium in a situation like this where they'd have to go off the pavement. Sorry." Garrett didn't seem that sorry.

"Fine. I'll call," I grumped. There was no way Garrett calling would actually be better than me doing it. He and James hadn't exactly hit it off. "Just give me a minute to talk myself into it," I said.

He obliged by leaning back on his seat and looking away from me. I appreciated the space as I dialed the number Hannah had given me for James. I simultaneously crossed my fingers that he'd answer and prayed he wouldn't. I had no idea what James did on weekends other than sometimes drive the two hours to see his mom and drop by our place with bridal magazines.

It took enough rings that I was beginning to give up when his voice came over the line sounding kind of muted.

"Hello?" he said.

There was laughter and something that sounded like a rock beat in the background. I wasn't sure where he was, only that it was obvious he wasn't sitting around bored at home. I'd interrupted him somewhere. My heart sank down into the mud below us.

"Oh, um, you know what . . ." I began morosely, getting ready to pretend it was a wrong number.

"Rachel?" He sounded surprised. He wasn't the only one. I was shocked he could still recognize my voice over the phone, especially with all that noise around him. "Um, hold on. Don't hang up. Give me one second." His voice became more muted, and I figured he was talking to someone there with him.

"He answered?" Garrett said from his seat next to me.

I'd practically forgotten he was there since he'd been so quiet while I'd wrestled with myself. I nodded and gave him a thumbs-up.

"Sorry, Rachel. You still there?" James was back, and the background noise was mostly gone.

"Yes. I'm so sorry to bother you. It's not really—" I started to say, but he interrupted me a second time before I could finish.

"What's going on?"

I took a deep breath and debated if I should tell him what was going on, or if I should just ask him a lame wedding-type question and let him get back to what he was doing. I must have hesitated too long, because Garrett nudged my hip with his hand and James started talking again.

"Rach? Are you there?" he asked.

He'd called me "Rach." Something in me broke a little hearing it. In that moment, I missed being that girl more than I could express. Calling him for help, hearing his voice over the phone—it was nerve-wracking. I'd thought I felt things with Garrett, but they were nothing like the feelings James had once created in me—feelings that wanted to creep back in even now.

"Yeah, it's just . . . I'm trying to decide what to do," I blabbed out in my surprise over his familiar use of my nickname.

"About what?" he pressed.

"Do I really tell you why I called or generously let you get back to what you were doing?" I giggled awkwardly. "Because if I tell you, then you might feel obligated to help, and I don't want to ruin your night."

"Ah. So everything is okay with Hannah then?"

Oh, duh! Of course he'd think there was a problem if I was calling. "Oh, sorry, yeah. She's totally fine."

"Why don't you just tell me why you called then?" he said reasonably. He didn't sound annoyed, which was a relief.

"Yeah, so I'm on this date, and well—" I began.

"Are you okay?" he jumped in, surprising me and interrupting yet again.

"Yes, yes. It's just that he took me up the mountain and we're stuck here now. So, I'm wondering if you have a truck that could maybe come pull us out?" I was embarrassed just saying it out loud.

He was quiet for a second before he replied. "You're stuck up the mountain with a guy you're on a date with?"

"Yes. It's Andrew's cousin, Garrett." For some reason it was important to me that he didn't think I'd let a complete stranger take me up the mountain, even though I wasn't sure him finding out it was Garrett was going to help matters.

"And you need me to come pull you out of . . . ?"

"A giant mud puddle."

"Okay."

I couldn't read his tone and was feeling more unsure by the minute. "You know what?" I said. "It's not going to be dark for a while. We can hike back down to the highway and get some help. I suggested that earlier, and Garrett, um, he thought it was too far, but, um, I think it's fine," I added in a fake cheery voice, wanting so much to take back the phone call. I wished I hadn't agreed to come up here at all.

Garrett tapped my shoulder and gave me a look like I was crazy. "That's seriously a pretty long hike," he said to me.

"Is that him?" James must have heard Garrett's voice.

"Yeah," I replied.

"Let me talk to him," James said.

"Uh, how about no on that. Go back to what you were doing and—"

"Rachel, let me talk to him." James sounded stern, and I was too flustered to argue.

I looked at Garrett. "He wants to talk to you."

"And who is this guy?" Garrett asked.

"Hannah's brother, James," I answered. Best to keep it simple.

Garrett nodded once and took the phone from me. The rest was guy chat, and I was so uncomfortable that I was able to forget about my squishy shoes and mud-soaked pants for the duration of their conversation.

In the end, it was decided that James would come get us. Garrett gave him directions and told him what he thought we'd need by way of tow straps and tools to get the job done. Then they hung up before I had another chance to talk to James.

I spent the next hour freaking out in my head. James was coming. I kept thinking about how Diana had said her first date with Jordan had been a bust. This date had been going fine, and I'd been so excited when Garrett had called. It was too bad that things had gone downhill. Pulling James into the date was making everything unravel. Garrett tried to go back to our idle chitchat, but I was too tense.

Eventually the silence descended. There was nothing to do but wait it out. We were trapped inside his truck, going nowhere, and done talking. I wiggled my toes around and tried to get more comfortable in my soggy clothing, but it wasn't happening.

Finally, I heard the sound of an engine and turned to see a full-size black truck bouncing up the trail toward us. The truck skirted around the mud puddle and came to a stop in front of us, the rear of the truck facing us. The engine shut off a second before James hopped out of the driver's side.

"That's him," I said to Garrett.

"Yep, I remember him," Garrett acknowledged. He sounded none too happy about it as he looked out the window at James.

"Hey, man, if you could just—" Garrett called out to James.

"Just a second." James held up a hand to Garrett. He stepped into some waders—who knew he fished these days?—and came around to my side of the truck.

It felt like our gazes physically collided when he came to stand at the edge of the giant mud puddle. He stood facing me, his expression giving nothing away, yet I could feel the vibes of something nameless across the distance. I was trying to apologize with my eyes, but my heart sped up in joy at seeing him—traitorous little thing. It wasn't supposed to feel anything for him still.

I leaned out the window. "Hey, James. Thanks so much for coming up here."

"You okay?" he asked.

"Yeah, I'm good." I nodded.

"I'm coming to get you," he stated as he waded into the water.

"What is he doing?" Garrett sounded annoyed as James got closer to the truck.

"Coming to get me," I said as surprised as Garrett was.

I was glad James had the waders. At least he was staying dry as the water rose to his knees. When he got to the truck, he opened my door and reached in a hand.

I hesitated, scared of making contact with him but wanting so badly to be rescued. My heartbeat increased at the thought of taking his hand and going with him. Oddly, at that moment, it felt like Garrett was safe and James was dangerous. After a blink of hesitation, I grabbed my purse and looped it around one shoulder before taking his offered hand and starting to jump down. His hand felt big and warm as it closed around my smaller one, but before I could swing my legs all the way out, James stopped me.

"What are you doing?" he asked.

"Coming with you," I stated.

"You'll get soaked if you just jump out." He huffed out a breath letting me know he thought I was being dumb.

"I'm already soaked." Using the hand that wasn't already in his, I pointed down to my legs and shoes as proof. He scowled down at my legs first and then past me at Garrett, who was suspiciously dry.

"Why is Rachel wet and you're dry?" James asked him in a dark tone.

For a moment, that tone didn't register with me. I was too busy thinking about how James was still holding my hand and I should really stop enjoying it.

Garrett laughed. "It's a funny story, actually," he said, not knowing James well enough to read the irritation behind the question.

James opened his mouth to say something, and it jolted me out of my daydream. "I'll tell you all about it later," I quickly said, pushing at his shoulder to get his attention refocused.

James gave me a look I couldn't quite interpret and then scooped me up into his arms. I couldn't make a sound as my arms grasped for his neck and my side was pressed up against him. He used a shoulder to slam the truck door shut as he turned and walked back out of the puddle. I was very aware of his too-long hair tickling my arm as he walked. He was broader than he'd been the last time I'd been held this close by him. I wanted to lay my head on his shoulder and soak up his strength, but I held myself rigid. I was positive that my still-damp pants were probably getting his arms and shirt wet, but he acted like he didn't notice. He set me down on dry ground and looked me over before walking toward his truck.

"There's a towel behind the passenger seat," he said as he turned and headed toward the bed of the truck.

"So that I don't get mud on your seats?" I teased, uncomfortable and off balance.

"So that you can get dry," he replied, already fishing around in the bed.

I didn't reply but squished over to his truck and opened the door, leaning the seat forward to find an old, orange-colored towel on the floor. I pulled it out and was grateful to see that it was relatively clean as I wrapped it around my waist before turning back to see how things were going with the trucks.

James was back in the middle of the puddle connecting a tow strap to Garrett's truck and talking to Garrett, who was leaning out his window. I heard enough to know that they were annoyed with each other. I thought I understood why James was annoyed. I was annoyed too. It was more than dumb to get yourself stuck like that, and James had been pulled away from his Saturday night plans to fix things.

I figured Garrett was annoyed because he'd gotten stuck while showing off for a girl, and now he had to rely on another guy to get him out. It didn't occur to me until later that maybe he was also mad about watching that same girl being carried off by the other guy.

When the tow strap was connected, James sloshed back out of the puddle and stepped out of his waders, which he then picked up and put into the back of his truck. He grabbed another towel out of the truck and hurriedly wiped his hands and arms before turning to me.

"Stand out of the way in case that tow strap snaps. I don't want it to hit you," he said. I nodded my understanding.

I walked to the side of the clearing to watch as Garrett started his engine and James climbed into his truck. The sound of two engines working hard broke the quiet of the mountain as they worked to get Garrett out of the mud. It took a few minutes, but before long, after a loud sucking noise, Garrett's truck began to creep forward. His truck was able to get traction after a couple of feet. In a show of masculine pride, he gunned it and pulled up alongside James, giving it a last rev before shutting off the engine.

When the trucks were both turned off, I figured it was safe and joined the guys at the vehicles. James was unhooking the tow strap from his truck and Garrett did the same to his.

"Hey, Rachel," Garrett called to me as he carried his end of the tow strap over and handed it to James. "Looks like we're good. I'll take you home now."

I was hesitant to ride home with Garrett, but I felt I'd already asked enough of James and didn't want to impose any more. Okay, honestly, riding home with James sounded scary like how a rollercoaster is scary. Garrett was the much safer bet. In the end, my thoughts didn't matter, because as I opened my mouth to let Garrett know I'd be coming, James shook his head.

"I've got her," he said. The words did a little dance in my head.

Garrett had started walking over to get me but paused. "I'm not sure you understand that we're on a date."

James nodded, still looking down at the strap he was rolling up slowly. "I understand."

"Well, I've never ditched a girl, and I'm not starting now. Especially a girl like Rachel."

"Like I said, I've got her." James put the last of his things in the bed of the truck and looked at Garrett briefly before turning to me. I was surprised at the inflexible look on his face. I knew better than to argue. Besides, there would have been no point since I actually wanted to go with James regardless of everything. Guess I was in a rollercoaster mood.

"Yeah, thanks, Garrett for an—um—interesting day. I'll go with James though." I smiled at Garrett, trying to take away some of the sting.

"You sure?" Garrett took a step closer to me, but James was there first, lightly blocking him. He gently put his hand at the small of my back and turned me toward his truck. I felt his touch down to my toes. Some things really hadn't changed at all.

"I'm sure," I said as I looked over my shoulder and gave Garrett a farewell wave.

I willingly went along and climbed into James's truck. He shut the door behind me and nodded before walking back around his truck and saying a few words to Garrett. I had no idea what he said, and I didn't care much. I just wanted to go home.

James joined me and got us headed the right direction, before following Garrett back down the trail. I wanted to ask James where he'd been and apologize again for pulling him away from his plans, but I wasn't sure how to approach him at that moment. Finally, I decided to just jump in and hope for the best.

"Uh, James?" I started. He gave me a quick glance, and I supposed that was an opening, so I walked through it. "I'm sorry again to have dragged you out here. I know you were busy doing something when I called, and you had to leave that and go home and get your things and then drive clear up here. I ruined your night."

He gave me another quick glance, keeping his eyes on the road as we bumped back down the trail. I couldn't help but notice that he did his best to avoid hitting too many bumps. It was a nice reprieve after Garrett's driving.

"Nah, you didn't ruin my night," he said.

"But I know you were out somewhere," I tried again.

"My roommate, Chad, had talked me into going out to dinner with some friends of his. I didn't really know them, so it was okay to leave."

"Oh. So you didn't get dinner either?" I chuckled. "That's just great." As if I didn't feel guilty enough already.

James didn't reply. I took my cue from him and settled in for a quiet ride.

Once we hit the pavement, it was actually pleasant to just drive along. James wasn't interested in chitchat, and neither was I. The windows were open, and the warm summer evening air blowing through the cab felt great. Some music was playing, and even though I was almost painfully aware of the man sitting next to me, I was able to sit back and enjoy the ride.

James drove straight to my apartment and parked his truck. By this point, my pants were mostly dry, even though my shoes were still slushy. I jumped out of the truck and folded the towel in my nervous hands.

"I'll wash this and get it back to you," I said as I leaned back in to gather up my purse.

I risked looking up at him and found his green eyes locked on me. I didn't want him to go, but I didn't want him to stay either. I was tied up in knots. How could I still feel so much for this man when it had been my choice to leave him? Hadn't enough time passed now for us to both move on? How had he moved on?

"Thanks again for everything tonight." I swallowed hard around the yearning I felt as we faced each other. "Do you want to come up and get a drink or a sandwich or something?" I was surprised to hear the words burst out and felt my breath seize with nerves.

James continued to hold my gaze, and I could see a few things flicker in his eyes as he thought about it. "I'm not sure that's a good idea," he finally said in a low voice.

There was no mistaking his meaning. He may no longer be in love with me, but that didn't mean he wanted to hang with me over some sandwiches.

I nodded and pressed my lips together in an impression of a smile. "You're probably right," I agreed and straightened up.

"I'll walk you in," he stated, opening his door and hopping out—a gentleman to the core.

I was shaking my head as we met around the front of his truck. I smiled sadly up at him, saying what he'd said just moments before. "I'm not sure that's a good idea."

He returned my smile with a small one of his own, and an understanding passed between us. I knew in that moment that neither of us had fully healed from our past relationship.

"James, I'm so sorry . . ." I felt compelled to say something. We both knew I wasn't talking about tonight.

"Please, don't," he stated flatly. "It's been a really long time." He looked away toward something in the distance.

His words silenced me. He wasn't interested in hearing more apologies from me, whether it was about tonight or our past. I'd apologized to him so many times that he probably didn't believe it anymore. It was one of those hurtful truths. He was right. No matter how bad I felt for the things I'd done, the end result was the same. All the apologies in the world couldn't change a thing. He'd wanted to marry me. I'd said yes, and then I had handed him back the ring and walked away.

Our eyes met again, and I gave him a tight nod. He did the same back to me as he turned and walked around to the driver's door of his truck. I didn't want to watch him drive away, so I turned and climbed the stairs to my building. I was grateful for his rescue that night but wondered who would rescue me from myself. I was in need of my own personal hero.

Chapter 14

Love is the master key that opens the gates of happiness.
~ Oliver Wendell Holmes Sr. ~

I moped around feeling wounded for a few days after spending time with James. My emotions ranged from anger, to sorrow, to determination. I was angry that I was still attracted to him physically and emotionally, and the sorrow of knowing I couldn't fix things or ever be with him again was overwhelming. Our relationship had been so all encompassing that it had been like splitting apart a pair of conjoined twins.

When the anger and sorrow would fade, I would roll into determination. I was determined to carry on with dating some more. I knew it was the only way to close that door forever. James wasn't interested in talking it out or trying to truly be friends, which meant I had no choice but to leave the past where it belonged.

The week after my date with Garrett and James's rescue, Hannah, Andrew, Val, and I had enjoyed an uneventful drive to my parents' house the night of July third. Val and I strongly voted for Andrew to drive. Our motivation was that if one of us drove, then Andrew and Hannah would probably get a little too snuggly in the back seat, and we'd have to deal with that for the entire three-hour trip. With Andrew driving, the worst that could happen is that we'd suffer at the hand of Hannah's DJ skills, or rather her complete lack of.

Her taste in music had become strangely influenced by the stuff they played in her trendy salon. She was always trying to get us to listen to bands with names that sounded suspiciously like grooming tools. I swear there was one called Buzzcut who did nothing but scream or hum. I had yet to decipher any actual language coming out of their shrill musical stylings. Still, it was better than kissy face in the back seat.

After a great night of sleep at my parents' house, we'd all gotten up for the local parade. Andrew, my dad, and Diana's husband had gone down early to get us seats in the shade at a local church. We didn't mind sitting back from the street if the tradeoff was the sun at our backs rather than in our faces as it came over the hills. A few years ago, Diana had come up with the idea of getting her own bag of candy for the twins. When floats would come by throwing candy, Diana would toss some in the air for her girls to gather up. It kept them willingly out of the street and away from all the candy wrestling that went on at these affairs. It was ten dollars well spent in my opinion.

After the parade, we returned to my parents' house for our traditional brunch. Seated outside on the covered deck, chomping down forkfuls of Mom's famous omelets and Dad's perfectly cooked breakfast meats, I entertained them with tales from my dates. When I laid them all out that way, even I couldn't believe some of the strange things that had happened. I was careful not to mention my date with James or his rescue in front of my parents, and my friends were kind enough to keep it to themselves as well. I couldn't live with the look I'd see in my mom's eyes when she realized he was back.

Sitting outside in the cozy, filtered sunlight, surrounded by my favorite people, elbows resting casually on the white wicker table, it all became hilarious. As I watched all of their faces light up with laughter and heard their words of encouragement cheering me forward, I was so grateful for this moment and the courage it gave me to not give up. I had survived some pretty amazing things, and I could survive anything else that might come my way. In the sharing of it all, the date with Garrett took on a different hue, and I decided that I would give him a second chance if he called me again.

When I ran out of stories, Mom announced that it was clearly time for her to get a shot at setting me up. "You know, sweetie," she said to me, "I think it's time you let me set you up with someone."

I wasn't a huge fan of this idea. She would set me up with "*just the nicest boy,*" and I'd have to pretend I'd enjoyed myself. Not to mention the fact that we lived hours apart. She couldn't possibly know anyone near me.

Diana saw the look on my face and jumped in. "I'd be happy to help," she offered.

I was honestly surprised that she hadn't told Mom she'd already looked over my online options. It was somewhat gratifying that she'd come up blank too.

I shook my head. "I don't think this is a great idea," I hedged.

"Of course it is. Everyone else has had a chance, and it ended up being terrible. You know, the season of failure is the best time for sowing the seeds of success." Mom threw out one of her favorite gems. "Is that not true?" she pressed when I rolled my eyes.

I pulled a face, but I nodded knowing she'd expect me to agree.

"Well, I think it's only fair that I get a turn. Diana can help me. We'll find someone wonderful!" Mom was getting really excited. "I'll get in touch with some of my friends—"

"Speaking of friends, have you had a chance to talk wedding with Hannah yet?" I said to Mom in an effort to distract her.

It worked like a bear to honey. My mom had loved Hannah ever since the day they met when we were both moving into the dorm our freshman year of college. They were similar in their interests and personalities and had quickly hit it off. In fact, the two of them had set up my bedroom and arranged things for me while I sat nearby watching them. I realized at that moment that I was somehow still going to be living with my mother.

When James and I were engaged, Mom had been thrilled with the idea of Hannah becoming family. After the breakup, Mom and Hannah had remained close, and I knew Mom's head was exploding over the joys of a marriage coming up.

Hannah, knowing my mom as well as she did, had only been too happy to bring fabric swatches, pictures of the bouquet and the reception hall, a sketch of her wedding dress, and the playlist of music we'd come up with. She jumped up from the table at my suggestion and returned quickly with her binder full of information. Mom was in heaven as they sat with their heads bent together and pored over the details.

I met Diana's eyes across the table and mouthed a *"thank you"* to her for jumping in. I hoped that with her helping, Mom wouldn't get too crazy about it.

"What about the honeymoon?" Mom came up for a breath after awhile. She looked at Hannah with a tender, dreamy smile on her face that made her look much younger than her sixty years.

"Well, we're still trying to decide for sure where to go." Hannah looked at Andrew and smiled. "We don't have a ton of money, but we also know you only get one honeymoon."

"Oh, yes." Mom put her hand to her chest and sighed happily. "You have to get it right. Somewhere romantic and cozy, with just the right . . ." Her voice faded away mid-sentence and her eyes took on a glazed look.

"Dad, you may want to consider a second honeymoon," I teased Dad, who was seated next to me. He nodded with a look of wary amusement on his face.

"Where did you and Mr. Stevens go on your honeymoon?" Andrew asked.

"Oh, Don and I didn't get much of a honeymoon, I'm afraid." Mom smiled sadly at dad like someone who'd had to make a choice and understood why but still wished things had been different.

"Oh, sorry," Andrew said awkwardly.

"Nothing to apologize for, son," Dad said. "We were very young, and I was still in school. We just went to a hotel the next town over and stayed for two nights. Don't let her make you feel bad for her." Dad smiled like a man who had accepted that this topic would come up on occasion. "Beverly and I had a great time," he added. "It wasn't Hawaii, but we were in love and happy. Same goes for you two. You'll be happy wherever you go." Andrew nodded, clearly in agreement with him.

"Oh, don't listen to Don. He's always been too practical to understand a woman's romantic nature." Mom waved a hand at Dad and looked back at Hannah. "We did have fun, but when you get older, you realize that you only get one shot at some things. Your honeymoon is one of those."

Dad chuckled. "I think she's starting her campaign for a romantic vacation."

"I warned you," I said, grinning.

"Where would you go if you could go anywhere?" Mom asked Hannah.

"I don't know. That's half the problem!" Hannah smiled and shrugged.

"Well, don't worry too much about location. You'll be so tired after all the wedding planning and the wedding day that you'll end up spending half your time in your room anyhow," Diana added.

"She's right," Jordan said with a grin. "We ordered room service and slept for at least half of our honeymoon."

"I like the idea of a smaller honeymoon and then going on a big trip for your first anniversary. That's what we should have done," Diana stated.

"Oh, hush all of you," Mom chided jokingly, throwing a reproving look around the table. "Don't listen to any of them. They aren't romantics like you and me, Hannah. Ladies like us need a little more."

"Romantic needs aside, ladies also need money to pay for these things," Val teased. Everyone but Mom and Hannah nodded.

"There's no room for logic in romance," Mom pronounced.

"She's right," Dad jumped in. "I've never known her to be logical."

Mom playfully rolled her eyes at Dad. "Come on, Hannah." She stood up and gathered her plate. "I have some travel brochures inside that we can look through."

I laughed as Dad's amusement sputtered out. He turned to me. "She has brochures?"

"It's worse than we thought!" I said, pulling a silly face.

"Oh, and Rachel," Mom said, turning to me from just inside the doorway. "I haven't forgotten about you. We'll be in touch about setting you up."

My big smile faded as the others chuckled at Mom's pronouncement. I should have known that Mom had willingly been distracted. I'd only bought myself a short reprieve by getting her to look over Hannah's wedding plans.

Dad stood and hurriedly gathered his dishes as he followed Mom inside. "Bev? Bev! What brochures?" he called as he followed.

We all cracked up briefly, and then we stood and started clearing the table. A trip back home had been just what I'd needed.

Chapter 15

Love makes your soul crawl out from its hiding place.

~ Zora Neale Hurston ~

My mother is not a woman who makes idle promises. Because of this, I was not surprised at all when a mere two weeks after our Fourth of July brunch I was told to expect a phone call from a guy named Mitch.

Mitch, it turned out, was a member of the gym that Diana and Jordan went to. Jordan had befriended him a few months back and introduced him to Diana as a prospective setup for me after Mom had announced it was her turn. Diana had chatted with Mitch a bit and then told Mom, who had agreed with Diana that he'd be a good candidate. However, she'd insisted on meeting him first.

So, Mom drove the hour to Diana's gym and attended a yoga class that Mitch was teaching. I had no idea Mom did yoga. I thought her exercise mainly involved walking the neighborhood to gather intel.

Mom had heartily approved of Mitch but wanted to leave no questions. According to Diana, after the class ended, Mitch had endured a lunch date with Mom before she gave the thumbs up. I cringed inside at how awkward that interview must have been. It may not have been done with style and grace, but Mom always got the job done.

I was actually eager to meet this guy after hearing about the lunch date. Anyone willing to go out to lunch with an older lady

Blind Dates, Bridesmaids, and Other Disasters

and then manage to impress her enough to get her daughter's number sounded like someone worth getting to know.

The only downside to Mitch was that he lived two hours from me. I wasn't sure how dating him would work. In the end, the timing had been perfect. He called, and during our visit, he told me he was coming to Pine Ridge the next weekend and wanted to meet up. I quickly agreed, selfishly happy to not have to drive the long distance myself or meet at a roadside diner in the middle.

Mitch arranged to pick me up at 7:30 a.m. on Saturday and asked me to wear athletic clothing. I could handle the early hour if it was our only option to get together, but I wasn't super thrilled about it. Also, I needed to go shopping for some athletic wear. He was clearly a gym regular, and I doubted he would consider my pajama pants athletic enough.

Eventually the date rolled around, and I spent a good fifteen minutes squatting and lunging in my new black yoga pants, trying to stretch them out a bit. I wasn't used to things being skin tight, so I was doing the whole jeans-fresh-from-the-dryer routine to loosen those babies up.

"They aren't going to get any looser," Hannah said in the early morning quiet as she entered the living room.

I jumped an inch in surprise and tugged on the crotch a bit to loosen the wedgie it had caused. "So I'm learning," I grunted.

"Where are you off to with Mitch?" she asked as she moved into the kitchen to get some breakfast before heading into work. She had to work a lot of Saturdays since it's such a busy day for salons.

I shrugged. "No idea. Should I be worried that I have nothing to go on but 'wear something athletic'?"

Hannah's face grew thoughtful. "He's friends with your family?"

"Sort of, I guess. He's my brother-in-law's workout buddy."

"I mean, your mom interviewed him and all. I think you're good."

I breathed a sigh of relief that her thoughts had followed the same track as mine. "Thanks. Also, check out this shirt. The tag says it's moisture wicking. I've never owned anything like this before." I smiled and held out the front of my pink workout shirt so she could get a better look. "I seriously think these should be standard issue to anyone working with children!"

"It's nice," she said, nodding and smiling.

"And check out my hoodie." I snagged the black and white printed hoodie off the couch and slipped it over my head. "It has thumb holes in the sleeves. It's genius!" I wiggled my thumbs at her.

"A really impressive feature, for sure." Her eyes smiled.

"Do you think I should do my makeup?" I asked. I'd debated all night about what to do for my look. I knew Mitch was an athletic guy who had asked me to dress athletically. Did that mean makeup free?

"Yes. When in doubt always do your face," Hannah, the cosmetologist, said as she nodded.

"You're right." I slipped back out of the hoodie and ran into my bathroom, leaving Hannah alone in the living area.

I took note of myself in the mirror. My long straight hair was pulled up in a high ponytail as shiny and black as ever. Unfortunately, my face was shiny too. I decided to keep it simple and just put on some light mascara and lip gloss. It was too early to do full makeup. My face wasn't ready for it yet. Besides, with athletic activity, there was a chance of getting sweaty, and I didn't need raccoon eyes from runny eyeliner on my first date.

A knock at the front door signaled that my date had arrived and primping time was over. I hurried out of my bedroom to meet him—and sputtered to a stop. There in the doorway stood probably the best-looking person I'd ever seen off the movie screen. He was wearing basketball shorts and a workout tank that showed off to perfection every hour of exercising he'd ever done. His light brown hair was cut and styled perfectly, and his eyes were an amazing color that Bob Ross would have fawned over. Just . . . wow.

A blush immediately rose to my face as I thought about my lightly applied make up and my skin-tight pants and how I sometimes jumped around in bounce houses. How could my family possibly think I was in the same league as this Greek god?

"Rachel, Mitch is here." Hannah smiled, clearly amused at my reaction.

I pulled my mouth shut with some effort and made busy gathering up my hoodie, while reminding my face to look normal. Only when I had the dreamy smile wiped off my face did I look back up to where he was still standing framed in the doorway. My stomach swooped.

"Hi, Rachel," Mitch said in a low voice.

I shuffled over to the door and managed a smile with a squeaky, "Hi. So nice to meet you." I cleared my throat.

He laughed. "It's pretty early for a Saturday," he said, obviously thinking I still had sleep in my voice. "We'll grab a drink on the way to get that frog out of your throat."

I managed to relax a little and smile larger. "Sounds great."

Mitch stepped out into the hallway, and I turned to face Hannah, my back to him as I reached to close the door. I widened my eyes to express my awe and said in a normal voice, "Thanks, Han. Have a good day at work. I'll catch you later."

"Have fun." She kept her face perfectly straight, not wanting to give me away, but her eyes crinkled up.

Mitch hopped down the stairs and walked backward, facing me, into the parking lot. While he chatted easily about the beautiful morning and what a pretty city Pine Ridge was, I couldn't think of a single thing to say. I was a little embarrassed about being so tongue tied, but a part of me knew I wasn't getting a second date even if I had been a chatter bug. Don't get me wrong. I wasn't down on myself or anything. I knew I was no slug, but I was definitely not in his league. Of course, my mother in her blind adoration of her baby would never have thought that anyone was too good looking for me. I felt a tug of love for her.

Mitch was relaxed and confident as we drove, and as the reality of no chance of a second date seeped in, I began to relax too. He was entertaining, and I saw no reason why we couldn't simply enjoy the morning together. We stopped at a gas station and grabbed some water bottles before getting back in his SUV and heading toward the foothills.

"So, what's the plan for today?" I asked after chugging down at least half of my water bottle.

"Have you heard of the Pine Top Fun Run?" he asked, smiling in my direction.

Unfortunately for me, I had. Even more unfortunate, I had a feeling I'd be participating in said fun run. Only it would not be fun at all for me. As my date, Mitch was also in for some suffering. I nodded and busied myself by taking another swig of water. I should have kept the drinking down, because I didn't love doing bathroom stuff in the forest, but sudden nerves insisted I gulp.

"I'd already entered the race when your mom gave me your number. I thought it would be fun to do it together," he continued. "I hope that's okay. I figured with as fit as your family is that you'd be up for it."

"You bet," I coughed out.

A misconception about my size is that I'm fit. Not true. My stature was totally a result of genes and not of machines. I tried to make good food choices, but I didn't regularly exercise, even though teaching school could be considered marathon training.

"Great. So it's a 10K through the foothills. It's really pretty," he explained happily. "They close off the canyon and we actually run on the pavement, so it isn't really rocky terrain and tight spaces. It should be fun."

"Great," I echoed out loud, but in my head, things weren't so great. What if I tripped? What if my new shoes gave me a blister? Would my yoga pants constrict blood flow too much or keep creeping up with no thought of modesty? Even worse, what if I just dropped dead from the exertion? What had my mom and Diana been thinking?

Before long we entered the foothills and began seeing cars parked alongside the road. Mitch parked in the first place he found and said we'd be hiking up to where the trail started. Great, so it was more of an 11K then.

"We can use this short hike as a chance to warm up our muscles and get ready for the run, okay?" he said as we climbed out of the car.

I put on my hoodie and mimicked the stretches he was doing. I had a feeling his muscles weren't screaming over the stretches like mine were.

"Ready?" he asked.

"Yes, ready, I am, yes, ready." I nodded overenthusiastically and sort of muttered out some words as I continued to stretch.

He thought I was being funny and laughed. "Let's go. You can tell me all about yourself on the walk up." He motioned for me to fall into step beside him. "So you teach school?"

"Yes. Second grade," I replied.

"What's the name of the school?"

"Pine Ridge Elementary."

"How long have you been teaching?" Mitch's strides were now lengthening as he started to set his pace. I was scrambling to keep up, my legs so much shorter than his. At least that's the story I was telling myself.

"Um, about five years now," I huffed a little.

"What do you like about teaching?" His arms started swinging in big circles, and I was sure I'd be decked at some point. Why was he doing that with his arms? I thought just our legs would be involved. Was I going to have to crawl up a wall or something?

"Um, the kids. Definitely the kids," I said.

"What do you do in your spare time?"

"I don't know . . . normal stuff. Read, watch movies, hang out with my friends," I replied, pushing my legs into a half jog to match his pace. I thought we were warming up. If this was his warm up, I was in serious trouble.

"Yeah, I hear that. I feel like my job takes up so much time that I don't really have hobbies to speak of. It's probably the same for teachers, right?" He smiled down at me. Okay, he smiled down to where I should have been, but ended up having to look back to where I was falling behind.

I nodded. It was nice of him to be so relatable and interested in me, but it was time for him to do some of the talking.

"What do you do for a living?" I asked.

"Oh, I thought your mom or Diana would have told you. I'm a personal trainer, fitness coach, and I do a little soccer coaching on the side," he replied. Of course he did. He was probably voted Coach of the Year, like, every time.

Then the sweetest words I'd heard all morning came from his mouth. "We're here. This is the starting line. We'll just join up with the group and wait. I think we have a few minutes."

I stood next to him in the group of people and did my best to pretend I wasn't breathing hard. The people standing around me all looked fit and happy. They were cheerfully chatting, slapping backs, stretching, and taking sips of water. Oops, I'd left my water in the car.

"So, um, remind me how long a 5K is?" I asked Mitch. I thought it was something like three miles. I figured I could go three miles without water.

"It's about 3.1 miles," he replied, his tone sounding a little surprised that I didn't know that. "But we're doing a 10K. So a little over six miles."

"Oh, sorry, a 10K. Even better." I tried to joke it off. "I left my water in the car."

"Oh, shoot. Want me to run down and get it?" he asked.

I had every reason to believe that he actually could and would quite literally run down the hill to get it and still be back before the race started. It was kind of him to offer.

"Oh, no, of course not. It's only six miles. I'll be just fine." I lightly waved my hands to show how unconcerned I was.

"So your mom says your roommate is getting married and you're helping with the planning," Mitch said.

"Right. It's been kind of fun." I smiled as I thought about all the craziness that had gone on the past couple of months.

"What's her name?"

"Hannah."

"Was she the one who answered the door?"

"Yes."

"What's her fiancé's name?"

"Andrew."

"How did they meet?"

"Um, at her work. He came in for a haircut. She's a cosmetologist," I replied.

"Is it just the two of you living in the apartment?"

"No. We have a third roommate. Her name is Val. Well, Valerie."

"What does she do for work?"

I sighed softly. Mitch was seriously the question king. "She's a nurse."

"I'll bet having a cosmetologist and a nurse for roommates can come in handy at times," he said, chuckling. I smiled. He wasn't wrong.

"Rachel?" I spun around as a voice behind me interrupted our conversation.

"James?" My voice came out squeaky with shock.

I didn't know whether to laugh or howl in frustration as I looked up into his eyes. Why was he always showing up in the same place I happened to be in? And why did he have to walk up behind me and surprise me by suddenly talking?

To my disappointment, he looked every bit as good as Mitch did in his athletic wear. My heart pounded as his eyes ran quickly over me, taking in my clothing. It had been a little touch and go emotionally since he'd rescued me from the mud puddle, and I wasn't sure I could stand seeing him again right now.

My chest grew tight as an attractive woman stepped up beside him. In my dismay over seeing him, I hadn't noticed her at first. James's eyes briefly flitted over to her before coming back to me.

"What are you doing here?" he asked.

I gestured toward Mitch. "I'm on a date with Mitch here," I said with a slight lift of my chin. I had no intention of falling apart in front of James. Mitch moved to stand next to me. "Mitch, this is James. You met his sister this morning. My roommate, Hannah."

"Nice to meet you, man," Mitch smiled, and the two men slapped their hands together in a firm handshake.

James gestured to the woman standing next to him. Her exercise pants were as tight as mine. "This is Michelle," James said.

Michelle was curvy, tall, and blonde, and I had already started plotting to slash her tires before she smiled at us. After she smiled at us, I began thinking about the possibilities of cosmetic surgery. She was gorgeous.

Mitch and Michelle beamed at each other and shook hands, two fit little peas in a pod. When Michelle smiled at me and reached for my hand, I purposely went with the limp fish handshake. I hate the limp fish handshake. Her smile faded a little. One sad little point for me.

After introductions, James continued to stand there, and I drew my lips into a line of annoyance.

"So, is this your first 10K?" Mitch asked James before I could tell him and the beauty queen to pull up anchor.

"Nope," James so helpfully replied.

"I didn't know you ran races, or fun runs, or whatever," I mumbled, interested in spite of not wanting to be.

"Likewise," James replied with a raise of his eyebrows in my direction.

I gave him what I hoped was a withering look before I awkwardly said, "Well, you don't know everything about me."

"Obviously," he agreed. It flustered me.

It was probably not the best thing for me to say. I was stressed and out of my element. I was seriously admiring how James looked while despairing over this new Michelle person and what pedestal she'd stepped down from. It was too much at this time of day—or any time of day. Running a 10K was starting to sound like a great idea if it meant running away from James.

"I like your outfit," James said with a totally straight face.

Oh my heck. He was really laying it on now. We both knew I was wearing brand new clothes. I wouldn't have been surprised if he'd seen a forgotten price tag sticking out somewhere.

"So do I," Michelle agreed with a kind smile.

Mitch looked closer at me and gave me a nod. "You do look good," he stated.

For the forty-seventh time, I physically willed down a blush over how tight my pants were. "Oh, these old things?" I tried to play it cool.

James didn't give me away, but I was taken by surprise to see a grin teasing the corners of his mouth and his eyes crinkling up. I had to put a stop to this. I was determined that the only thing getting my heart rate up was the jog I was about to go on. With Mitch.

"Are you two here alone, or did you come with a group?" I asked, hoping they'd take the hint and head back to some super fit gym buddies they'd come with.

James's smile grew. "It's just the two of us. Michelle and I like to try out different races on the weekends."

"Yeah, we always have so much fun." Michelle smiled at him. "I think this is our tenth, isn't it?"

James nodded and smiled back at her. "At least."

I was seething now. James could tell and seemed to be getting more amused by the minute. I started rotating my ankle, warming it up for the shin kick I was about to deliver.

"That's cool that you've got a running partner, man," Mitch joined in. "Until Rachel's mom set me up with her, I was going to run it solo."

"Oh, so Rachel's mom set you two up?" James latched onto this tidbit with more interest than it warranted.

"Yeah. She came to the gym where I work and made it happen." Mitch laughed and shared a look with James that I did not understand.

"I see," James replied. It was apparent that he did understand the look, because his face grew cold for an instant before going back to a casually interested expression.

"How funny," Michelle jumped in. "James and I met at a gym too. Although, since he moved here, it's been harder to get together as often." James nodded and smiled again.

I couldn't help but be interested by that little nugget. So she didn't live in town. But no, I wasn't going to get interested in nuggets about James. Good grief, lady! Focus.

"Anyhow, good luck this morning." I smiled at the two of them, dying for them to leave.

James grasped the hint but took his sweet time moving off. As they walked away, he turned back to look at me at least twice with a grin on his face. I managed to avoid giving him a nasty look, because Mitch was looking at me and talking.

"They seem nice," Mitch was saying. "But you and James must not be good friends if he didn't know you run."

"Right, right. I mean, I mostly know him because he's my roommate's brother, so . . ."

Mitch nodded and suggested that we move into place since the race was about to start. I didn't feel guilty at all about keeping Mitch in the dark regarding James. The chances of seeing Mitch again after this were nil. The thought was oddly entertaining as I realized that this time the date fail was going to be my fault. It wouldn't be because the guy was nutso or we couldn't get along. Nope, this time it would be me letting the other person down. Mitch was about to be extremely unimpressed.

As the starting time arrived, Mitch announced that he wanted to be at the front of the crowd. I followed him with heavy feet. How was I supposed to look all athletic and charming while moving my body in a way it wasn't familiar with? Not to mention my lungs. My poor lungs were about to have the fight of their life.

I was saved having to overthink it by the sound of a gunshot. My first thought was to duck, but others around me took off running, and I managed to keep from embarrassing myself thanks to my instinctual herd mentality. When everyone around you is running, you run.

Mitch was kind enough to let me set the pace. It was a mistake on his part, but it was kind. After a minute or two during which I applauded myself for pulling off a steady jog, Mitch finally spoke up.

"All warmed up?" he asked.

Oh heavenly days. He thought I was just getting started when in reality I was at my peak performance. Still, I nodded. My mom always warned me that pride cometh before the fall.

"Great, let's go."

Mitch poured on the juice and moved ahead of me on the road as he zigged and zagged between other runners. I pushed myself harder and managed to make a respectable showing while dodging people. When I caught up to him, he started asking me more questions.

"Where did you go to college? How did you meet your roommates? What's your favorite kind of food? Favorite vacation spot?" He fired questions faster than I could answer them.

I was trying desperately to respond, to appear fit as a fiddle, to be charming and lovely. In the end, it wasn't meant to be. I don't know if a rock caught my toe or if my foot gave out, but one moment I was cheerfully telling him I loved Mexican food and the next I was eating asphalt.

I heard Mitch make a sound as he looked back and saw me on my stomach. I was trying to catch my breath as he hurried back to my side and rolled me onto my back. A stinging sensation on my chin told me I'd hit it too. I hoped it wasn't scraped too badly. I reached up trembling fingers to test it. They came away with some blood and gravel. I winced and put my fingers back on my wound.

"Did you get the wind knocked out of you?" Mitch asked. It was a perfect excuse for my heavy breathing, so I nodded and let him think that. "Are you hurt anywhere? Can you move your legs? Did you hit your head or just your chin?" he asked. What was with him and a zillion questions all the time? This time I shook my head.

"Rachel?" Suddenly James's face came into view above Mitch's shoulder.

I let my eyes slide closed, my fingers still covering my chin, as I felt a lump rise in my throat at the sight of him. Kind of like how you're always okay with getting hurt until your Mom shows up, and then you're a sobbing mess.

"She fell," I heard Mitch say to James as if looking to him to take over.

"I saw. It looked like it hurt," Michelle's concerned voice stated. Of course, she had to be nice. It just made it worse.

"You cut your chin." I felt James kneel next to me as his hands gently turned my face toward him for closer inspection. He pulled my fingers away from the wound and tilted my chin up to get a better look. "You scraped it pretty good, but nothing major. Other than that, are you okay? Did you twist your ankle?" James asked.

I opened my eyes and shook my head. "I'm okay."

"Your hoodie is torn," Michelle stated as she pointed at my stomach.

I glanced at Mitch and noticed his eyes watching all the other runners pass us, and I knew it was killing him to stand there while his race went on without him.

"Guys, I'm fine." I tried to stand up.

James jumped up first and then four hands were thrust in my direction. I decidedly took Mitch's and let him launch me into a standing position, but he was so distracted that he barely even noticed what was going on. I wiped my chin on the sleeve of my hoodie as I tapped his shoulder.

"Mitch, go on without me. You can still catch up. I'll go wait for you back down by your car." I smiled, and the motion tugged at my chin, making me wince before I could stop it.

"You can't go on?" he asked, but his heart wasn't in it. I sensed definite relief from him.

"I'm sorry, I can't." I pulled a face that I hoped looked disappointed.

He sighed. "I can't let you walk down alone."

"You can, I promise. I'll be totally fine," I insisted. "By the time the race is over, I'll be back to rights."

"He's right," Michelle said. "You really shouldn't have to troop down by yourself after laying it out on the pavement like that."

At her words, Mitch sighed again. He'd already wasted a full minute talking to me. He was dying. I knew the halfway point wasn't far, and then he'd be out of chances to be in the lead pack. It wasn't fair of me to keep him trapped there, so I walked in a tight circle to show that I was fine.

"See? Just a little scraped up. Nothing I can't walk on. I scraped my knees, so running will hurt though. And I should probably get a bandage for my chin. Please, you said you were going to do this race alone. Just finish it, and I'll see you when you're done," I pressed with a smile.

James was watching me closely as I spoke. Michelle was watching James. I felt bad that they were caught up in my little accident too. Poor James had just wanted to run a race that morning with Michelle—and move to this city for a great new job and not be thrown back into my life . . .

Mitch finally caved when some of the stragglers came into view. "If you're sure?" he asked one last time. I smiled and nodded.

He was off like a rocket and out of sight before I could wish him luck. The sight of him running away from me as fast as his legs could carry him was absurdly ironic. Usually I was the one running away from a date.

Now to get rid of James and Michelle. I turned to them and made a face. "I'm fine, and I don't need you to stick around." I made the mistake of reaching up to wipe some more oozing blood off my chin as I said it.

James wasn't fooled so easily. "There are a lot of things I want to say right now . . . ," he began, and I couldn't help suddenly feeling very entertained by the thought of just what it was he wanted to say. A huge smile lit my face at the thought, which stopped him.

"Oh, I'm sure there are," I agreed with a smirk.

He surprised me by smiling back. "I can't let you hike down all by yourself."

"Yes, you can."

"Why don't I at least walk you to the starting line?"

"You won't finish the race if you do that," I replied as I started pulling my torn hoodie off.

When my face reappeared from under my hoodie James held out his hand to take it from me as I pulled my arms the rest of the way out.

"She's right, James. I think she's okay, and we're never going to finish if we don't get going." Michelle was now looking up the trail the same way Mitch had.

I'd almost forgotten she was there and started at the sound of her voice. James turned to face her. He was still holding my hoodie as their eyes met. I tried to grab it out of his hand, but he held firm.

"I'm sorry, Michelle. I just . . . I've known Rachel a long time. She's Hannah's best friend. I just feel like I should—" James shrugged.

For a moment, Michelle's eyes were tight before her face smoothed out. In that moment, I understood a little too well how she felt. She'd probably come a long way to spend the day with James, and I was interloping. And because I was like an injured baby animal, this round wasn't one she'd win.

"Okay," she breathed out. "Want me to come along?"

"Why don't you finish the race and I'll meet up with you back at your car?" James replied. "I know how much you were looking forward to this one."

What James didn't seem to be picking up on was that Michelle had wanted to run the race *with him*. However, she had the grace to realize she'd lose this battle, so she cheerfully smiled, waved, and turned to chase up the trail the same way Mitch had gone. Based on her gazelle-like build and speed, I had every reason to believe she'd do fine. I also had every reason to believe she was not pleased with this development. Happy people don't run like that.

"I know where the first aid station is. I'll walk you there," James said as we watched Michelle disappear around a bend. I begrudgingly walked next to him. After a minute of quiet, he asked, "What made that guy think you wanted to run a 10K as a date?"

"What makes you think I wouldn't want to?" I said. He gave me a look letting me know he didn't think I'd changed *that* much. I gave up the pretense. "I guess because he met my mom and sister at the gym. He said he figured I'd be fit too." It sounded funny when I said it out loud.

"Assumptions aren't great for blind dates," he said, chuckling. The sound of his laugh warmed me in a way that running definitely had not.

"He and I aren't meant to be anyway, so it doesn't matter. I mean, did you see that guy?" I shook my head and waved my hands.

"Yes. Why?"

"He's not going to be calling me back. We don't belong in the same dating circles."

I stepped lightly around a stick that had been knocked into the path and bumped my shoulder against James's arm. He reached out to steady me. His hand was warm, and I quickly moved back into my space.

"There are dating circles?" His voice sounded confused, and I glanced at his face.

His expression said he had no idea what I was talking about. Leave it to James to be the only good-looking guy on the planet to not realize there were leagues within dating.

"Of course. He dates women who are much more fit and driven than me. We won't see each other again. I will give him bonus points for being nice though. He's not a snob."

We had slowed down to a stroll at this point, and it took on the feel of a leisurely Sunday walk for all the effort we were putting into getting down to first aid.

"Wait, so you think he's too good for you?" James asked.

"Not too good for me. Just in a different social circle. I'm not the type of girl he's looking for. He's too kind to acknowledge it, but he doesn't need to. I know it, so I don't expect anything from him."

"That has to be the biggest load I've ever heard," James said, and he started laughing. Hard. Hard enough that I stopped walking and turned to face him.

James laughing was a sight to see. Eyes dancing, that generous Redmond mouth pulled wide, head tilted slightly back. The tingle it caused ran straight to my toes. I looked away and started walking again, a little faster this time.

"You can laugh all you want." I added some speed to my steps and was relieved to see the starting line up ahead and the first-aid tent nearby. "But I'm telling the truth."

"Come on, you can't really think that," he argued as he caught up.

"Trust me. If I were you, I'd be worried about Michelle catching up to him and lighting his fire. She is exactly the kind of girl Mitch would normally date."

"Light his fire?" James grinned and shook his head. "I'm not worried about Michelle."

I didn't see how continuing this conversation was going to get us anywhere, so I stopped talking. That did not mean I stopped thinking. Why wasn't he worried about Michelle? Did he not care enough to worry? Or maybe he knew Michelle's love for him was stronger than the pull of Mitch's biceps. That line of thought was horrid.

Thankfully the first aid tent came into sight before my thoughts could go downhill any further. He drew to a stop next to me, the last of his smile still on his face. I felt flustered, frustrated, and all sorts of emotions. "It doesn't matter if you agree or not, but thanks for walking me down," I said. "I'll see you later. You'll have to hurry if you want to catch your date."

I spun and half jogged toward the first aid tent before he had a chance to respond. Both James and I knew there was no way he was going to catch the runners. I doubted he'd even try. That didn't mean I wanted to kill time with him until Mitch and Michelle got back. Actually, the fact that I *did* want to kill time with him was enough to annoy me. I desperately needed to get that man out of my head.

Later that night, I was lounging on the couch with my roomies and Andrew when James showed up unexpectedly. I was still in my athletic wear, with a bandage on my chin, my glasses on, and my makeup washed off. Despite the fact that I'd wanted nothing more than to get away from him earlier at the race, an involuntary flutter spread through my chest when I opened the door and saw him standing there. He was alone. My heart fluttered a bit harder.

He looked good all cleaned up and dressed in jeans and a T-shirt. His hair was falling down into his face, and I wanted to reach up and brush it back.

His eyes studied me closely, warily. I did the same. We were both on high alert, and it caused a spark to flow between us that neither of us seemed to want to extinguish by being the first to break the spell.

We must have stood there staring at each other like idiots and measuring each other up for more than just a moment, because the door was wrenched from my hands and thrown wide open by Val.

"Oh hey, James," Val said with a confused look. She looked from James to me and back again.

I jumped an inch and quickly broke the connection. What in the actual heck had I just been doing? I walked into the living space, putting distance between James and me.

"Hey, Crabby," James replied easily, and I saw him grin a little at my reaction to Val's intrusion.

"What brings you here?" Val asked.

"I brought Rachel's hoodie back."

He walked into the room, where I was leaning awkwardly against the back of the couch, and presented me a freshly laundered and folded hoodie. I had all but forgotten it even existed. Mitch hadn't said a word about my outfit change when we met up at the car after the race. Not even while we sat and ate a pleasant breakfast together or on the drive home. How funny. Proof that he really had already written me off and wasn't paying that much attention. It was okay. My heart wasn't exactly breaking.

"Oh, thanks. You washed it," I held it up and sniffed it.

"Do you always sniff clothes that people bring over?" Val teased as she went back to where she'd been sitting on a chair in the living area.

"You can never be too careful." I smiled as I moved away from the group. "It probably wasn't worth washing with the big hole in the front." James just gave me a half smile. "No Michelle?" I added. I regretted it the moment the words slipped out.

"Michelle?" Hannah and Val both echoed. I took pleasure in knowing Hannah didn't already know Michelle.

James shook his head. "Nope." Okay.

"I'm going to put this away," I blurted awkwardly.

I escaped with the hoodie, grateful for the chance to settle myself down. What had made me stare like a fool at James? I already knew every line and shape of that face. Yet I was finding it more and more fascinating, especially as I noticed the subtle changes that time and maturity had wrought. Even more important, why had he stared back? And where was Michelle? Was she back home? Would they see each other next weekend? I wanted to bang my head on the wall to get the thoughts to stop circling.

My room was quiet, and I took some deep breaths before I decided to go back to the living area. I hadn't heard the front door close, so I assumed James was still there, and I wanted to present a calm front when I saw him again. Regardless of my wound-up emotions, I was not going to hide out in my room like a wimp.

". . . watching *Clueless* if you want to stick around," Hannah was saying to James from her seat on the couch. Andrew nodded and jumped up from his seat to plant himself on the floor and lean against Hannah's legs.

"What's *Clueless*?" James asked as he walked around and took the seat Andrew had vacated.

"Only the best, most classic movie ever," Val interjected from her seat. "It's not chick flicky at all. You'll love it."

James turned to Hannah. "So I'll hate it?"

Hannah laughed. "No, it's pretty funny. I think you'll like it." She saw me out of the corner of her eye, standing in the hallway behind James and smiled at me.

I returned the smile as I walked in. "Popcorn, anyone?" I asked.

Everyone said they'd like some, and I welcomed the opportunity to lose myself in the sounds and smells of popcorn popping in the kitchen while they chatted in the living area. I was having a hard time trying not to melt like the butter over the fact that James would be staying.

Too soon, a big bowl of popcorn was ready, and I returned to the seating area. The only seat left was next to James on the couch. It would have been terribly obvious and rude if I'd sat on the floor, so I thanked my lucky stars for once that I was small and could squish myself against the arm of the couch to avoid contact in any way.

Even the movie *Clueless* didn't have enough pull to keep me from being aware of every single move James made on the couch next to me. It seemed like he shifted an awful lot. I could smell his shampoo and the scent of clean clothing that matched how my hoodie had smelled. The tension was so great that I felt like I was sweating buckets—more buckets than I'd sweat that morning during my first 10K. Well, technically, I'd probably only run a 2K, but still, I'd been sweaty.

I got up to get a drink. Then I needed to pop more popcorn. Then I had to use the bathroom. Then I needed another drink. Then I thought I'd change the Band-Aid on my chin.

"Rachel!" Val finally yelled when I'd settled back on the couch for the fifth time. "What is your problem tonight?"

"Probably sore from her all her marathon dating," James cracked. It was supposed to be a joke, I knew, but for some reason his voice had an edge to it that made it sound cruel rather than funny.

"What is that supposed to mean?" I was more than happy to have something to aim all my nerves at.

"It means you've been on some crazy dates lately. Maybe they're making you go nuts," he said with a smirk I'd never seen on his face before.

"Oh, this from the guy who never even dares to date?" I shot out.

"And whose fault would that be?" James said flatly.

That statement, blaming me for his single life, sucked the air right out of the room. Everyone was silent and watching us. In the background, I could hear the dialogue of the movie, but no one was looking at the TV. I was sure that Val, Hannah, and Andrew were exchanging looks. I didn't care.

"You said yourself that was years ago," I ground out. "At least I'm brave enough to try. You're a coward, too afraid to take a chance." My heart was racing and my palms were beginning to sweat.

"Again, whose fault would that be?" James's tone started to shift a bit, and I could feel a reckless energy between us.

"At least I'm not afraid to move on!" I cried.

James only smiled, but it wasn't in humor. "You met Michelle today, right?" Gut punch. "And how is moving on working out for you? Don't forget I've had to rescue you from two dates now."

"You did *not* rescue me today. I'm not a wimp, and I did *not* need rescuing! If anything, you were in the way!"

"Of what? Your one true love match?" James's voice had a cynical edge to it. "Please. You said yourself that you'd never see Mitch again, that you weren't in his league."

There was a gasp from the two other girls as he said that. I could see the instant regret in his eyes. James was not a cruel person, and underneath my anger, I knew he hadn't meant it how it sounded. He was just repeating words I'd said myself, but I was too mad to care. It was fine for a girl to say it about herself. It was not fine for a guy to say it about her.

"And you, James Redmond, aren't in *mine*!" I stood up and dumped the entire bowl of popcorn in his lap and over his head, letting the bowl clatter to the floor. I spun and walked down the hall to my room, followed by nothing more than the sound of the clock ticking.

The slam of my door echoed down the hallway, and I flopped facedown on my bed. Why had I gotten so riled up about his stupid comments? Why had he gotten so riled up about mine? What was going on? Why was today so full of questions?

After taking a few deep breaths, I could hear voices outside my door. It sounded like Hannah and James. I was sure she wanted to come after me and make sure I was okay. I wasn't sure what James wanted, or if I even cared what he wanted. In the end, what I wanted didn't matter. James won whatever conversation they were having, and I heard his voice after a quick knock on the door.

"Rachel?" he called softly.

It would do no good to pretend I wasn't there and hadn't heard him. I stood up and slowly opened the door. Hannah had left, and it was just James standing there looking as unsure as I felt.

It was so puzzling to have had an argument with him, even more so to now have him standing outside my bedroom door. A lot had certainly changed in the past few months. Over the years I'd grown comfortable in the knowledge that he didn't live close and wasn't in my life. Yet now we were constantly being thrown together. With the intensity of my emotions when I was around him, it was inevitable that something would eventually blow up. In some ways, it had felt good to let it vent.

Our eyes met, and he lifted up one side of his mouth in a hesitant half smile. This was new territory for us both. We hadn't been a couple who fought much when we were together, and it had been a long time since we'd been together. What wasn't new was the pull I felt toward him. Fighting it was making me cranky. Knowing I couldn't change anything, combined with meeting Michelle that morning, had made me downright miserable.

"The good news is that I didn't put extra butter on that popcorn, so you shouldn't have grease stains on your pants," I said, offering my version of an olive branch.

A slight puff of air escaped from his lips as he leaned against my door jamb and folded his arms. "The more important news is that I'm a jerk." His voice was low and quiet.

I sighed and shook my head. "No. You're not."

"Not usually, but what I just said out there was completely out of line." He took a deep breath and let it out slowly. "It's hard to be around you," he admitted. He sounded exhausted and frustrated with himself.

My heart pounded at his admission. I knew exactly how he felt. "I know."

We looked quietly at each other for another minute. "I thought I was over it," he said half to himself as though he couldn't believe it.

"Me too," I confessed quietly, still facing him, too afraid to move.

He blinked a little as my words jolted him to his senses. He pushed away from where he was leaning on my door and stood up straight.

"Well, I'm sorry for how rude I was out there. You know . . . I mean . . ." He cleared his throat and swallowed. "That's not what I really think about you." He pushed out the last words quickly. I knew he was anxious to be gone. He wasn't alone in feeling awkward.

"You're forgiven," I said softly, releasing him with the two words I'd give anything to hear him say to me.

I think he understood the deeper meaning, but he said nothing more as he turned and walked back down the hall into the living area. I watched him disappear and gently closed my door.

As I changed into my pajamas, I tried to convince myself that everything was going to be okay. Yet, as my mind slowly drifted to sleep, it was images of past James that came to me—James laughing, James dancing with me, James holding me close and promising forever.

Chapter 16

There is only one happiness in life: to love and be loved.

~ George Sand ~

As the days slowly rolled into August, Hannah became suspiciously quiet about setting me up on another date. Even though I had officially completed her challenge, having done more than the minimum of six dates, she had continued to encourage me to try again. Not anymore. All I could figure is that she knew me and James well enough to guess that something was going on between us.

Val, for her part, seemed to be fascinated by watching Hannah backpedal. Hannah never backpedaled. However, in the end, Val's heart must have softened—either that or she was tired of the unspoken tension around the topic—because she found a way to come to the rescue and set me up. We all breathed a silent sigh of relief. I was thrilled to have another shot at finding a spark big enough to blast James out of my heart. Hannah was happy to avoid the topic of James and to see that I hadn't given up. And Val—well, it was anyone's guess what she was thinking.

The guy's name was Shawn, and he was one of Val's coworkers. Shawn was into sports, and, according to Val, he was one of the best phlebotomists in the hospital. I tried not to focus too much on the fact that it was a sad state of affairs when a man's ability to draw blood gently was seen as his best selling point.

Shawn had invited me to attend a baseball game on a Saturday afternoon. When the day arrived, I went to a lot of effort to look sporty. Not being sports-minded myself, I even went so far as to look online at what was appropriate baseball game attire. I went with a fun graphic T-shirt, shorts, and tennis shoes, with a baseball cap I'd stolen from Val to top it all off.

Andrew and Hannah were sitting at the kitchen table looking over their seating chart for the wedding dinner when I came out of my room carrying my tennis shoes. Val was working, and that was fine by me. She always made date pick-up time stressful, and I wasn't interested in hearing them swap bloody stories before we headed out. She had, however, given Shawn our address herself and insisted he was trustworthy.

"So where is Shawn taking you?" Hannah looked up from the chart in front of her and threw me a smile.

"To a baseball game," I replied as I sat down to tie my shoes.

"That's odd. I don't think any teams are playing today," Andrew said with a confused look on his face. "Plus, it's like three in the afternoon. Kind of early."

I shrugged. "I didn't ask a lot of questions. He just invited me to a baseball game, and I agreed."

"I'm sure it'll be fine," Hannah encouraged.

"There's really nowhere to go but up." I did a fist bump in the air as I stood up and went to get my purse from near the front door.

"But, I really don't see—" Andrew began before a knock sounded at the door.

"That'll be Shawn." I crossed my fingers in the air at Hannah, and she did the same back. "Wish me luck."

Even though I was standing right next to the door, I wasn't about to throw it open and appear like I'd just been sitting there waiting for him. Any self-respecting woman knows to at least count to ten first before throwing it open—which is what I did.

Shawn was not what I'd expected. He was small, which was fine since I was too. He had a nearly hairless appearance. His head and face were cleanly shaven, and if I wasn't mistaken, I'd say he even had his eyebrows waxed into perfect shapes. He awkwardly waved at me, and I couldn't help but notice how small his hands were. Well, that explained the gentlest blood draw.

"I'm assuming you're Rachel?" he said in a ridiculously low voice. How that low, deep voice could come out of that small frame was a mystery to me.

"And you must be Shawn." I smiled. "I'm ready." I held up my purse and waited for him to back up a step so I could walk out the door.

We walked down the hallway and to the stairs in relative silence, the only sound being my tennis shoes squeaking lightly. When we got to the parking lot, there was a green minivan parallel parked next to the curb. The only reason I noticed was that we didn't get many minivans in our apartment complex. It was mostly young, single professionals.

I assumed we'd walk on by to his car. But nope. As we got nearer, the sliding door closest to us automatically opened. A woman in the driver's seat leaned back so that her head was in view past the passenger seat headrest and smiled at us.

"Hi there. I'm Jenna. I'm so glad you could join us today." She waved a little, and her smile was broad.

I looked at Shawn for guidance as two little kids in the back row of seats waved at me too. Shawn smiled and motioned for me to climb in before him. In a state of shock, I took a half step back rather than follow his invitation, unsure if I should really be getting into this family's vehicle.

My hesitation must have been obvious, because an older girl, probably thirteen or fourteen, rolled down the front passenger window and leaned out with a big smile on her face.

"Hi, Rachel. I'm Kelly. This will be so fun," she chirped.

I raised my eyebrows a bit and smiled back at her. It wasn't her fault I didn't share her excitement. And how did she know my name? While it was clear that this was our ride, I turned to Shawn expecting some answers. Did he not have a license? Did he not own a car? Were we being chauffeured?

Shawn had the decency to look a little sheepish as he gestured around to the people who were patiently waiting for me to come aboard.

"So, um, Jenna is my aunt, and these are my cousins," he said pointing to the three kids in the car. "They're going to come too, so I thought we could all ride together."

I took a deep breath and smiled back at all of them. Not ideal, not by a long shot, but beggars can't be choosers. I climbed in the van and plopped myself down on a slightly sticky middle seat. Yay for kids.

I heard the clank of the van door closing as Shawn sat in the seat next to me and gave his aunt the signal to go. Jenna did so in a zippy manner.

Shawn turned slightly to face me and threw out this little zinger. "Yeah, so I always go to my cousin's baseball games and thought it would be fun to have you along."

Cousin? As in relative? As in this better not mean what I think it means? It simply could not be happening. My heart pounded with an emotion very closely related to anger. I was not going to meet my one true love at a kid's baseball game while being driven around in his aunt's minivan. It was going to take me a minute to be able to speak without sounding like an evil banshee, so in the meantime, I simply nodded at Shawn's explanation and looked out the window.

After a few minutes of talking myself down, I felt a little foolish for my reaction. Maybe I needed to relax. Actually, it was nice that family was so important to Shawn. Anyone who spent his free weekend time supporting his cousin and cruising in minivans couldn't be all bad. Perhaps this cousin played for the minor leagues, and we were going to a stadium. There was a chance I'd jumped to the wrong conclusion here.

I shook off the last of my irritation and asked, "What team does your cousin play for?"

He smiled. "I think they call themselves the Batty Batters."

Well then . . . that begged another question that I sure didn't want the answer to. "How old is your cousin?"

"Oh, uh, Tyler is . . . um . . . six, I think?" Shawn paused for a minute. "Is that right, Aunt Jenna? Tyler's six?"

Jenna smiled at us in the rearview mirror. "That's right, hon."

I swallowed hard. "Six, huh?" I cleared my throat. I had been right. I was on my way to cheer for Little (stinking) League.

Okay, all was not lost. Still cute and sweet that he supported his little cousin. Liking kids was good. If my nieces lived closer, I'd go to their recitals and school plays. This was kind of the same thing, right? I wouldn't have taken a blind date to one, but hey.

"Yep. They're so fun to watch. You're going to love it." Shawn patted my knee. The unwanted contact made me flinch.

"So, I guess my chances of getting a hot dog and a pretzel at this thing are pretty slim then," I cracked in an effort to keep things light. I was in a family van, surrounded by kids who had no idea why I'd be upset. Thankfully Jenna and Kelly laughed.

Shawn smiled and shook his head like he thought I was the cutest thing ever. "I guess we'll see how good you behave. Good kids get to have a slushy afterward," he teased.

Slushies. Hoo boy. I shaved my legs for the promise of slushies. I sank back into the seat and wondered how bad it would look for me to start texting Val strongly worded messages. I typically left my phone in my purse during dates, but this might be one of those times I'd break my rule. Hannah could come pick me up.

Thoughts of Hannah naturally led to thoughts of James, and I firmed my resolve. It would do no good to have a bad attitude. I would give Shawn a fair shot. Just as I'd talked myself into sticking it out, Aunt Jenna pulled the minivan into a community center parking lot and the doors slid open. The two back seat kids jumped out before Shawn and I had even unbuckled.

"Come on, Shawn. We won't get the good seats if we're late," one of them said.

Aunt Jenna turned and smiled at us two lovebirds in the middle seat. "Take your time," she said with a conspiratorial wink. "I'll hurry ahead with the kids, and we'll save you two a seat."

"Thanks." Shawn blushed a bit but smiled back gratefully.

When Aunt Jenna, Kelly, and the two nameless kids were out of hearing distance, I unbuckled and turned to Shawn. "Um, this is kind of a surprise. I didn't realize we were going to a Little League baseball game."

Shawn looked a little embarrassed. "I didn't think you'd come if you knew," he admitted.

"Possibly, but you still should've asked." I swung my legs out the door and stood on the pavement waiting for Shawn to follow. "And why does your aunt think we need alone time?"

"I kind of let her believe we've been dating awhile." He kept his eyes averted as he pushed the button to close the door behind us.

"Why?"

"Because I don't think she'd have let me take a first date to her son's baseball game. Then I would've missed it. I've got a perfect record so far of being at every game."

"That's because your aunt knows that this isn't a great idea for a blind date." I said it kindly, but I wasn't letting him off the hook. He shifted uneasily. "We could have gone out another time, you know," I continued.

"I'm on at the hospital for the next six nights," he responded as we started walking toward the baseball diamond.

"I could have waited," I said, sighing.

"Well, Val kept telling me how great you are, and I couldn't wait to meet you," Shawn declared. It was a nice thing to say.

I took a deep breath and let it slide off my shoulders. "Okay. Well, we're here, so let's go see what your cousin is made of."

As a teacher, I definitely love children. You can't teach if you don't like kids. It just doesn't work, and everyone is miserable. But just because I love kids doesn't mean I get excited about sitting for two whole hours cheering for a group of kids I don't know.

At first it was fine. The boys were cute in their too-big uniforms and baseball helmets that seemed to hide the ball from their view. They tripped and struck out, tried to run the bases backward, and occasionally got distracted by a butterfly or an airplane flying overhead.

After an hour, it was painful, and you started hoping they'd get at least one hit. After ninety minutes, you wanted to curse the gene pools that bred these kids who weren't ever going to amount to anything. After two hours, I was plotting the murders of both Shawn and Val.

Shawn hadn't said much to me the entire time, although that hadn't kept him from occasionally putting an arm around me, or a hand on my knee. The feel of his skin against mine wasn't exactly making the birds sing, and I did my best to shimmy away. I suppose he thought that watching a failing attempt at sports would keep me entertained without conversation. His aunt Jenna spoke to me a lot, and I really liked her, even though it was clear that she saw her son and his teammates through rose-colored glasses. I wasn't going to be the one to point out that her sweet Tyler was wearing his pants backward.

I didn't know it was possible to tie for zero. At the end of the sixth inning, I was almost in awe of the disaster that was Pine Ridge Little League. I couldn't believe they kept the charade going. When I made a comment about no one winning and wondering if they did overtime in Little League, I got an audible gasp from some mothers around me. It didn't matter what the scoreboard said. There were no winners and no losers. It was all about the fun. They were right about one thing: there were definitely no winners on that field.

Mother Nature hadn't been on my side either. The blazing August sun was a scorcher, and someone had planned the baseball field just right to give us a heavy dose of direct sunlight streaming down on us for the entire two hours. I'd be burnt to a crisp for sure. I was grateful I'd worn a cap that had kept the sun out of my eyes for the most part, but I wished Shawn had warned me to wear some sunscreen. Of course, that would have required Shawn to warn me about any of this, and that clearly hadn't happened.

After the game was over, we walked slowly back to Aunt Jenna's van while she gathered her tiny super star. Shawn got chatty at this point, totally animated about the delights of baseball and how his cousin had a shot at making it big if he kept it up. He was totally delusional. I let him yammer on, grateful he'd remembered I was there and was keeping his hands to himself.

"Who's up for a slushy?" Aunt Jenna said as the last seatbelt clicked into place.

"Me!" All four of her children cheered. She looked at Shawn and me, who had remained quiet.

"You two want to join us? Or did you have other plans?" Aunt Jenna winked at us for the second time. I pasted on a smile.

"Actually, I was wondering if you could drop us off to see Dad?" Shawn replied cheerfully.

What now? First a Little League game and now meeting his father? "Uh—" I started to hedge a bit.

"I think that's a lovely idea." Aunt Jenna turned back around and fired up the engine, cruising out of there before I could really process what was happening.

I turned to Shawn. "Um, you want me to meet your dad?"

Shawn smiled and nodded. "He's actually really close to your apartment, so I'll have Aunt Jenna drop us off, and then we can walk back to your place whenever you want."

I decided to shut my big mouth. I wasn't going to bother to ask how he was planning to get home. I figured that if I went for slushies, then I was trapped at the mercy of this family for a while longer. If, however, I was dropped within walking distance of my apartment, then I could ditch and dash at any time—like as soon as Aunt Jenna pulled away and before I'd stepped foot into his dad's place. I'm a monster, I know.

Ten minutes later, I wanted to cry, or scream, and then cry some more. There were no words for my horror as I stepped out of the van and into a cemetery. Aunt Jenna happily waved goodbye as she sped away, the van door still sliding closed behind Shawn. What was going on here?

"He's over here." Shawn took my elbow and turned from the pavement onto some grass. He let go when I started following him.

I looked around and saw a couple of homes across the street from the cemetery, but it didn't make sense that his aunt hadn't dropped us off in front of one of the homes if that was our destination. I started taking deep breaths as I realized that we were going to visit his father's grave.

Shawn was cheerfully talking as he wove in and out of headstones, careful to not step on any. I followed slowly behind, my eyes scanning the roads around the cemetery to make sure I knew where I was and didn't take off running in the wrong direction. I'd lived in Pine Ridge for the past couple of years but hadn't had a reason to visit the cemetery before.

"Here we are." Shawn stopped suddenly, and I bumped into his back hard enough to make him take a step forward.

"Oh, sorry," I mumbled. I didn't step out from behind him though. I was still looking for my getaway route.

"So, this is my dad's place. Pretty nice, huh? All this open space with the beautiful trees and flowers." He turned to face me and stepped aside so that I could see the headstone.

Yep, there was his dad.

Shawn was looking at me with expectation in his eyes. Wait, what had he just said? Oh, yeah. "Um, yeah. The city really keeps it up nicely," I mumbled, my jaw practically frozen shut. Inside I was screaming. It was hard to keep that from happening on the outside.

"They should. We pay enough taxes, right? I call them my dad's HOA fees." He laughed at his own joke.

"Ah, yeah." I raised my eyebrows and nodded my head, hoping that would be enough for him. It was.

"I just knew Dad would love to meet you today. I told him I had a blind date, and he always likes to meet whoever I'm dating."

"Um-hmm."

"Anyhow, why don't you tell Dad a little about yourself?" Shawn put a hand on my back and propelled me forward to where I was standing right in front of the headstone.

I looked down at it and read the name and dates. I had nothing—absolutely nothing—to say to that piece of cement. I understood that this was a special thing for Shawn, and I did not want to be disrespectful or hurt him, but holy cow! Did he hear how crazy this was?

"Come on, just a few things. He can already see how pretty you are," Shawn coaxed.

I cleared my throat. "Um, I'm sorry, but are you serious?" I looked at Shawn.

His eyes were wide with excitement, and he was completely serious about me having a word with his dad.

"Of course!" His smile faltered just a hint. "Why wouldn't I be?"

"Uh, well, it's just that I didn't know your dad before he passed and so . . ."

"Well, that's why we're here. For him to get to know you." Shawn's face fell a bit more, and he seemed exasperated. I wasn't feeling too bad about that, because the feeling was mutual.

"Okay." I didn't actually mean "okay." I really meant, *Either you're on medication or you're off of it, but either way, it's a problem.*

"Do you not believe in life after death?" Shawn asked in an appalled voice.

"Sure I do," I replied firmly.

I did. I wasn't lying. I just didn't believe his dad actually lived in his grave and waited for Shawn's visits. I especially didn't believe that his dad wanted to meet me at this moment. I was pretty sure he was busy in heaven with more heavenly pursuits. I mean, if you think about it, who wants to pass from this life only to be stuck hanging around a headstone for eternity? Not this girl.

"Then why don't you want to say something to him?"

"Because I don't believe he's here waiting to speak to me," I finally retorted. I felt totally backed into a corner.

Shawn looked surprised, then hurt, then tired, and then mad. Wow. A lot of emotions had flitted across his face. He looked up at the sky and mumbled something so softly that I couldn't hear what he'd said. He waited a beat before looking back at me.

"I'm sorry, Rachel. I tried. But Dad and I both agree that this relationship isn't going to be able to progress to the next level," he pronounced.

"I'm . . . sorry?" I was so confused.

"I am too. Really, I am." He mistakenly thought I was apologizing rather than asking a question. "I thought I saw something in you, but the more I get to know you, the more I'm sure we just wouldn't work."

Shawn was looking at me now like he sincerely pitied me. In his mind, I was bad goods. And what did he mean, the more he got to know me? This was the longest conversation we'd had all day.

"I did not see this coming," I muttered.

"I'm sure you're hurting right now." Shawn put a comforting hand on my arm.

I was definitely *not* hurting. I was stunned. I felt like a person who had just had a grenade land nearby and was recovering from the aftershocks.

"When I'm upset, I like to pray," he was saying. "Will you pray with me, Rachel?"

Another grenade launched.

"I just want to leave," I said, not really thinking through my words, just wanting to run away as fast as I could.

"Of course. But I think we need to end this properly. Will you please offer a closing prayer on our relationship?" Shawn was already folding his arms in front of him as he said this.

I gulped. Then I sputtered. Then I just stared at him. What was he talking about? A closing prayer? What relationship? I could not process all of this at once.

"I'm ready whenever you'd like to begin," Shawn said with an edge of impatience.

I felt like he was looking down on me for everything that had just happened, even more so for not jumping straight into a prayer. Not just any old prayer, but a closing prayer on our *relationship*.

"I'm not comfortable with this," I finally stated.

"Fine. I'll pray. I wanted to offer you the opportunity. But if you don't want to take it, then I will." Shawn had barely finished that condescending statement before he launched into a prayer.

I didn't even try to fold my arms, or hands, or anything. I didn't close my eyes. I bowed my head, but it was more in defeat than anything. I'd been raised to be respectful during prayers, or else I'd be stomping away right then.

As I listened to Shawn talk about how he hoped I'd be able to move forward from this and be more open to others, I felt tears burning behind my eyes. My throat felt clogged. I knew that crying was imminent, and it made me angry.

This—*this*—was officially my last date. I felt his closing prayer was the symbolic closing of my entire dating journey. As Shawn finished up, I turned on my heel and walked away. I didn't look at him or say a word. I was out of there.

And I wasn't just out of the cemetery and the craziness that Shawn had thrown my way. I was out of dating. I had endured some of the most ridiculous, terrifying, insane dates anyone should have to endure. I'd sat next to a guy who had his jaw wired shut and listened to him slurp a meat shake. I'd listened to hours of Disney love songs and been invited to play strip poker. I'd been sprayed with Lysol and asked to have less opinions. I'd eaten at Tasty Taco for both lunch and dinner, been asked to order off the kid's menu, left without a meal, picked up frozen dead animals, and gotten stuck in the mud. I'd run a 10K and—perhaps the real winner—actually been hit by a car! I didn't care anymore about all the pep talks and hopes I'd had. I was so done. Done, done, done.

The tears that had threatened earlier were burned out by sheer anger as I left the cemetery grounds and turned toward my apartment. I was grateful that daylight was fading into dusk as I walked for several blocks hoping that no one could see my face. I probably looked like a homicidal maniac the way I was stomping down the street.

I had tried! I'd tried, and tried, and tried. I'd gone out with every guy that had been put in my path, and I had done it while maintaining some hope that I'd find someone. Soon, any clear thoughts fled my brain as I indulged in a total rage-fest. I was due to have one.

When I reached our apartment complex, I still wasn't done fuming. I didn't want to go in and risk getting asked questions until I'd gotten myself under control, so I sat on the steps leading up to our floor and leaned one shoulder against the wall. I worked really hard at taking some deep breaths and tucking everything back away into that place where I could ignore the hurt. The only problem seemed to be that this time the hurt was just too big.

"Rachel?" A voice broke through my fog and my head snapped up.

It was James. As if things could get any worse. Standing above me was the one thing I couldn't have. I'd ruined it. These dates were my penance. The knowledge that I'd be alone forever was my just desserts.

"I'm not going to ask if you're okay, because I can see the answer," he said.

It was said so matter-of-factly that it made me chuckle, which of course made me suddenly sob. I made a strange hiccupping sound as tears sprang from where I'd muscled them down.

He sat next to me, and it was the most natural thing in the world to lean into his side and rest my head rest on his shoulder. I let all thoughts flee from my mind as I absorbed the warm comfort of him. After a small hesitation, he lifted one arm to wrap around my shoulder and pulled me in close. I couldn't have possibly told him how much I loved that he wasn't saying anything. His smell was the same, the rhythm of his heartbeat against my ear familiar. It felt like a slice of heaven in the chaos my life had become.

After a few minutes, he cleared his throat and said softy, "Rach, someone is coming this way."

Saying this was the only thing that could have penetrated the daze I was in. I started to pull away, but he moved his arm to my elbow and helped me stand. As we began climbing the stairs, he reached down the hand that had been on my elbow and curled his fingers around mine. I held on to his larger hand like a lifeline, letting the warmth seep up my arm and make my heart rate increase.

When we reached the apartment door, he looked down at me again, his eyes hiding what he was thinking. I felt vulnerable as I clung to his hand and gazed back through my tears.

"Should we go in?" he asked.

I nodded, and a tear plopped down onto my upper lip. I licked it away as he released my hand and once more put his arm around me, pulling me in tightly to his side, offering support. I melted into him, allowing him to brace me as we walked through the door, my head ducked down, and my footsteps unsure. James held me securely.

"James, hey—" Hannah said, but paused when she caught sight of me. "What's going on?"

"I thought Rachel was on a date with Shawn," Val's voice joined in. I could see her shape on the couch as James walked me past it. "Why is she with you now?"

"And why is she crying?" Hannah stood up from her seat at the kitchen table.

"Just leave her alone. She'll tell you when she's ready," James replied.

"What? James . . ." Hannah started to follow.

James walked me quickly through the living area and into the hallway while talking to the two other girls. "She just needs some space," he stated in a warning voice.

"What suddenly makes you an expert on Rachel?" Val's voice sounded angry as she joined in.

Val clearly did not appreciate James telling her what to do where I was concerned. I understood her frustration. We'd been a little family of three for a long time.

I could hear both Hannah and Val walking toward us as James guided me through my bedroom door and closed it partially behind us. I came to a stop in the middle of my room and just stood there sniffling quietly, hugging my arms around myself, while James leaned his head back out the door to talk to them. All I could think was how much I hated that he'd let go of me.

Their voices were muffled as they whispered fiercely back and forth. Although I could hear them talking still, I didn't try to understand what they were saying. Hannah's voice was high pitched with worry, and Val's was gravelly with irritation as James responded concisely to their questions. For a minute, I was struck by how strange it was to hear the lower timbre of his voice as it echoed in the hallway of our all-female household.

I almost smiled at the thought of Hannah and Val standing outside my door, wondering what was going on and being blocked by James from entering my room. I was sure it irked them to have an outsider involved in the problem. Add to it their knowledge of my history with James, and they were most likely in a tizzy.

They must have come to some decision, because their voices trailed off as James let go of the door and turned back to face me, closing the door behind him and leaning his back against it. It struck me as I looked at him that this was the second time in weeks that James had come to my room.

"You want to talk?" He finally broke the silence. His voice was soothing, and it drew me to him.

"No talking," I replied shakily.

He watched me for a minute, uncertainty in every line of his face before pushing away from the door and opening his arms. I was in them as fast as my feet could move, terrified he'd change his mind. I understood his hesitancy. I deserved it.

After hugging me tightly to him, he loosened his hold and guided me to the chair in the corner of my room. He sat down and pulled me onto his lap. As we settled in together, me still a little weepy, I reached up and threw my baseball cap off so that I could snuggle in as closely as possible. My head rested heavily on his shoulder, one arm around his neck and the other resting on his forearm as he loosely held my waist.

His body was warm and calm, his breathing slow, and his heartbeat steady. He ran a warm hand up and down my arm once, yet still said nothing, allowing my emotions to run. As I settled down a bit, I let the first thing I thought pop out of my mouth.

"Who's Michelle?" I cringed at the question, even though I desperately wanted to know.

James let out a soft breath that sounded somewhat amused. I felt him shake his head. "A friend. An old coworker. The building I used to work in before I moved here had a gym. We both worked out there in the evenings. We struck up a friendship."

"She isn't your girlfriend?"

He just shook his head. I snuggled in deeper, almost lightheaded with relief. As the weight of that particular worry began to lift, I started rambling.

"I just got taken to a cemetery and asked to speak to the guy's dead father. When I wouldn't, he asked me to pray over the end of our relationship. I didn't want to do that. So he prayed for me. Then I had to walk home, and it all just felt like too much."

"He asked you to talk to his father's headstone?" He sounded as shocked as I'd felt. I nodded my head against his shoulder.

"He said his dad wanted to meet me." I knew it sounded funny and would probably be hysterical to rehash later, but for now, I couldn't work up any laughter over it.

We were quiet for another moment, him letting me take my time, me gathering my thoughts. His presence was so comforting, demanding nothing. I took that feeling and let it fill me.

"The thing is," I finally felt brave enough to share, "I wanted this challenge to work out. I really did. But it's only been one disaster after another. I guess it caught up to me today."

I felt James nod against my head, but still he said nothing, waiting for me. The stillness he projected gave me time to think, which may have been a mistake, because I felt myself coming full circle back to the state he'd found me in, simmering and angry on the stairs.

The emotions welled up again, this time without the tears. With the anger came heartache as I felt James pressed against my side. The years melted away until it was simply James and me sitting in my dorm, cuddled close, whispering forevers.

I thought of all the times James had been there for me and I for him. From the moment he'd come to check in on his baby sister that first week of freshman year, we'd been like two magnets slammed together. I'd felt like the luckiest girl alive. I'd made a best friend in my new roommate and found love with her brother. It didn't matter if it had been in our plans or not. We were helpless against the tide. Within a month, we were exclusive. Almost two years later, James had proposed to me at his graduation. I had said yes, but then the doubts had crept in.

They weren't doubts about James, but doubts about me. The more James applied for jobs and we talked about different cities to move to, the more I felt myself shrinking up inside. I still had two years of college left. I was only twenty years old, and I wasn't sure I was ready for marriage or to chase him around the country and possibly lose my dreams in the bargain. I'd been too scared and immature to realize that we could have shared my dreams and worked on them together. "His" and "mine" could have become "ours." The doubts took root, and I'd broken off the engagement.

There had been so many tears, so much arguing. He'd begged and begged. I had shut him out. Hannah had cried and begged too. I'd shut her out. My mom had been inconsolable. Val had been my only friend for almost three full months until Hannah finally forgave me. Even all this time later, I wasn't sure she'd ever truly understood how I'd felt.

Looking back, it was easy to see that it had been the biggest mistake of my life. I'd broken both of our hearts when there were so many ways we could have stayed together. We could have put off marriage until I was ready. He would have waited. He had never asked me to give up my dreams, only to let him be part of my life. In my young mind, it had been so black and white, so all or nothing. I'd given in to the fear alone rather than having faith in our strength together.

"James?" I finally said.

"Yeah?" His voice was a rumble on my cheek. I could feel him turn his head to look down at me.

I leaned my head back against his shoulder and returned his gaze. Seeing his face so close, his eyes that shade of green I'd loved so much, made me forget what I was going to say. A fresh wave of emotion rose, making my throat feel thick.

I broke eye contact with him and almost mindlessly lifted my hand from where it had been resting on his shoulder to run my fingers through his hair. His hair was longer now than it had been when we'd dated. I watched my hand as it played through the layers hanging down to his earlobe. They were so soft. I was sure Hannah had gotten to him with some fancy salon products. I didn't remember his hair being this silky.

Under my tentative explorations, I could feel James tense up, but he made no move to stop me or push me away. His hands slowly flexed on my waist, yet he maintained what little distance there was between us.

I knew he was trying to meet my eyes, but I couldn't bear to have him delve that deeply, so I shifted my gaze to his chin—which was a mistake. I should have avoided looking at his mouth. His lovely, generous, tantalizing, kissable . . .

Before I could think it through, I closed my eyes and leaned up to press my lips softly to his. It was a butterfly kiss for how lightly I pressed, but that didn't stop it from setting off stars behind my eyes. I only held the contact for a moment before pulling away. I was humiliated, exhilarated, and terrified all at the same time.

"Rachel . . . ," he breathed my name as he let his forehead press against mine.

Both of us had our eyes closed, and I could feel the questions radiating from him. "I know. I'm so sorry again. That was a mistake," I said even as I found myself nudging our faces up and pressing my lips to his again. This time it was firmer, and I allowed both of my arms to wrap around his shoulders.

He tightened his hold on me, pulling me in that last bit until we were pressed together fully. He deepened the kiss, the strength in him making my heartbeat accelerate. For that brief moment, time stood still, and my world shifted in a bittersweet way.

"Rachel? James?" A firm knock on the door made us jerk apart. "Is everything okay?" It was Hannah.

I felt James's fingers tighten briefly on my sides before I jumped away and up into a standing position. My fingers flew to my lips, and I looked at him in alarm. I could hardly believe I'd done that.

He cleared his throat and stood up too, motioning with his head for me to go into my bathroom. "Yep, we're good. Rachel just went into the bathroom to wash her face," he said as he walked to my door. "You're timing is great, I was just on my way out."

His voice sounded totally unaffected, even somewhat bored. I didn't know how he pulled it off. My heart was absolutely racing, and I couldn't have said a word. When he looked at me one last time, I couldn't read his expression.

He opened the door, smiled at Hannah, and said, "I'm sure she'll be ready to tell you all about it after she's relaxed a bit." He let himself out and joined her in the hall, closing the door behind him.

I could hear their voices getting softer as they entered the living room, and then it was quiet. I was trying desperately to catch my breath as a new wave of tears fell down my cheeks.

That kiss! That kiss had been a bad idea. How much more proof did I really need that I was *not* over James? And what must he think? This day called for a whole lot more than a change of clothes. I was going to sink into the tub and not come out for at least five years.

Chapter 17

To love and be loved is to feel the sun from both sides.

~ *David Viscott* ~

With two more weeks left until I had to report back to school, I decided to take Diana up on her kind offer for me to come stay at her house for a weekend. I was happy to have a little one-on-one time with my sister and my nieces during their summer break, and I really needed to get away for a while before I accidentally threw myself at James again.

It had been a full week since I'd kissed him, and I hadn't seen or heard from him at all. The more I'd replayed the scene in my mind—which happened about every two minutes—I wasn't actually sure if he'd really kissed me back or if the romantic moments were entirely my imagination. I knew he hadn't pushed me away, but I was beginning to be afraid that it had been completely one-sided.

I had been too chicken to face my friends the same evening, so after James left I'd taken a shower and crawled into bed with a good book. When I'd emerged from my room the next morning, Hannah had acted totally normal, which meant she knew nothing about it. Val had grilled me for details about Shawn and my crying and James being in my room, but I'd had answers for everything, and she'd backed down. Although I was sure Shawn was going to hate his next lunch break with Val, I couldn't seem to work up any feelings of pity for him.

As I made the two-hour drive to Diana's house on a Thursday morning, my plan was to stay through Sunday. I needed to be back to help Hannah with some final details for the wedding now that it was barely a month away. I was hoping that three nights away would do me a world of good. I was also hoping that a sister's understanding would help me get myself back together. I wasn't used to living in a place of doubt, and I didn't like it at all.

When I arrived at Diana's house, it was lunchtime. Heather and Hailey were standing at the counter, wearing their swimsuits, and spreading pizza sauce and toppings on pitas. Diana was wearing an apron and welcomed me in with a big hug. I felt a sense of relief spread from my head down to my toes. I hugged her back tightly. I was so happy to be there.

"Aunt Rachel, do you like olives or pepperoni?" Hailey asked as she made a pita pizza for me.

"Definitely both." I smiled and kissed the top of her blonde head.

I leaned over to Heather, who was standing next to her identical twin, and gave her a kiss as well. They looked so grown up. It had only been a month since I'd seen them, but it seemed as if they'd shot up a foot.

"You two are adorable." I squeezed them both into a hug. They squealed and tried to smear pizza sauce on my cheeks. It was perfect.

We enjoyed lunch in the backyard at a shaded table next to the pool. Conversation was light as I asked the girls about their summer so far and how they felt about school starting up again. They giggled a lot and talked so quickly I could barely keep up. Diana smiled as she watched us interact.

After we'd eaten, Diana had the girls clear their places and jump straight into the pool. Seeing Diana's method of "feed them something messy and then make them swim" made me think that every school cafeteria could use a water trough.

I finished my lunch while watching the girls play in the pool. They were having a grand time. Their grins and squeals convinced me that a swim would be a great idea. I helped Diana clear away the rest of the dishes and changed into my suit. I announced my arrival with a cannonball that made the girls scream. Their big blue eyes were wide as they wiped their faces dry and looked back at me before we all dissolved into laughter.

Squealing little girls became the theme of the weekend as I fully wrapped myself up in them. We played board games, yard games, and video games. I helped them bake cookies and then brownies. We watched a couple of movies and colored. Every day we swam, and every night I slept with them in a fort we'd built. While I listened to their breathing and their sleepy sighs, I did my best to keep my mind from wandering to James.

It was impossible to do. He was in everything I saw from the pancakes at breakfast to the setting of the sun. An old and familiar ache to be with him had wormed its way back into my life. I beat myself up over the fact that I'd ever let him go. I beat myself up even more over kissing him. Things had been so much easier when I'd stayed in my comfort zone and routine.

I felt like I was grieving a second time for the loss of our relationship. The first time I'd missed him deeply but was firm in my decision. This time I missed him, but with missing him came the added weight of knowing exactly what I'd lost. Knowing I could never undo it was like a fresh wound. The regrets ate at me constantly.

I was stacking up Jenga blocks with Hailey on Sunday morning when Diana walked into the family room and put her hands on her hips. Whatever it was, she meant business.

"Let's go. Jordan is watching the girls. Get your tennis shoes," she said as she pointed me toward the guest room where my luggage was sitting next to the unused bed.

"What the—" I started to argue.

"Now!" Diana pointed a stern finger in the direction she wanted me to go. "Aunt time is over. It's sister time now."

I changed into my yoga pants and pink exercise shirt, happy to have a reason to wear them a second time after my 10K date, and met Diana in the front foyer of her house. She was dressed similarly.

As we strolled along through her neighborhood, I felt myself tense up a bit. I hadn't set out to avoid my sister during my visit, but I also hadn't been ready to answer her questions when I first arrived. I knew this walk was not about exercise.

"So, thanks for not making me jog," I joked as we waved at a neighbor. "Last time I tried to do that, I scraped my face on the pavement."

Diana chuckled. "Sorry about Mitch. Guess that didn't work out like we'd hoped."

"He was actually one of the nicer guys I went out with, so don't stress over it."

We walked in silent contemplation for maybe thirty seconds when Diana abruptly said, "Okay, enough chitchat. That's all we've done all weekend, and you have to go home this afternoon. Look, I know I invited you, and I'm so happy you accepted, but I thought you were just coming for a casual visit. I was clearly wrong. Hailey and Heather are loving this time with their aunt, but I know there's something more going on with you."

Leave it to Diana to cut to the chase. I blew out a puff of air. It was only natural that she would be the first person I told about my rediscovered feelings for James. I certainly couldn't tell Hannah—James was her brother. And telling Val was almost worse than telling Hannah. Lisa had set me up with James, not knowing who he was, and had been the victim of a lot of "we're just friends" speeches on my part. Mom—just no. So that left Diana. In my heart, I'd known that. I think it's why I'd raced off so willingly to her house, jumping a little too high at her invitation. The problem was, I wasn't sure where to start.

"So, it turns out that . . . well, there's a chance I'm . . . uh . . . I think I may still be in love with James," I said at length.

She turned to look at me, most likely to judge if I was teasing or not. What she saw in my face must have convinced her I was telling the truth.

"Oh?" was all she said.

"Yep." I made a face.

"When did this happen?"

Big sigh. "I'm afraid it's been going on forever. I just didn't realize it."

"What made you realize it now?"

"We keep running into each other and getting thrown together."

"Oh," she said, this time with more understanding.

I nodded. "Then last week I was having a horrible day, and he happened to come along and was really nice about it."

"James was always really nice," Diana stated. It was true.

"So nice that I kind of kissed him," I groaned out the confession. It was the first time I'd said it out loud.

"Oh!" This one surprised.

"Uh-huh."

"Did he kiss you back?"

"I can't be really sure," I replied sadly.

"How is this up for debate? He either did or he didn't."

"We got interrupted."

"Oh." This one sad.

"I think it's a good thing. I have no idea what would've happened if we'd been left alone," I exclaimed. "I'm still so embarrassed when I think about it. At least this way there was no awkward conversation where he had to tell me he'd gotten over me and to stop throwing myself at him."

"*Has* he gotten over you?" Diana asked.

"He sure acts like it. He's so cool and calm all the time. He even told Hannah he was totally over it when she asked him about being part of the wedding party."

"Oh." This one flat.

"And he had a girl with him one of the times we ran into each other. She was seriously intimidating and obviously totally into him."

"Oh." Another sad one.

"It was the worst. I made a total fool of myself over her. I even asked him if she was his girlfriend."

Diana shook her head and smiled. "Please tell me you didn't."

"Oh, I did. Yep. While I was sitting on his lap, crying."

"Oh?" Diana's eyebrows shot up. "Wow. It's worse than I thought."

"Right! I don't know what to do."

"So, is she his girlfriend?"

"No," I replied.

"Have you seen him since?"

"No. I don't want to either," I said and added, "I'm glad he's avoiding me," which I firmly believed he was doing.

"So . . . you ran away to my house?"

"No. I did not run away. You invited me, and I was happy to come," I stated firmly. Diana gave me a look. I sighed. "I ran away just a tiny bit, yes." I was sad again. "Diana, what am I going to do?"

"First step is you're going to pull up your big girl pants and go home. Stop moping around like you did something wrong. There is nothing wrong with you kissing a man you're interested in." Diana paused to chuckle lightly. "Especially after you've taken the time to make sure he isn't dating anyone."

"I'm humiliated just remembering it," I moaned. "Never mind that seven years ago I broke off our engagement," I reminded her. "Seven years is a really long time! Half the kids I teach were born the year I broke his heart. Besides, I already had my chance with him, and I threw it away."

"Rach, you need a little perspective here. You were twenty years old, in college, and probably still didn't know how to balance your bank account," Diana said in a patient voice. "Now you're a grown woman with a career and a life who knows what she wants."

"That may be true, but I broke his heart, Diana."

"His heart wasn't the only one broken," she replied gently and reached out to squeeze my arm.

"Okay, that may be true too, but at least it was my choice. He was the victim." I felt that familiar guilt creeping in. "Now he probably thinks I'm toying with him. I don't think he trusts me."

"Do you want James back? I mean, really, for keeps?" she asked.

"I'm not sure how to answer that," I said morosely. I was depressingly sure that no one else would do for me, but I was uncharacteristically torn on what to do.

"Well, you'd better be sure. Until you know it with all your heart, you leave that poor man alone."

"And what if I decide I do but he doesn't want me back?" I asked in a quiet, vulnerable voice. "I don't exaggerate when I say Michelle—the other girl—was gorgeous."

"Stop worrying about Michelle. If he wanted to be dating her, he'd be dating her. No matter what James wants, you'll survive the same way you always have," Diana stated.

"Can I run back here if I need to?" I grinned at her, feeling my heart lift a little at her total unwillingness to let me wallow or worry. She also had a valid point about Michelle.

"Of course you can. But next time, tell me what's going on instead of avoiding me in my own house," she scolded gently. "Oh, and one other bit of advice?"

"Shoot."

"Do not breathe a word of this to Mom. I think she's still in love with James too."

It was the best advice she could have given me, and I felt happier as our conversation flowed on to other lighter topics. As far as not running away went, this had worked out just fine.

The next night, Hannah and I were sitting around the kitchen table, sorting through all the RSVPs that had been sent back for the wedding. Val, who wasn't getting dragged into more wedding prep, was flipping through a healthcare magazine on the couch. We were all comfy in our loungewear, with our contacts out and our glasses on, our makeup washed off, and our cute hairdos relegated to rubber bands and messiness. Some light, jazzy background music played from the living room.

I had a stack of envelopes next to me, my job being to open them and check names off a list, noting if they were coming or not, before passing them to Hannah. She was jotting down their dinner selection, along with making notes and adjustments on the seating chart based on if that particular guest was coming or not.

Because it required a certain degree of focus, conversation was limited and sprinkled throughout with silences. However, it was nice to be sitting there with just the three of us together in the apartment. It struck me once again how much I'd miss this when Hannah was gone. I wondered if Val and I should consider getting another roommate. . . . Never mind. The idea of breaking in a new girl sounded awful.

"Oh, I just remembered. James asked me if you were back in town yet." Hannah looked up from her chart, one finger pushing her glasses up onto her face and another holding her place. "Were you two supposed to get together or something?"

My heartbeat increased, and I tried to play it casual as I looked back at her through lenses of my own. "Um, not unless I've forgotten some kind of wedding event we were working on together." I shrugged and made an innocent, confused face.

"Nope." Hannah looked back down at her paper. "Well, I told him you were home now."

"Okay," I replied, grateful she'd bought my look.

"Doesn't he have your number from the day he helped you and Garrett get unstuck?" Val asked from the couch. I nodded. "Why wouldn't he just ask you himself then?"

I pulled the same confused face and shook my head. There was really nothing more to say without causing a major halt in our production line. I didn't want to cause a halt. I just wanted to keep my head down and avoid inviting questions.

I couldn't get my mind to slow down though. I wondered how James had even known I was gone. More important, why had he wanted to know if I was home?

My answer came thirty minutes later with a knock at the door. Val, who was apparently tired of poring through articles, jumped up to get it. I heard James's voice before I saw him. I wasn't prepared for the look on his face when he walked in the door.

In the months since I'd first seen him again, he'd never looked anything other than totally put together and somewhat aloof. Now, as he stood there, he looked as though something in him had unraveled a bit.

"James, are you okay?" Hannah asked, obviously seeing the same thing I was seeing.

He just nodded at her before looking at me, piercing right through my armor and making me feel like I was vibrating on the inside. I swear my glasses actually fogged up.

"Rachel, can I talk with you?" he said. "Alone."

It was as if the entire room shrank down to his face. Hannah and Val could have been in another time zone for all I noticed them. I stood up and gave him a quick nod. I turned without looking to see if he was following me and did everything possible to keep from running to my bedroom. I was trying to remember what Diana had said about being sure how I felt and that there was nothing wrong with wanting to be with him again. It was all jumbled in my mind, and I wasn't sure if I was supposed to lock him out or drag him in.

He was right behind me, his longer stride quickly eating up the space between us. He managed to pass by me and walk straight into the middle of my room as I followed him through the doorway.

"Close the door," he said as he turned to face me. "Please."

I obeyed and leaned against it for support. I had no idea what was coming, but I was terrified that based on his expression, it was going to be a scathing dialogue. He came right at me, and I had no time at all to process what was happening before he wrapped one arm around my waist and used the other to pull my chin up to meet him as he pressed his mouth to mine.

He said nothing. He just kissed me like I was the thing he needed most in the world. I kissed him back the same way, throwing my arms around his neck, toes barely touching the floor, knowing he was it for me. The kiss wasn't nearly as long as I would've liked. He pushed me to arm's length and drilled his eyes into mine. I raised a shaky hand to straighten my glasses, which had been knocked askew.

"This doesn't change anything," he grumbled before I could clear my head. I nodded as I pulled my limp arms off his shoulders and let them drop to my side.

"Okay," I managed to say as I looked up into his eyes. "But you should know—"

"Nothing," he said again as he leaned in for another kiss. This one was soft and tender, a whisper compared to what the other had been. It raised butterflies everywhere inside of me. I raised my hands to rest on his shoulders, keeping my touch light even though he'd wrapped me securely back in his arms.

After two or three soft kisses, he straightened and stepped away. The look on his face didn't invite conversation, so I reached behind me to grab the doorknob and let him go, even though I had so much I wanted to say. He sailed past me the same way he'd sailed in, leaving me with shaky limbs and tears pressing at my eyelids.

Five excruciatingly long days later was Hannah's bridal shower and engagement party. It didn't make sense in my mind to have them combined. Engagement parties were typically done when people got engaged, right? Not one month before the wedding. And I'd never heard of it doubling as a bridal shower.

But Hannah had explained that her family had handled things in this way for two reasons. One, enough cousins in her extended family had called off their engagements so that her relatives now preferred to wait to spend the time, money, and effort until it was a sure thing. Second, with the family being spread out across several cities, they now tried to combine activities whenever possible. You can't beat logic.

I tried not to let it sting knowing that James had been one of those family members to call it off and I may have played a part in the Redmond family's decision to wait before celebrating.

I had not heard so much as James's name since he'd pressed me up against my door and kissed me. It made me wonder if he'd really meant it when he said it didn't change a thing. I wasn't sure that I believed anymore that he was immune to me. I mean, how could I feel such an electric pull and he not feel at least a little tingle? There was no way he wasn't at least thinking about me. I was reasonably confident he wasn't showing up at girls' houses all over town and kissing them like that. However, maybe it had been about wanting to get the questions out of his system, and he had no intention of anything redeveloping between us.

I was a bundle of nerves leading up to the party. I asked Hannah no less than 592 times what I should wear, how I should do my hair, and for any makeup tips she could offer me. She was more than happy to help and was excited that I was showing some interest in getting fancy. Val had determinedly stayed behind her bedroom door during all conversations and tutorials.

Hannah wasn't the only one I consulted. I spoke with Diana a few times, updating her on what had happened with James and how I felt about it. We analyzed and overanalyzed and finally decided that the night of the engagement bridal shower party would be a good time for me to tell him what was in my heart. James would obviously be there. He was not only the bride's sibling, but he was also one of the groomsmen. I was sure we could find a private place to talk.

When the day arrived, I curled my long hair and did my best to copy the makeup steps Hannah had taught me, all the while pondering how the party would go. I imagined how amazing he'd look in his suit, being lean and muscled like he was. I was doing my best to look equally amazing. I had plans that didn't involve glasses and yoga pants.

I felt a sting on my wrist, and the smell of burning called me back from my daydreams, reminding me to focus and get my head in the game. I quickly set the iron down and ran my arm under cool water, an angry red welt already forming on the soft, pale underside of my arm.

"Dang it!" I said through gritted teeth.

The water soothed the pain away, and I returned to my primping. When I felt confident that I could do no better, it was time to slip on my dress. Hannah had taken me shopping the day before to choose just the perfect thing.

Because of my fair skin and dark hair, Hannah had sold me on a flirty red dress. It had a scoop neck and a tightly fitted bodice, but it flared out at the waist, almost like a ballerina tutu down to my knees. I had strappy red heels to match. I was out to make an impression.

Hannah hadn't asked me about the night James stormed in and right back out. After he'd left, I'd taken a few minutes to collect myself before rejoining her and Val in the living area to finish RSVPs. They'd both looked at me with questions in their eyes.

"What was that all about?" Val had finally pressed when I'd remained silent.

"He had a message he needed to deliver," I finally replied, forcing a calm nonchalance into my voice.

"Looks to me like it was received," Hannah had cracked.

Her joke made me smile, and I nodded. We'd gotten back to work after that, but I wondered if Hannah's insisting on taking me dress shopping and being overjoyed about giving me makeup tips was an indication that she was aware that things between her brother and me were possibly sparking again.

I stepped into my dress and picked up my sandals, leaving my room to find Val and get help zipping up the back of my dress.

"Val?" I called into the hallway, unsure if she was still in her room or in the living area.

"My room," she replied.

I turned down the hall and knocked softly on her door before walking in. Val's room was a total reflection of Val as a person. A disaster. Her bed had probably never been made, her clothes hung on various furniture pieces, and her bathroom counter was cluttered with every medicine you could get without a prescription . . . and probably some that required one.

She was standing in front of her dressing table mirror, putting finishing touches on her makeup. Val looked great in a dress of deep purple. It was floor length with straight lines and a floaty material that didn't hug anything but definitely teased.

"Wow, you look amazing!" I said to her.

Our eyes met in the mirror and she smiled. "You look pretty hot yourself," she replied.

"Can you zip me when you're done?" I asked.

"Yep."

I sat on her bed and put on my sandals while I waited for her. It didn't take long for her to finish, and as soon as I was zipped, she slipped on her own shoes. We stopped in the living area to gather our purses and gifts as we left the apartment.

The drive to the Florentine Banquet Hall where the party was being held would take about an hour or so. It was in a location that was central for Andrew and Hannah's family and friends. Since the wedding would be in Pine Ridge, they didn't want to make people travel the distance twice.

The long drive wasn't exactly helpful. It gave me plenty of time to worry. What would James do when he saw me? What would I do when I saw him? Would I be able to eat? Would any of the extended family recognize me? What had Diana said I should do again?

"Rach, settle down," Val reached over from the driver's seat and tapped my knee gently. "Just play it cool. He's probably nervous too." My eyes swung to hers in surprise. The corners of her mouth lifted slightly. "I'm not blind, and neither is Hannah. I'm just brave enough to say it. Something is going on with you and James."

"I really don't know," I replied honestly.

"Well, whatever it is—or isn't—you need to get a grip. Don't go in there looking like you're going to barf all over him."

I smiled at her. "That visual is actually helping," I said, laughing.

"You look great. You'll knock his socks off!"

With Val's faith in me, I began to have faith in myself. I was not a scared, young college student. I was a grown woman who could make decisions and didn't need to be living in fear. I mentally straightened my shoulders and puffed up my chest.

By the time Val and I walked through the doors to the banquet area, I was ready to take on the world. I played it cool by purposely not looking around to see if James was there. Instead,

I handed Val my gift to take with hers and walked straight to the bar to order a soda. While I waited, I leaned against the bar and looked around.

I spotted Hannah across the room, looking gorgeous in a simple white summer dress. I thought it was cute that she was wearing white. It wasn't her wedding dress, but she looked lovely. Andrew was standing by her side, an arm around her waist, smiling and talking with the group of people around them. The music playing in the background was upbeat and lent a festive feeling to the evening.

"Wow, you look amazing!" a voice close behind me said just as the bartender handed me my drink.

I spun around to come face to face with Garrett. He was smiling warmly, and an immediate smile spread across my face in reply. He put a hand lightly on my waist and leaned in to kiss me on the cheek. I hadn't seen him since our date and was grateful that he seemed unaffected by how it had gone.

"You don't look too shabby yourself," I said cheerfully as I took him in. He was wearing a beautifully tailored gray suit.

"I try," he replied, letting his hand drop back to his side. "I'd ask if you just got here, but nobody could have missed that red dress walking in the door. Really, you look great."

I fought down a blush. "Thank you. Have you been here long?"

He shook his head. "Just long enough to get all the greetings out of the way and add my gift to the pile. Now I'm ready to eat. Care to join me?"

I hesitated for a moment and scanned the crowd again. I still didn't see James, so I smiled back at Garrett and said, "I'd love to."

Garrett held out his arm, and I slipped my hand into the crook of his elbow as we walked to the buffet line. Hannah and Andrew had planned a formal wedding, so they wanted their engagement party shower to be the total opposite. Dinner would be served buffet style with no assigned seating. People could come and go as they pleased and as time permitted. They would visit with guests and open gifts during conversational lulls. I was happy with the choice and could tell by the atmosphere that others were too.

Garrett and I joined the line at the buffet table, and he casually flirted with me as we filled our plates. Our date ending on a sour note hadn't lessened his playful nature with me, which I was grateful for. I hadn't laughed so much in weeks. I began to feel the tension over James fade and be replaced by calm. I was going to be fine.

"Why don't we sit over there?" Garrett pointed to a table near the back. "We can visit a little better in the quiet." He wiggled his eyebrows. I chuckled and followed him with my full plate.

Even though I'd been thoroughly entertained by Garrett, I was still scanning the room out of the corner of my eye. Just because I wasn't feeling tense didn't mean I didn't care where James was. As we got to our table and Garrett pulled out my chair, I finally caught sight of him. He was standing near the buffet table chatting with someone, which gave me a minute to casually notice how incredible he looked.

Just like Garrett, he was in a well-tailored suit. Only his was navy blue with a slimmer fit that accentuated everything worth accentuating. Seeing him was all it took to zoom right back to sweaty palms and a fluttering heart.

He must have felt my gaze across the room, because he suddenly looked to where I was sitting. Garrett was chatting away at me, but I didn't hear him over the pulse in my ears. James's expression didn't change, but he nodded once at me. I did the same back, remembering Val's advice to play it cool.

However, Diana had told me to stop playing cat and mouse, so I tilted my head toward the seat next to me at our table and raised my eyebrows in question. He got the message, and after a brief hesitation, he nodded again. Good. He'd be joining me when he could. I was already anticipating the sound of his voice and the warmth of his nearness.

". . . camping at Yellowstone National Park this summer. It was great," Garrett finished.

I tore my eyes away from James, picked up a piece of fruit with my fork, and smiled. "Sounds amazing," I said.

"It really was. I'd love to show you sometime."

"Show her what sometime?" A pretty younger brunette pulled out the chair next to Garrett and sat down with a plate of food.

Garrett looked up at her, and the strangest expression crossed his face. I got the impression he was uncomfortable with her joining us. It was flattering to me, but not fair to her. She probably just wanted to hang out with her cool older cousin.

"Hi, I'm Rachel. I'm the maid of honor," I said to the girl.

She smiled, completely unaware of the vibes Garrett was giving off. "I'm Maddi. So you're who Garrett will partner with then?" she asked.

I nodded. "I'm just glad he's as great as he is."

"Seriously. You lucked out." She smiled again and nudged Garrett on the shoulder with her arm. The smile he gave her was genuine, but it seemed smaller somehow than the smiles he'd been giving me.

"What have you been up to lately?" Garrett asked me.

"I feel like all I've done is wedding planning even though it isn't my wedding," I joked. "I've spent some time visiting family though, so that's been fun."

"Rachel here is a teacher," Garrett said to Maddi, "so she's been off for the summer."

Maddi nodded her understanding as she started digging into her plate. "That's great. What grade?"

"Second. In Pine Ridge. It's a great job," I replied.

"Are you ready to go back?" Garrett asked. "The summer really flew."

"Next week is my last free week before I have to go back and get the classroom ready," I said, sighing. "I'm always excited to start the year and I'm always happy when it's over."

Garrett picked up the conversation from there for a bit, and I let my eyes wander, trying again to catch sight of James. He was at the end of the buffet line now with Val. Both of them were carrying plates of food and were comfortably chatting.

When they reached the end of the line, Val turned to James, and it looked like she asked him where he wanted to sit. His eyes met mine from across the room again, and he motioned toward me. Val turned to me and smiled as she followed James to our table. I was both grateful and a little anxious to see them heading my way. Just because I'd invited him and was trying to exude calm didn't mean I wasn't practically choking on my food. Was this how guys felt when they were approaching a girl they liked?

James slid in next to me, and the familiar scent of his cologne washed over my senses as he adjusted his chair. I put my hands in my lap and folded them tightly to keep from reaching out to touch him. This was possibly the definition of sweet suspense. I couldn't wait to find my chance to talk to him. This night felt heavy with possibility for me.

"Hi, James." Garrett leaned across me to shake hands with him, apparently truly over our experience in the mud puddle.

"Garrett," James replied, taking his hand.

"This here is Maddi," Garrett pointed to the cute girl sitting next to him. "If I remember right, this other pretty lady is Val."

Val nodded but barely gave him a glance before looking at Maddi. "Nice to meet you, Maddi. How are you related to Hannah?"

Maddi started to reply, but Garrett cut her off. "She's not really an official member of the family," he stated smoothly. Maddi laughed as if it was their little joke, and they both left it at that. It was odd, but I didn't care enough to delve deeper. Maybe she was a distant cousin, neighbor, or childhood playmate.

Instead, I turned to James and saw he was looking at me too. No time like the present to jump in and see what would happen.

"You look great," I said quietly to him.

His lips raised in a slight smile. "Thanks. You too," he replied.

I could tell by the look in his eyes that he meant it. James had always talked about how beautiful I was to him. I was hoping that hadn't changed.

"Hannah appears to be happy with how this has turned out," I said in an attempt to settle into comfortable conversation.

"She should be happy. The place looks great," Garrett responded even though the remark was made to James. "Almost as great as the girls are looking tonight," he added, giving me a knowing smile.

I saw James's face tense. Maddi's did too. Uh-oh. I hoped she didn't have a crush on Garrett, because he wasn't giving her the time of day.

"Wait . . . Rachel . . . ," Maddi said, studying me for a minute. "Are you the friend Hannah's mom was talking about who has gone on all sorts of dating adventures lately?"

I was a little bothered to find out Hannah's family was discussing me, but I forced a self-deprecating smile. "That's me," I replied.

Her timing couldn't have been worse, bringing up my dating adventures in front of the man I was planning to talk to about how not flighty I was with my affections.

"Yeah, sounds like it's been pretty crazy," Maddi said to Garrett as she picked up her fork and started eating again. "I'll bet you could tell some stories. Is it true you've gone on like fifteen blind dates over the past couple of months?"

Wow! That had really been blown out of proportion. "No. Definitely not fifteen." I shook my head and tried to brush it off. "Only like six or seven."

"Really?" Garrett seemed a little put off by that.

My annoyance took it up a notch to indignation over his reaction. My dating life shouldn't be fodder for family gossip, nor should he get to judge me about it. I felt heat crawl up my neck.

"That makes it sound worse than it is," Val jumped in. "Most of them have been set up by Hannah and me, or Rachel's family and other friends." The irritation in her tone was obvious. I was grateful to her.

"I'm surprised. I'd think you wouldn't need any help catching someone's attention." Garrett flipped back to his flirty self, and I smiled even though my shoulders felt tight.

Maddi looked at Garrett. "They said she had a bad breakup a few years ago and decided to stop dating. But when Hannah got engaged, she realized she didn't want to be alone forever, so Hannah challenged her to jump right back into the dating world," Maddi continued as if I wasn't sitting right there, burying me as she chewed her food innocently.

"Oh, a bad breakup?" Garrett sent me a sympathetic look. "You must have really cared about the guy if you didn't date for a few years afterward."

I nodded stiffly, unable to work out the right words to respond with. I felt myself melting in place. This conversation could not be going worse. This night was supposed to be about me opening the door with James and talking to him about our future. Now they were unknowingly reminding him about our breakup and making it sound like I'd date just about anyone. The message Maddi was sending was that I was only interested in dating because I was jealous of Hannah and didn't want to be lonely. My stomach clenched.

"I mean, there's, you know, more to the story than just that," I half whispered through the lump forming in my throat.

"So have you found anyone interesting?" Maddi asked with a final slurp of noodles, acting as though she didn't hear me.

"The problem is that they've all been a little too interesting," Val inserted drily. She gave Maddi a smile and added, "The world is full of odd ducks. I bet you could tell us some stories about dates you've been on."

I shot Val a grateful look, and her eyes told me she understood. Maddi took the bait and jumped in with more chatter as the subject changed to her life.

Not being interested in more attention coming my way, I focused on eating. Unfortunately, some of the tension had returned. I hated talking about this dating thing in front of James. I didn't want him to remember that I'd been dating everyone under the sun. I wanted him to think I was only interested in him. The problem was that I didn't know if he was only interested in me.

I sighed softly and rolled my shoulders a bit as I smiled at a joke Garrett told. I jumped a bit in my chair as I felt a warm hand close over mine under the table.

"Nothing to get upset about, Rach." James's soft voice filtered to my ear through the louder conversation going on around us.

"This isn't how I wanted this night to go," I whispered back earnestly.

"Oh?"

"I've been wanting to talk to you all week. I was hoping we could find some time. . . ." I glanced at him and turned my hand to intertwine my fingers with his. My meaning couldn't have been clearer.

His eyes searched mine, but just as his hand began to close around my fingers, Garrett's voice interrupted.

"James, what do you think of Rachel's dates?" His voice was boisterous compared to the quiet side conversation we'd been having. It felt as though we'd been literally yanked back to the table. "You'd never guess from looking at her that she has a secret life as a serial dater." Garrett shook his head and smiled playfully, thinking he was teasing, having no idea what was actually happening here.

James's fingers suddenly pulled away as if he'd been shocked. The connection between us severed completely as he looked away.

"It's really none of my business. Rachel is a grown woman." James put an exclamation point on his statement by shrugging and taking a swig of his drink.

It felt like a knife to my gut, especially after I'd told him we needed to talk. I knew he'd understood my meaning. A shuddering, shallow breath filled my lungs as a part of me crumbled inside. It took massive effort to look natural.

"Well, I think we can definitely agree that Rachel is all grown up." Garrett's hand landed on my knee under the table. It was a quick and light touch, hardly anything. I gave a weak smile back.

The remainder of dinner was taken up with light conversation. Maddi chatted cheerfully, Garrett cracked jokes, and even Val surprised me by holding up the conversation that I just couldn't face.

As I listened to the ebb and flow of their chatter, I forced each set of muscles to unclench. James didn't have much to say. I hated to see the return of his aloofness but figured at least I could stop wondering where he stood.

A strange sort of peace descended on me as I let it sink in. My path shouldn't be dictated by anyone but me. I'd been thrown around at the whims of fate and well-meaning people for the past six months, and it had gotten me nowhere. I'd decided to acknowledge my feelings for James and been rebuffed. As an adult, I could either wallow in the failures or take the bull by the horns and create my own destiny. The path I wanted to take was closed to me, so I would forge another.

Eventually Val excused herself, followed by James, who appeared only too happy about being called away by family duty. When Maddi saw someone she really wanted to catch up with, just Garrett and I were left at the table. He was all smiles and compliments, and I made a conscious effort to soak in what he was drizzling over me.

My eyes wandered to James a few times as Garrett talked, and each time I saw him, I felt an odd mixture of longing and submission. I didn't know how long it would take me to stop wishing for him, but I understood that it had to be a two-way street.

Garrett's hand landing softly on my arm interrupted my thoughts, and I looked at him questioningly.

"I was wondering, would you like to go out again sometime?" he asked quietly, changing from being a flirt to being sincere in the blink of an eye.

My initial reaction was to cringe away. I didn't want this. I wasn't looking for something. My heart was hurting. But... I had also just finished reminding myself that I could take charge. Garrett was nice enough. Why not?

"I would love that. I'm tired of blind dates." It was my turn to smile at him. "I'm taking control back," I stated.

"Name the time and I'm all yours."

"How about next Monday night?" I asked. It was only two days away, but I was suddenly filled with a reckless energy that had never heard of wisdom or patience.

"I'll count down the days." He leaned over and kissed my cheek.

Shortly after that, he was called away by some acquaintances, and I was left alone for a few minutes before I went to visit with Hannah and Andrew. During those heartbeats of quiet time,

I discovered that it was possible to live with opposing emotions banging around in your body. How could I be so distraught and so resolved at the same time? If this was what it felt like to finally be an adult, then I wanted nothing to do with it.

Chapter 18

> Being deeply loved by someone gives you strength,
> while loving someone deeply gives you courage.
>
> *~ Lao Tzu ~*

Sunday night found me pondering the mysteries of life while soaking in a bath. I felt a little battered and bruised after the rollercoaster ride at the engagement party the night before. Garrett had been friendly and by my side much of the evening. So had Maddi. And while I had initially been hurt by her remarks, I realized that she couldn't have known how that topic of conversation would affect me. She'd clearly thought my dating challenge was common knowledge. She seemed like a decent person the more I got to know her. Garrett had vacillated between being annoyed at her presence and then accepting it the next time she showed up. It amused me to pretend that he wanted me all to himself. At least someone did.

Garrett walked me out to Val's car at the end of the night and wrapped me in a hug so all-encompassing that I had struggled to breathe. Yet somehow it felt as if he'd squeezed a part of me back into place. I'd ridden home knowing—or at least hoping—I could push through.

James had been friendly when we were thrown together throughout the evening, but for the most part, I could feel him avoiding me. I knew the space between us wasn't accidental separation, like what can sometimes happen in big groups. It was purposeful. I caught him looking at me a few times during the course of the evening, and I eventually stopped looking back when I felt his gaze. It hurt too much to think about what was going on in his head.

Now that I'd had overnight to think over things, I was trying to decide if it was fair to Garrett to go out with him the next night. I really liked Garrett, but my heart didn't race when I saw him, and my mind easily slipped away from him rather than fixating on him like it did on James. I knew I wasn't interested in an actual relationship with Garrett. However, I wanted to prove to myself that there were other options, and, dang it, I wanted a date with a fun guy to wash away the sour taste left from my train wreck of a dating life.

I sunk lower into the tub and let the water tickle at my earlobes and lower lip. I wanted the bathtub to magically wash away the past years. I wanted a chance to make the right choice where James was concerned.

Yet, even as I thought that, I wondered what good it would really do. The seven years in question had been a time of growth and independence for me. I'd settled into the life I had chosen. I'd learned, grown, and had great experiences. I definitely regretted losing him, but I didn't regret the growing up I'd done.

I sank all the way into the tub and cleared my mind as the water covered my head. This swirling thought process wasn't going to help me at all. I could not go back. I could not change the past. All I could do was look forward and forgive myself, which is what I'd been struggling to do all along.

To that end, I sat up and scrubbed my hair. As I did, I thought of myself symbolically scrubbing away my guilt. I'd done the best I knew how as a twenty-year-old. I had not been out to purposely ruin anything or destroy anyone. I was a good person then, and I still was now.

I dunked back under the water to rinse, and as I came up out of the water, I sucked in a huge breath. I knew what I had to do. A good person wouldn't go out with Garrett tomorrow night. He thought I was truly interested. I knew I wasn't. I needed to get out of the tub, dry off, and call him.

Once I was in my comfy pajamas, sitting cross-legged on my bed, with my head wrapped in a towel, I grabbed my phone from the nightstand and—dropped it as a loud banging sounded on my bedroom door.

"Rachel!" It was Hannah.

I jumped off the bed and flung the door open to find Hannah standing there with a shocked look on her face. She shoved her own cell phone into my face like she thought it would start transferring information directly to my brain. Val was standing right behind her with a disarming look of delight on her face. That expression on Val's face worried me more than the shock on Hannah's. Something big had gone down.

"What in the world?" I looked back at Hannah, whose mouth was working as she grasped for words.

"Oh, just spit it out." Val tapped Hannah on the back and it seemed to reboot her brain.

"Garrett is engaged!" Hannah practically shouted at me.

"Garrett? As in Garrett, Garrett? Andrew's cousin?" I asked.

"Yes, him," Val said, the look of delight still on her face.

I took a step back. "What? But I was just about to call him!" I pointed at my phone on my bed as evidence.

Hannah and Val both stepped into the space I'd just deserted and nodded their heads in unison. "It's true. Garrett is engaged!" Val stated happily.

"I'm still . . . wait . . . he's engaged?" My voice rose to the same desperate caliber that Hannah had used. "To whom? When? How is this . . . ?"

"To Maddi!" Hannah dropped another bomb. "For the past three months!"

Total explosion. I had no words. Sweet little naïve Maddi was Garrett's fiancé?

"Isn't this the best?" Val wiggled around in a celebratory dance.

"I know!" Hannah joined her in some sort of spastic bunny hop around my room while I stood there dazed.

"That snake!" I finally said. "We went on a date, and he was engaged. We had another date tomorrow night."

The bunny hopping stopped in front of me, and they were both still smiling. "We know," Hannah said, giggling.

"He flirted shamelessly with me!" I said, my stomach dropping with each new realization of what, exactly, this meant.

"He's a total jerk, for sure!" Val cheered.

"I was just about to call him and cancel our date," I announced.

"You must have felt the universe telling you to stay far away from that creep," Hannah offered.

"I mean, I spent half the evening last night with him and Maddi. Not a single word." I walked to my bed and flopped down. "Would you two quit with all the cheering and dancing already?"

"It is so messed up," Val agreed as she sat in my chair and Hannah joined me on the bed.

"How did you not know?" I asked Hannah.

"Hey, don't blame me. He's Andrew's cousin. You've spent more time with him than I have," she replied, still beaming.

"How did you find out?" I was trying to fully catch up.

"Andrew just called and told me. He didn't know either."

"You two seem awfully happy about this," I mumbled.

"He's not right for you," Hannah replied. I agreed with her, so there was nothing to argue about there.

"Poor Maddi," I sighed.

"Oh, her life is going to be the worst with him." Val nodded as she pursed her lips. "I don't know how she stood by watching him flirt with you all night."

I groaned as I thought about how much I'd been hamming it up with Garrett the night before. "Poor Maddi. I'm so embarrassed."

"Why?" Val asked. "You had no idea they were engaged. You can't be held accountable for things you didn't know."

"She's right," Hannah added. "Besides, the worst part about it is that poor James had to watch it."

Evidently, we were now acknowledging the James situation even though I was still muddling through the Garrett revelation. Regardless of the information drop I'd just received, my thoughts snagged on the mention of James, as they always did.

"Trust me, James didn't care," I replied sadly.

"Oh, so you *do* care that James didn't care!" Hannah smiled slyly.

"James really, truly, did not care," I said firmly. "He made that clear."

"How? By staring at you like a sad puppy all night?" Val quipped.

I rolled my eyes. "You were there, Val, when James all but told Garrett that I am a free woman and he doesn't care who I date or what I do," I said in exasperation.

"That's true. I did hear him say that. I almost punched his lying face. But actions speak louder than words. He had his eyes on you all night. He cares," Val replied.

I didn't respond. I couldn't allow even the tiniest sliver of hope to enter my heart where James was concerned. I wasn't going to bank on hearsay. I was going to accept what he said at face value.

"So . . . Garrett's engaged?" I changed the subject with a deep breath and a shake of my head.

"Garrett is indeed engaged," Hannah agreed.

"Best news I've heard all day," Val declared.

"Man, I really am back to square one." I collapsed back onto my bed and stared at the ceiling.

"I don't think that's true," Val's voice floated thoughtfully through the quiet room. "I think you may actually be worse off than you were before this whole challenge started."

There was silence for a heartbeat before Hannah snorted and full-blown laughter rang out. Tears streamed down our faces, and our sides ached as we gulped for air. Val was right. The challenge had been a bust. Tears would have been useless. Laughing together, however, was the best thing I'd done for myself in a long time.

Now I can't exactly say that this is a scientific fact, but I have a strong suspicion that every school building in America smells the same. As I pulled open the front door of Pine Ridge Elementary School for my first contracted day of the new school year, I was greeted with that special whiff of scent that brings with it a thousand memories.

I could almost hear all the little voices, phones ringing in the front office, footsteps in the hallways, balls bouncing in the cafeteria/gym, pencil sharpeners humming. I was always happy to start a new year, but this year the return felt even more welcome. I'd had an adventurous summer and was ready to settle back into my routine. Too much free time was making my mind feel like a merry-go-round.

I, of course, bypassed my own room and went straight to Lisa's. The downside of not teaching over the summer was that I never saw Lisa. We texted a bit here and there, but for the most part, we were work friends—happy to be together, but rarely crossing paths in our "real" lives.

Her blonde head was bent over a stack of papers coming from her printer. She'd chopped off her long curls and was sporting a cute curly halo. I let out a little chirp as I entered the room.

"We're baaack . . . ," I singsonged as I walked in.

She spun around and hurried to where I was standing to give me a hug. "Reunited at last," she singsonged back to me.

"How was your summer?" I said, smiling.

"A few weeks ago, I got the crazy idea to do a bunch of DIY home improvements. It was a mistake. I'm thanking the heavens to be back at school. It's sad that coming back to teach feels like going on a vacation." She pulled an animated face. "Help me move desks around, and I'll tell you all about it."

She pointed to a drawing she'd put on her white board that showed how she wanted desks arranged. I helped her move them as she told me how she and her husband had remodeled their kitchen and living area. When we finished moving her room around, she asked about my summer.

"Same deal for you, lady," I teased. "You schlep desks, and I'll spill the beans." She cheerfully agreed, and we went to my room to make some changes there.

It was satisfying to hear Lisa's reactionary sounds to my stories. Rationally I understood that some terrible stuff had gone down, but having her confirm it was amazing. There is nothing better than having your sanity validated.

"What are you going to do now?" she asked.

We each pulled out a tiny chair at a tiny desk and sat down. I rested my elbows on the desk and my chin on my hands as I thought about it—for the millionth time.

"Well, it wasn't all for nothing, I suppose," I mused. "I mean, some things haven't changed. I would still like to find someone and create a life together, but I also know that I can't just throw myself at anything breathing and hope to make a go of it."

Lisa chuckled. "I don't know. Shawn and his dead father sounded truly appealing. Maybe if you'd prayed more with him you could have learned to love him."

My lips curved upward in amusement as I replied, "It's hard to believe I turned that down."

"There are some good guys out there, even though nothing that's happened to you over the past months has proven that."

"I know. I'm going to need some time, but if someone asks to set me up again in the future, I'll say yes. I'll be more outgoing and try to get out more to meet people. However, I'm not going to force it, and I'm not going to be upset if it doesn't happen immediately."

"Sounds smart. You should teach people stuff," Lisa said, nodding playfully.

"I really should. I have a lot to offer," I said, grinning. "Actually, Lisa, there is something I've been meaning to tell you," I added.

My tone must have tipped her off, because she sat up straight in her chair. I told her the whole story of James. Her jaw hit the floor as she raptly listened to everything.

"Oh wow. I had no idea. Why didn't you tell me after I set you two up?" she asked. I was grateful she wasn't angry.

"I had no reason to think it would matter or go anywhere." I shrugged.

"But you still love him?" she asked.

I nodded. "Yes, I still love him. Which is why I'll need some time before I go on another date."

Lisa made a sound of agreement. "Sounds like school starting was the best thing for you too," she teased.

"Oh, definitely. I'll be so busy this week getting the room and lessons ready that I won't have a second to worry about any of it. Then when the kids show up next week—*whoosh*—who was James again?" I forced out a carefree giggle that I wasn't really feeling.

"No one said love comes easily," Lisa said as she stood up and put a comforting hand on my shoulder. "Give it time." She squeezed my shoulder lightly and headed back to her room. I waved as she left.

My gaze traveled slowly around my domain. There were stacks of new books, paper, and school supplies in the corner where they'd been left upon delivery. The endless work of setting up a classroom was before me, and I allowed it to pull me in, grateful to have my mind kept busy.

Many long hours later, I let myself out the front doors of the school and headed to the parking lot. I was hot and dusty but satisfied with the work I'd done and the feeling of accomplishment it gave me. I was equally glad the kids weren't back in school yet so I'd been able to wear a T-shirt and shorts with sandals. The school district didn't usually turn on the AC until the week school started, and it had been a scorcher.

The sun was past its peak, but the heat remained, and I was thankful I'd found a tree to park under. I fished through my purse for my keys, eyes down, as I walked toward my car, hoping upon hope that it wouldn't be too awfully hot when I got in. I found my keys and looked up just as someone sitting under that shady tree rose to stand.

My breath caught as I recognized him—James. Would I ever stop reacting to him this way? I tried to force down the awareness and sudden rush of happiness that involuntarily rose as he stood up. It wasn't working. My nerves hummed as he drew near. He stopped a few steps away, probably wanting to maintain some distance. It was all I could do to keep my features cool.

"Hannah said I could find you here." His voice sounded a little rough, like he hadn't spoken much yet. He cleared his throat. I nodded. It didn't take him long to realize I wasn't going to start talking. He cleared his throat again. "Did you go out with Garrett?" he asked.

I hadn't known what he would say, but I definitely hadn't been expecting that. How did he even known I was supposed to go out with Garrett?

"I didn't think you cared about my dating life," I replied calmly.

"Did you, or didn't you?" he pressed.

It would have been easy to just tell him no and stop punishing him with non-answers. In fact, somewhere inside I was absolutely thrilled that he was so worried about my date with Garrett that he'd tracked me down at school. Yet, somewhere else inside I was seriously ticked that every time I started to make peace regarding James he'd show up again. Right or wrong, I didn't feel like being easy when I was hurting still.

"Why does it matter? You said I'm all grown up, remember?" I pushed back.

He groaned and drove a hand through his hair. "Look, you said you wanted to talk," he redirected in a calmer tone.

"And you made it clear that you didn't want to," I replied matter-of-factly.

"Well, I want to talk now," he retorted.

I smiled a little on the inside. "About what?" I asked.

"I need to know if you went out with Garrett or not." He was getting more agitated, and I was eating it up. Someone who was totally unaffected by me wouldn't have cared.

"James, why do you care if I went out with Garrett? And why do you want to talk now? What changed? You didn't care to hear what I wanted to talk about last weekend," I reminded him.

"That's not true," he replied heatedly.

"Yes, it is."

He didn't respond immediately but looked at me in a way I couldn't decipher. Even though I could see he was jealous and frustrated, it appeared that he wasn't going to open up. I couldn't emotionally afford to engage with him. If he didn't want to get the ball rolling, I certainly wasn't going to do it.

I sighed as I turned and moved to open my car door. "I don't think we need to talk. I'm just going to move forward."

He shook his head and pushed out a frustrated breath as he moved a step closer to my car. "Do you realize that everything doesn't always have to happen on your timeframe?"

I turned back and frowned up at him. "What is that supposed to mean?"

"It means that seven years ago you basically told me that I didn't get a vote on how things were going to go. We talked when you wanted to talk, and then when you were done, you walked away."

He may as well have slapped me across the face. I took a step back and stared up at him. "This is not the same. I'm not the same. I wanted to talk to you, and you shut me down."

"Well, can you blame me? Last time you wanted to have a talk, it ended up with me being hurt." I saw the truth of that in his face, and my anger deflated a little. "And you were the only one who had any say in that," he finished.

It hurt to hear that. It hurt even more to know it was fair of him to be cautious around me. After another pause and a deep breath, he asked me again.

"Did you go out with him?"

I shook my head. "Garrett's engaged."

It was his turn to be surprised. "He is? To whom?"

"Maddi," I stated.

"Maddi? The girl who sat with us at the engagement shower thing?"

"Yep."

"Huh." He looked off in the distance for a moment, like he was trying to put some puzzle pieces in place. I waited. He shook his head and looked back down at me. "You said you wanted to talk."

"I'm not sure it matters anymore what I wanted to say," I replied honestly. I was no longer angry, just tired.

"I want to hear it," he said softly. "I'm ready to hear it," he added.

I watched his face closely and saw nothing but open curiosity there. I remembered again that I was an adult and there was nothing wrong with telling him how I felt. The worst that could happen would be rejection. I was already living with that reality, so I didn't think it could get worse.

I took a deep breath and looked directly into his eyes. As I did, I thought of all the words I'd planned to say to him, all the apologies and arguments about why we should be together, about how I'd changed. I'd scripted out the entire thing.

But more than that, I thought about what Val had said about James's actions on the night of the engagement party. She'd said that actions speak louder than words. So, I turned and set my purse on the roof of my car, letting my keys fall back in. Then I turned back to where James was waiting.

I walked up to him, raised both of my hands, and gently took hold of his face. His skin was scruffy from his beard growing in, and it tickled my fingertips. I tugged very gently, keeping eye contact with him as I lowered his face. Then I closed my eyes and kissed him with all the tenderness in my heart. He leaned into me, returning the affection as his hands came to rest lightly on my waist. My entire body tingled and moved toward him.

After a breath-stealing moment, I pulled away, dropping my hands to hold one of his, and whispered, "I will be sorry forever that I hurt you and pushed you away. I miss the life we could have built together, and I want you to give me another chance." I decided to keep it simple and direct. I had no reason to add words that were pointless. It all boiled down to this one truth: "I still love you."

I stepped back, dropping my hands from his. He didn't respond straightway. First, he looked at me, and then away for a few moments. I didn't push, but I felt the weight of the moment like an elephant on my chest. I was sure he had feelings for me too. He'd been jealous of Garrett. He had stormed into my apartment and kissed me. He'd held me when I cried. He had returned my kiss just now. Would any of these things be enough for him to be willing to take a chance on me again? I had no idea.

After what felt like an hour, he looked back at me, and I could see the battle raging within him. He was physically standing close but felt miles away as he fought whatever it was my words had done.

"I don't know what to say," he said on a sigh.

Say you love me too, my heart was crying out. What I said instead was, "I told you it probably didn't matter anymore. I know you don't trust me. I know I don't deserve a second chance." My voice shook, and I cleared my throat and willed away the emotion. I was not going to use my distress to sway him in any way. "But, well, I wanted you to know how I feel."

He continued to watch me, his eyes raking over my features. Other than the muscle I saw tightening in his jaw and the agony in his eyes, he seemed to be carved from stone.

I pushed the rest out on a painful breath. "I also want you to know that I only went on all those dates because I couldn't get you out of my heart, and I thought the only way to do it would be to find someone new. It didn't work. You're stuck in there." I tapped my chest lightly over my heart. My voice shook again on the last part, but I swallowed hard and kept the emotion from breaking free.

As I gazed up at him, I knew I needed to give him some space. He'd had a good point about me always being the one in control of our relationship. He now knew, without a doubt, how I felt, and where I stood. It was time for me to step out of the driver's seat and allow him to have a say in where things would go—or not go—from there.

With my heart bleeding on my sleeve, I turned back to my car, grabbed my purse from the roof, and opened the door. Heat wafted out, and I paused before getting in to let some of the hot air escape. I had my back to him, but he made no move to say anything or close the distance between us. I could feel every heartbeat pumping heavily through my body. My breathing felt tight. I couldn't look back at him. I knew I needed to drive away, but it was physically painful to do so.

As I sat down in my car and closed the door, I dared a glance in his direction. He was still standing there watching me. He hadn't moved one single inch. He looked like everything I could ever dream of. I loved him. I realized I'd always love him. I also realized there was nothing I could say in that moment that would make things better, so I gave him a small smile and I started my car.

When I'd backed out and put the car in drive, I looked at him once more over my shoulder before pulling away. He was still standing there, looking as shell-shocked as I had felt so many times over the past months. He reached up a hand in a stiff wave, and, grateful for that tiny sign of life from him, I returned the gesture. With my heartbeat filling my ears, and tears burning my eyes, I watched him grow smaller in the rearview mirror as I drove away.

Chapter 19

Love is life.
All, everything that I understand,
I understand only because I love.

~ Leo Tolstoy ~

As Lisa had predicted, the timing of school starting ended up being a major blessing. I threw myself into setting up my room and reworking some lesson plans. I only had to be at the school for eight hours a day in order to meet my contracted time, but I worked twelve-hour days for the rest of the week leading up to the students arriving.

My roommates were concerned. Not only had it had never taken so much time to set up my classroom, but I was distracted and moody at home. I lied and told them there were some curriculum changes that had come last minute. They bought it, but I was sure they could see it was something more than that.

Hannah made me swear that the last Saturday before school started I would come with her for her final dress fitting. I had agreed, but sitting there, watching her glow in her wedding dress, hadn't been easy on my heart. I'd made sure to ooh and ahh over how lovely she looked. It had all been genuine. She was beautiful, even if my voice hadn't sounded quite right.

After the fitting, we'd gone past the salon where Hannah worked to pick up some of her supplies. She wanted to practice wedding hair and makeup over the weekend. As I watched other cosmetologists and clients together, I thought maybe having a makeover myself would be a good boost. After all, when you can't change your circumstances, you can always change your hair!

"Hey, Han, would you have time tomorrow night to give me a full do-over?" I'd asked as she packed up a box of things.

Her head snapped up and a huge grin filled her face. "Back to school in style?" she said, smiling. I smiled back and nodded. "Absolutely. I'm so glad you said something while we were here already. Let me add in a few more things that would be great for you."

I sat at the kitchen table Sunday night with a black salon-style cape around my neck and Hannah staring at me with a pair of shears in her hand. My hair was freshly washed and, after warning me to remove my contacts, Hannah scrubbed my face with some sort of exfoliation thing that smelled like a dead rhino and burned a bit. My eyes were still watering, and my skin felt raw. My glasses were dangling from Hannah's fingers as she thought about my new style. I couldn't put them on until she'd captured the vision. My glasses, which I only wore at home, would mess up her creative flow.

"What is she going to do?" Val asked from the couch where she was watching from a safe distance.

"I'm not sure," I replied in amusement.

"I don't feel good about how much it stinks over there," Val added.

"I've purged all the darkness out of her soul," Hannah quipped without taking her eyes off me.

"Please tell me you didn't give the beast free reign," Val whispered to me in mock horror.

"I can't remember what I said or why," I teased, pulling a face.

"I knew you'd done something wrong when I saw her slather than concoction all over your face. It's still bright red. There's a good chance you've got a second-degree burn going on over there," Val said.

"Shh, both of you. Rach is going to look amazing when I'm done." Hannah walked a slow circle around me and reached up to move pieces of my hair in a few different directions.

"Are you sure her face is going to bounce back?" Val asked. She sounded so honestly concerned that I began to worry. "She's got really pale, sensitive skin, you know."

"Do I come into your hospital and tell you how to fix people?" Hannah gave Val a look.

Val just shook her head and shrugged her shoulders. She'd lodged her complaints but wasn't willing to get herself firmly in the crosshairs.

"Okay, I think I'm ready. How do you feel about the length of your hair?" Hannah asked.

For the past several years when she'd asked me that, I'd told her to leave it alone, but this time I hesitated before answering. I'd been growing it for a long time. I suddenly felt like it was time to cast off old things. Giddiness filled me as I looked back at her.

"I'm good with whatever you want to do," I said, smiling widely at her.

Her smile grew to meet mine, and she gave a little cheer. "I've been waiting for this moment. Oh, the ideas I've had! Okay, I'm not going to whack it all off, so don't flip out, but let's make some serious changes."

"I can't watch," Val groaned.

"Oh, stop it, Valerie. You know you love your choppy hair style," Hannah retorted. "It fits your choppy personality perfectly."

I looked under Hannah's arm to where Val was sitting, and she pulled a face at me. Hannah was right—the style suited Val to a T.

An hour later, Hannah brought out her gigantic hand mirror and showed me the results. I now had shoulder-length, layered hair with side-swept bangs and some caramel-colored highlights. Cutting off so much length had added some body to my straight hair. The redness on my face had faded, and Hannah had put on some smoky eye makeup that made my blue eyes look like they were lit from behind. I looked like an entirely new person. I didn't realize how young and, in some ways, unsophisticated my long, straight hair and minimal makeup had looked.

I'd always worn my hair parted down the middle and tucked behind my ears. My makeup was some light mascara and a coat of lip gloss. The change in styles and colors made me look like an adult—a put-together, grown-up adult.

"Oh my gosh. You look sort of . . . uh . . . sultry," Val said as she came around to look.

"Sultry?" I coughed in surprise.

"Oh, yes, so sultry!" Hannah clapped her hands together. "The sultriest of the sultry. Someone's eyes are going to fall out of his head," Hannah said as she played idly with a piece of my hair, laying it into the perfect position. I knew with a pinch in my heart that she was talking about James.

"Someone isn't going to care one little bit." I smiled sadly at her.

"Someone obviously hasn't seen someone else moping around for the past week. Someone hasn't had to take someone else's phone calls ten times a day and hear all about that someone else's worries."

"Someone kissed him and he didn't care," I admitted gloomily. "More than once."

My announcement was met with a beat of silence as they both blinked their eyes at me.

"Someone is an idiot," Val muttered, and I really hoped she wasn't talking about me.

"Someone is scared," Hannah corrected.

"This someone's head is spinning," I put my hands over my eyes. "No more. I didn't do this for James or anyone else. I did this for me. You've made *my* eyes pop out of my head, Han. Thank you. It's perfect!"

I helped Hannah clean up the kitchen and thanked her again with a huge hug. This updated look was just the boost I needed. Miss Fairy was switching out for a more grown-up look—a look that finally reflected who I was on the inside. That could only bring with it good things.

The first day of school flew by so quickly in a rush of backpacks and extra loud voices that I didn't have one second to think about anything. I trudged out of the school at 5:00 p.m. that night to a dusky heat that seemed to float off the pavement. I hadn't scored the tree parking space, and I knew my car would be hot. Not for the first time, I daydreamed about remote start as I flung the car door open and leaned in to turn on the engine. As was my habit, I stood outside the car door for a moment to let the heat filter out as the AC began to cool it down.

As I let my gaze travel around the now quiet schoolyard, my eye was drawn to a white envelope sitting under my windshield wiper. It had my name scrawled across the front. My heart did a little dip as a recognized the handwriting. My hands shook as I tore it open and looked inside. I pulled out a single 4 x 6 card with a few lines written on it.

*Sometimes all you can do is not think,
not worry, not imagine, or obsess.
Just have faith. Because where there is
love, there are always miracles.*

—*James*

My throat clogged as I read those words, and tears burned my eyes. I wanted to see him, but as I searched around, there was no sign of him. I didn't feel disappointed, though, as I climbed into my car and headed toward home. Instead, I felt hopeful. I was willing to let him do things on his terms. I was up for the adventure.

I never said a word to anyone as every day for the rest of the week I found something on my car when I came out. It felt like something that needed to be kept between just us, this fragile reaching out and opening up. It would have been ruined somehow to share it with others.

The things he left were all little things. A bunch of bright yellow wild chrysanthemums held together with a twist tie, a bag of cinnamon-flavored candies, a string of hearts cut from red construction paper, and finally, on Friday, a book of uplifting quotes and stories that I'd given to James years ago. Tears fell as I read the inscription still inside. He'd added his own for me underneath it.

I hugged it to my chest and let myself believe that this was really happening.

And yet, despite these gifts and sweet thoughts, I never actually saw him or had any other contact with him. I understood that he wanted to keep his distance while he worked through things, but it was killing me to not be able to throw my arms around him and talk through it all.

Saturday and Sunday passed in a blur of nerves. Every knock on the door and every chime of my phone sent me running. It was never James, and there were no little gifts delivered. I kept busy helping Hannah gather up the songs they'd selected for their playlist and burn them onto a disc to give to the reception hall. I must admit that listening to love songs for two days straight almost put me over the edge.

The little gifts resumed after school the following Monday. A picture of us from when we first met, all smiles and flashing teeth, with a note that said, "Thinking of you makes me smile." Tuesday it was a bag of bath salts from my favorite local boutique. Wednesday, a postcard from a trip he'd taken to New York after we'd broken up that he'd never sent, the message faded and the card bent. Thursday was a basket with three fresh apricots.

By the time Friday rolled around, I was giddy with excitement as I ran out to my car to see what he'd left. This time nothing was there. I looked on the ground all around the car, frantically wondering if it had fallen or was stolen. After five minutes, I had to admit defeat. I was surprised by how devastated I was. I'd come to treasure the time after work seeing what he'd left and imagining his handsome face as he selected things he thought would make me happy.

I didn't find anything when I got home either. I checked the mailbox, the kitchen, the hallway around my front door, my room, and Hannah and Val's rooms. I checked my cell for the hundredth time, but he hadn't called. All was quiet. There was nothing.

If this weekend was like the one before, he wouldn't be around. With it being Labor Day weekend, and with only eight short days until the wedding, Hannah and Andrew were off visiting her mother for the last big push of planning. Val always offered to take extra shifts at the hospital over holidays for the bonus pay. I had a feeling that she also did it to let those with families have the time off, but I never flat out asked her.

I was truly alone. Not just alone, but lonely.

I hadn't thought to ask Hannah, but I wouldn't be surprised if James had gone home with her and Andrew for a visit. It would have made sense for him to go along. Even though he'd been reaching out to me, we weren't actually talking, so he'd have had no reason to tell me what his plans were.

I felt the beginnings of a serious wallowing session tug at my emotions. I couldn't believe how much it had affected me to not have a gift waiting. When had I become dependent on James's attention again? In that moment, I made the decision to go home and visit my own parents for the long weekend. They were constantly asking when they'd see me again and there was no sense in moping around my apartment by myself, waiting for something—or someone—who wasn't coming.

With it being a three-hour drive, I needed to get moving, so I hurriedly threw together some weekend clothes and toiletries. On my way out, I scribbled a note to Val, letting her know I'd gone home, and left it on the kitchen table. I could have texted her, but sometimes it's nice to come home to an old-fashioned note, proof that other people are around.

The drive to my parents' house was uneventful. I grabbed a burger and a cola at the drive-thru on the way out of town, set some upbeat cruising tunes on the radio, and just relaxed. The past few weeks getting my classroom back up and running, helping new second graders remember how school worked, and riding the love rollercoaster had been insane. It was heavenly to have some silence as the miles sped by.

I hadn't told my parents I was coming, and when I walked in the door around 8:00 p.m. that night with a duffle bag over one arm and mustard stains on my T-shirt, my parents' faces made it all worth it.

"Rachel? What on earth?" Mom jumped up from her seat in front of the TV and ran to greet me. "Look at you! Your hair! It has Hannah written all over it. You look lovely. Why don't you have makeup on? I think you look fine in those glasses, but tired—definitely tired. You've probably been so busy getting school going again. Have you eaten? Come sit down. What are you wearing? Is that a mustard stain on your T-shirt? Where are your normal clothes? Did you drive all the way here in pajamas? I raised you better than that. Do you have shoes on at least? Flip-flops? I think there might be a law against driving in flip-flops. But that's not important. You're here safe. Don, look who's here!"

Dad had approached during Mom's greeting monologue and taken my duffel bag from me. He'd given me a hug, patted my back warmly, and was already halfway down the hall to my former bedroom to put my bag on my bed.

Mom looked around for him. "Oh, your dad, he always disappears at the worst times. I'm sure he'll be so happy to see you too." She took me by the arm and led me into the kitchen, where she pulled out a chair and gestured for me to sit.

"Dad's putting my luggage away," I said, laughing as Mom ducked her head into the refrigerator. "And I've had dinner."

Mom peeked back out over her shoulder. "Well, that was probably hours ago, and I've got some great stew left from dinner."

"How about just a drink for now?" I offered.

Mom popped out of the fridge and shook her head. "Always was impossible to feed you two girls. How about we make it milk, and I'll get some cookies to go with it?" Her smile grew at the idea of getting something in me. I nodded. Cookies and milk in the kitchen with Mom sounded perfect.

We chatted around the table for a little while before joining Dad in the family room, where he was watching a rerun of one of his favorite sitcoms. I told them about my first weeks of school. They told me about the trip they were taking to Fiji in October. Dad had picked up the hints Mom had been putting down ever since I'd visited over the Fourth of July holiday. I was happy for them.

Around 9:30 p.m., Dad stood up and stretched. "I'm glad you're here, Rach, but this old man needs his rest. I'll see you in the morning." As he started walking toward his room, there was a knock on the front door. He swerved toward it without missing a beat.

"Expecting someone?" I asked Mom. She shook her head.

We both watched the door as Dad swung it open. I couldn't hear what the person on the other side said, but in true Dad form, he opened the door further and looked at us like it was the most typical thing in the world to have James step into the house. To my knowledge, they hadn't seen each other since our break up, but you'd never know it by Dad's reaction.

"Rachel, James is here." Dad gestured for James to come all the way in before he closed the door and continued on his way to bed. "'Night everyone," he said as he disappeared around the corner.

Mom, however, reacted as though she'd been stung by a bee in her rear end. She shot off the couch and scooted directly over to James.

"Oh, what a surprise!"

She threw her arms around him, and after squeezing him with all her might, she grabbed his arm and drew him in to where I was sitting frozen in shocked silence on the couch. Giddiness and confusion were warring for space as warmth crept up from my toes to my hairline.

"Rachel, look who's here!" Mom was beaming.

I was surprised her face didn't crack. I could practically see her counting grandbabies as she looked back and forth between us.

James was a little reserved as I stood to face him. I didn't mean to sound harsh, but I blurted out the only thing going through my mind. "What are you doing here?"

His eyes crinkled up a bit as he grinned. "I'm trying to find you," he replied.

"Oh, this is just . . . I mean . . . I'm just so . . . well, silly me! I'll leave you two alone." Mom was flustered as she continued to watch our reactions to each other. "James, where are you staying?"

James smiled at her. "I'm hoping you'll let me stay here for as long as Rachel does," he replied.

He may as well have told her she won the lottery for how her face lit up. "Excellent. That's wonderful. I'll go make sure the basement bedroom is all ready to go." She scurried away.

James's eyes roved over me, and I self-consciously adjusted my glasses and played with my hair as I realized he'd not seen it since Hannah's makeover. He smiled at my fidgeting.

"You cut your hair?" he asked. I nodded. "It looks really good." His voice was low and warm with affection. It made my toes curl.

"Thanks," I said, smiling.

"Is that mustard on your shirt?" He chuckled as his eyes found the stain on my collar. I nodded again, feeling fuzzy at the sound of his voice.

"You came to find me?" I asked quietly. It was his turn to nod. "How did you know I'd be here?"

"Hannah gave me a key to your apartment. I was going to surprise you with dinner tonight. Instead I found a note saying you'd run away." His smiled grew warmer as he stepped closer to me. "My little chicken," he said softly.

I felt deliciously happy all over, like sunlight would pop out of my pores at any moment. "I'm no chicken," I insisted as I took a step closer to him. "Possibly pouty, yes. But not a chicken."

His eyes were warm as he closed the final distance between us and reached out to take my hands softly in his. They hung between us, the grip loose but sending light up my arms.

"I liked your gifts," I said, smiling up at him.

"I'm glad. I had one more I was going to give you tonight. I drove all this way because I thought you wouldn't want to wait." He released my hands and put his hands on my waist, pulling me in closer.

"Oh yeah?" I whispered as I reached up and put my hands lightly on his chest.

He nodded and moved his hands around to my back, pulling me into his embrace. To say we kissed makes it sound so ordinary. It was so much more than a kiss. It was a reunion of our hearts, an acknowledgment of our need for each other, a promise to love. It made my entire body burst into flame in a way I'd thought would never happen again.

When we finally pulled apart, I realized that my mom had joined my dad in their room and was probably doing a happy dance since she'd had to have seen that scorching kiss.

"So, you just thought you'd crash here, huh?" I asked as I happily gazed up at him, still warm and comfy in his embrace. He gave me a grin in reply. "Lucky for you, my mom is your number one fan," I added.

"She seemed pretty excited," he said, laughing. "Think she'll let your dad get any sleep tonight?"

I smiled and shook my head as I wrapped my arms around his waist, tucking my head under his chin. "I'm glad you're here." I felt so secure and peaceful that it was almost too much to stand.

"We've both done enough waiting," was his whispered reply. "I didn't want to waste any more time." At last, we were on the same page.

The next couple of days were filled with talking, laughing, teasing, joking, and getting to know the subtle changes that had happened in each of us over the years apart. The really remarkable thing, the thing our hearts had known all along, was that as we took down our protective walls, we still connected in the secret, quiet places, and that made any other changes feel superficial.

We went for walks every day around the town I'd grown up in. We sat on the swings at the park and talked. We played games with my parents, ate meals in dimly lit restaurants, and stayed up way too late each night, sitting on the couch after my parents had gone to bed, arms around each other, once more whispering together. It was like we quite literally could not get enough of each other. The years apart had made us greedy.

My parents didn't even try to conceal their happiness, but I saw questions in my mom's eyes. She wondered how we'd found each other again and what this meant for the future. Most of all I saw in her eyes planning weddings and giving grandbabies their first baths, singing silly songs and reading stories to them. I wanted those same things too, but the timing of it all was up to James. I was truly okay with that.

"Rach, are you sleeping?" I awoke at the sound of James's voice and sat up in bed.

My bedroom door was open enough to let some light in from the hall nightlight, but all I could see was his shadow as he stood over my bed. Even though I'd recognized his voice, I still gave a start and pulled the covers up to my chin—as if that would ward off an attack.

I cleared my throat and willed my heartbeat to settle. "I'm awake," I mumbled.

He walked around my bed to the window and pulled the drapes aside. The fall night was clear, and the moon was high in the sky and shining directly into my room. It gave us enough light to see by. Without looking at my clock, I knew it was still the middle of the night.

James was in his pajama pants and a T-shirt, his hair rumpled from sleep. I wanted to smooth it out, but he stopped a step or two out of my reach as he came around the side of my bed to face me. He said nothing for a moment, just stared at me sitting there in the moonlight, my own hair rumpled, hugging a quilt to my chest. I couldn't read the expression on his face in the dim light, but I could read the tension in his body.

I relaxed my hold on the bedding and let it drop as I held out my hand to him. He paused for a fraction of a second before stepping forward and taking it in his own, twining his fingers with mine.

"What is it?" I whispered.

He surprised me by kneeling on the floor and reaching for my other hand. I slid closer to the side of the bed, my legs crossed like a pretzel as I sat near him. With an almost imperceptible sigh, he lowered our hands together into my lap. I felt some of the tension drain from him as he bowed his head for a moment. I remained silent, patient.

"I wanted this to be perfect, but I can't wait," he said, lifting his head to meet my gaze. His face was finally in the moonlight, and his expression made my breath hitch. "Rachel, the other day you told me that you still love me. I never stopped loving you for even a second. There hasn't been anyone else, ever. It has been the longest, loneliest road finding my way back to you."

Tears stung my eyes as I let his words flow through me. He still loved me! I wanted to reach out and hold him close, but I held back, letting him set the pace.

"I am so sorry, James, for everything!" I let the tears fall but held firmly to his hands.

"I know you are. I've thought a lot about this over the years, but recently, seeing you again, I realized that you were also deeply hurt." He squeezed my hands and leaned forward to place a soft kiss on my lips. I leaned in, wanting more, but he backed away. "I know I was partly to blame. I shouldn't have pushed so hard. I should have listened when you tried to tell me you were scared."

"No, no. I should have understood that dreams don't have to be chased alone," I replied firmly. "I shouldn't have panicked."

"You were only twenty—" he insisted.

"An adult," I retorted.

"But still a child in so many ways," he said. He sighed and shook his head. "Look, we're getting off track here. The thing is, I love you. I was so crazy for you back then that I couldn't see straight. And regardless of how much time has passed, those feelings are still there. You've grown into the amazing, talented, and beautiful woman I always saw in you."

He leaned forward and pressed another soft kiss on my forehead. I reveled in the feeling. The darkness felt like a blanket wrapped around us in our private little world.

"I love you too," I said. "Can you forgive me?"

"I already have. And I promise that I always will," he replied.

This time he did seal it with a kiss. He released my hands, and I leaned into him, kissing him with all the love inside of me. He chuckled softly as he pulled away.

My heart stopped as I saw him reach into his pocket and pull out a little black box. Velvet. I saw the name printed on the outside of the lid and felt a new sob rise up in my chest. It couldn't be. He flipped the lid open with a soft click.

"Rachel Stevens, I have loved you since the moment I walked into your freshman dorm room to check on my little sister. I saw this tiny pixie of a girl sitting on the couch, smiling back at me, and I just knew. You, and only you, have had my heart from that moment forward. I will love you, protect you, tease you, laugh with you, and rescue you every day for the rest of my life if you'll marry me." His voice broke on the last part, which sent me over the edge.

"You still have my ring," I hiccupped.

He nodded as he pulled the same ring out of the box that he'd proposed to me with years ago. He held it up for me to see. I'd often wondered what had happened to it when I'd given it back.

"I never could manage to take it back," he whispered. "Will you marry me, love?" he asked again.

"Oh yes! Yes, yes!" I burst out happily through the tears and held out shaking fingers for him to slide the ring on. As soon as it slid over my knuckle, he pulled my fingers to his mouth and kissed where the ring rested.

"I can't tell you how much I love seeing that ring there." He smiled and wiped away a tear on my face.

I didn't have words to express how I was feeling, so I just wrapped my arms around his neck and pressed my cheek against his. He held me tight, and all was right in the world.

We talked softly for a few minutes, expressing our excitement and love for each other before he slipped away as he'd come, silently in the darkness.

After James went to his room, I stared at my hand in the moonlight. So many tears had been shed and so much heartache had been endured by both of us, but we had been called back to each other, and now was our time. I could hardly believe that after everything I'd gone through, I had come back home to James's heart.

The next morning, I snagged James as he came out of the bathroom. While I was absolutely thrilled about our engagement, I felt the celebration should be put on hold for a few days. I'd thought a lot about it overnight—because who can sleep after getting proposed to?—and I didn't want to overshadow Hannah's wedding in any way. It was now only five days away.

"I hope you don't take this the wrong way," I said as we whispered in the hallway, "but I don't want to do anything to take away from Hannah and Andrew. Could we wait to tell people we're engaged until after the wedding?"

He smiled at me and nodded. "I agree. We should let Hannah have her day. But make no mistake, I've waited seven years to get you back, and the second that girl leaves the reception hall, it's game on for us."

He snaked his arms around me and sealed his pronouncement with a searing kiss that left no questions before grabbing my hand and leading me to the breakfast table. My feet barely touched the ground.

I took off the engagement ring and tucked it into my pocket as we ate breakfast. I was sad to have to put it away, but I loved feeling it pressed against my leg, a reminder of what was to come.

After breakfast, James suggested a last walk around the neighborhood before we had to head back to Pine Ridge. We stepped out into a perfect fall morning, holding hands and walking slowly. I was sad to have to go back to real life. And the reality of us not being able to ride back together was disappointing.

"So, I've been thinking," James said as we strolled along hand in hand. "I'm not sure I want a big wedding."

I squeezed his fingers. "I feel the same way. Our relationship has been such a journey and so personal, I don't want to share it with everyone in the world." I sighed and then chuckled. "I wish we could just elope!"

James didn't immediately respond, but I could see the gears of that amazing mind shifting around. "Well, why not?"

"Why not what?" I asked.

"Why not elope?" he said, smiling down at me. "I'm serious. Nothing about our relationship has been typical. Why have a typical wedding?"

"My mom would kill us," I replied, loving the idea but not sure.

"Not if we promise to get right to work having babies!" He wiggled his eyebrows playfully as he turned to face me, growing more excited as he spoke. "She'll forgive us for anything when grandchildren start coming."

I giggled at his antics. But still. "I don't know," I said. "Are you sure?"

"Sweetheart, I've waited a long time for you. I already told you, I'm done wasting time."

Something about those words rang bright and true to me. In my heart, I knew that James pledging his life to me and I to him was all that mattered. The rest was fluff. I didn't need a large, traditional wedding. I'd been so involved with Hannah's that I knew how exhausting it could be. I just needed James.

"Could we invite a few people?" I hedged a bit.

"Like who?" He pulled a playfully annoyed face.

"My parents, Diana's family, your mom, Hannah and Andrew, Val, Lisa and her husband." I listed off the only people who really mattered to me.

James nodded. "Yes. And I want you in a beautiful white dress like you've always imagined."

I nearly cried, the joy of it flowing out of me. "I'll be in white."

"When?" he pressed.

"Well, Hannah's wedding is this Saturday, and then their honeymoon is a week long. So, how about in two weeks?" I teased.

"Done. In two weeks you'll be mine."

Suddenly the seriousness of what we were planning hit me, and I sobered. "Are you sure? Do you want more time to make sure you still feel good about this when we get back to real life?"

James pulled me close and kissed my worries away. "Being with you is my real life, Rachel. I don't need more time. I just need you."

Two Weeks Later

> Whatever our souls are made of,
> his and mine are the same.
>
> ~ *Wuthering Heights* ~

While it was still too early for snow on the mountainside around Pine Ridge, the cold air pricked at our eyes and cheeks as we looked down into the valley below. The only place warm was where James's arm wrapped around my shoulder and our bodies pressed together. The veil of my dress whipped across my eyes and made me laugh. I heard James chuckle as well as he reached over to untangle it from his tie. Our eyes met, and my heart leapt for the thousandth time. His smile was wide and warm. His eyes said what my heart felt.

We stood outside the cozy ski lodge restaurant where our wedding dinner would be held. Inside was a small group of our immediate family and closest friends. I wasn't sure if their shock had worn off yet.

"I'm trying to decide if my mom is mad that she didn't get to plan my wedding, or too happy that I got married to complain about it." I smiled at James as we turned toward the building.

"I'm going to remember the look on their faces for years to come," he replied as he squeezed my shoulders in a one-armed hug.

He was right. In the end, we didn't tell anyone anything. Hannah's wedding was beautiful, and the celebration large and festive. A week later, when she and Andrew returned from their honeymoon, we called everyone we loved the most in the world to let them know our wedding would be in two days.

It appeared that two days hadn't been quite enough time for the shock to wear off. They all had bemused expressions on their faces when they'd entered the room we were to be married in.

I was in the white dress of my dreams, and James was perfectly handsome in his suit. It was wonderful. With our small guest list gathered around us in their Sunday best, I felt the power of forever as our past and present collided.

I struggled with emotion as I quietly said my words of promise. As I listened to James's lower, gentle voice saying the same words back to me, something inside shifted like a puzzle piece settling into place. I felt whole, wonderful, and ready to take on the future with him by my side.

Those words of promise still rang in my ears as we walked together, arms around each other, across the chilly grounds. The wedding itself was so warm and peaceful, a true celebration. I wouldn't have traded that feeling for anything and was so grateful that James had insisted that we keep it small and quick.

James held the door for me and put his hand on the small of my back as I walked through. "After you, Mrs. Redmond," he said.

At hearing him call me that, my heartbeat skipped. And as I looked up at my wonderful husband, I knew, without a doubt, that there was no getting over James.

Epilogue

"... and then he took me on a tour of a waste treatment facility," the voice of our twenty-three-year-old daughter, Daisy, harrumphed along the invisible connecting lines of the phone. "I've learned more about poop and the disposal of it than I ever wanted to know." I tried to keep my amusement to myself as she told her father and me about her second bad date this month. "The worst part is that when he came to pick me up, he brought this incredibly gigantic zucchini he'd grown in his garden. I kid you not—it was the size of a horse's leg. After our tour, I jokingly asked him if he used 'special fertilizer' from the treatment plant to grow something so large, and he said yes! Guys, he said yes! Then he went on about how it's called biosolids, and it can be used safely."

At this, I finally did laugh out loud. "Oh, no! What did you do?"

"I hurried and texted my roommates, telling them to pick that thing up with gloves and run it straight to the dumpster," Daisy continued in a dramatic tone.

"Seems wise," James chimed in on the other line.

"Dating is just the worst," Daisy finally moaned. "You two are so lucky that dating wasn't this awful when you were my age."

"Oh, honey, dating is crazy no matter what generation you come from," I said, chuckling.

"Did your mom ever tell you about the time one of her dates hit her with his car?" James asked.

I could hear Daisy gasp. "Really?"

"Oh, yes. But that wasn't the worst one. One of my dates took me to a cemetery to meet his deceased father," I added.

"How is that possible?" Daisy sounded confused.

"That's what I wanted to know. When I asked him that same question, he told me we'd never work out. So I left and walked home."

"It worked out for me, because she left there and walked straight into my arms." James sounded pleased about how that had worked out.

"I'm going to die alone," Daisy whimpered.

"No, honey. If it ever gets to that point, I'll buy you a cat," I said kindly.

"Two cats," James amended.

"Guys, the last thing I need is to become a stereotypical cat lady," Daisy groaned.

"Then I guess you'd better keep on trying," James encouraged. "He's out there, Daisy. Be patient."

"You just have to hold on until you get your miracle," I added. "And when you do, it will have all been worth it."

> Love is the voice under all silences,
> the hope which has no opposite in fear;
> The strength so strong mere force is feebleness:
> the truth more first than sun, more last than star.
>
> ~ *E.E. Cummings* ~

Acknowledgments

My husband, Steve, who understands that some days need chocolate but others need Mexican food, who laughs at my jokes and dances with me around the kitchen, who offers to fill up the gas tank when I want to run away, and who shares my daydreams no matter how crazy. I love you.

My four kids: Even though some days I tell you to settle it the heck down, there is nothing better than having children who are happy. I love you and all the giggling, dancing, laughing, running, jumping, and teasing that goes on in our home! If I could freeze time, I'd do it . . . minus all the jokes about bodily functions.

My parents, my husband's parents, and our siblings and their spouses: Friends may come and go, but family is forever. I'm so happy that you're mine.

My friends: Man, I'm a lucky girl. You're too many to name, but you all make my life brighter. Thank you for sharing the journey.

The lovely people at Cedar Fort Publishing, for endlessly and kindly answering my questions and continuing to teach me so much! Thank you for giving me this chance . . . a second time!

And last, but in no way least, I'd like to thank my beta readers. As always, your input is invaluable!

About the Author

Aspen Hadley loves nothing more than a great story and has been busy telling them for as long as she can remember. She loves people and the crazy, romantic, defiant, dumb, risky, wonderful things they do. Aspen shares her life with a patient husband, four hilarious children, and one grumpy dog in the foothills of her beloved mountains. Given the choice, she'd happily road trip her life away, listening to classic rock and eating chocolate. Aspen is also the author of the Whitney Award–nominated novel *Simply Starstruck*.

You can find her on Facebook at facebook.com/aspenthewriter, on Instagram @aspenhadley_author, or on her website at www.aspenmariehadley.com.

Scan to visit

aspenmariehadley.com